SIN & SECRETS

A FORCED PROXIMITY MAFIA ROMANCE

THE PRINCE'S GUILD

SIERRA VOSS

Copyright © 2025 by Sierra Voss
All rights reserved.
No part of this book may be reproduced in any form or by any electronic or mechanical means, including information storage and retrieval systems, without written permission from the author, except for the use of brief quotations in a book review.

Under the smokey stage lights of my club, I watch an angle sing like she was made for sin.
She doesn't know it yet. But she's about to pay off a debt —with her total submission.

They call me ruthless for a reason.
I took this empire from my own father.
Rebuilt it in blood.
Now, it's time to claim my little angel—my '*Angioletta*'—and make her my queen.

Cassandra Bellini is torture in a Gucci dress.
With heat in her eyes.
And bruises that tell me another man laid his damn hands on what should belong to me.

Her bastard of a boyfriend owes me $101,000.
So I take her as payment.

101 nights.
$1,000 a night.
Until the debt is paid… or until she begs to stay.

The longer she's in my bed, the deeper I sink.
And she whispers the words that change everything.
"I'm pregnant… and I think you killed my father."

Now? I'll burn down the world to atone for my sins and rip apart her secrets.
Blood. Vengeance. Ruin. Nothing will stop me.

For her and our baby.

Sin & Secrets is book on of The Prince's Guild dark mafia series. It's a standalone with a delicious HEA. Be sure to also download Revenge & Ruin, book 2.

Warning: This mafia romance features a possessive alpha male, kidnapping, stalking, obsession, power play, steamy scenes, and a dangerous criminal empire. Not for the faint of heart.

1

ROCCO

"We need to deal with this quickly," I announce to no one in particular.

The unanswered texts from Daniela burn a hole in my pocket, but there's nothing I can do. I'm likely going to miss her performance again.

"The job always comes first," Martino mutters next to me. There's no judgment in his tone; he's merely stating the truth—a fact we all know to be relentlessly and unforgivingly true.

I made no secret of my priorities when I first engaged her, but now Daniela's resentment rages through those messages. Unfortunately for her, I can't bring myself to care.

I massage my forehead as the Mercedes comes to a sudden stop. Glancing over at Martino in the driver's seat, I note how his eyes dart across the scene before us, intent on finding what we came for.

Putting the messages out of my mind, I follow suit. This line of work has no room for distractions.

One moment, there's nothing there at all, just the eerie

quiet of the abandoned dockyard and Martino's shallow breaths next to me. The next, a shadow emerges from behind a shipping container.

Alessandro's eyes pierce through the darkness, the only part of his body not entirely cloaked in stealth gear. He gestures quickly and precisely.

"Shit."

Martino revs the car to life, not needing me to translate. Our target has company. Two more bikes are heading in from the north.

We take off at breakneck speed. I don't need to look back to know Alessandro has disappeared into the gloom. I can only hope he makes it to his next location in time.

"Clear at the rendezvous point." Teo's voice crackles into my earpiece. His eagle eyes are undoubtedly monitoring every available camera feed across the dock. "No SIL at the west exit."

I reach behind me, grabbing hold of the silencer for my AR-15. "I need eyes to the north. We have company."

Martino takes a corner so sharply I can feel the car begin to lift beneath me, but I have total faith in the man driving. His skills behind the wheel have made the difference between life and death on more than one occasion.

Teo curses in my ear. "Coming in hot. You'll intercept in T-minus twenty."

"Make that ten," I instruct Martino, his matching earpiece relaying everything Teo says.

I have to fight against the g-force as Martino hits the gas.

"We only have a small window of opportunity to intercept our target," I reiterate needlessly. "These bikes are likely some kind of distraction. Let's deal with them fast."

Tires screech as we make it around the final corner.

Warehouses tower over each side of the road—there's only one exit, and two motorcycles currently guard it, revving their engines. Their headlights are bright enough to blind us as we race toward them.

"They're armed, boss," Teo warns as I open the window.

"So am I."

I click the magazine of my assault rifle into place and maneuver out the window. I aim directly at the rider on the right—it would be a shame to shoot out the wheels on such nice Super Dukes. I make a mental note to ask Alessandro if he can salvage them later.

Bullets begin to bounce off the Mercedes' plated armor as we approach, but my aim is steady, honed over years of drilling and far too much field experience.

Zip.

The bullet shoots clean through the target's brachial artery in his shoulder. The bike beneath him wobbles, then flips, throwing the rider to the ground with a sickening crunch.

"Should have worn a helmet," Martino mutters. "Brace!"

It's all I can do to cling to the top of the car as Martino pulls off a handbrake turn behind the other bike.

The second rider takes off with a lurch when he realizes we are directly on his tail. He shoots at us blindly, focusing on jerking his bike across the road in random zig-zags to throw us off, making my job that much harder.

"I'll cut him off at the next intersection," Martino barks.

I jam the stock into my shoulder to keep it steady as Martino maneuvers us into position. For a single beat, I allow myself to breathe out.

"INCOMING ON YOUR LEFT!"

Teo's warning couldn't have come a moment too soon. I

turn in time to see the headlights tearing toward the intersection and jump on instinct. I hit the unforgiving tarmac in a roll just as a spray of bullets pounds into the car door.

A third bike swerves to avoid T-boning the Mercedes, clearing it by less than an inch.

I gasp into the throbbing pain in my side as I force myself to stand.

"Teo. Tell Martino to take out the second bike," I order as I pat myself down, cursing at the tear in the side of my new suit. "I'll deal with this."

The Mercedes takes off to give chase to the second rider as I haul up the assault rifle I had cradled against the impact with the floor. This time, I'm squaring off against my opponent on foot.

Finally recovered from the near collision, the third bike turns back to me just as I begin my approach. A spray of bullets blows up dirt from the tarmac a few yards in front of me. I check my gun as I continue to walk forward.

The bike accelerates. The bullets are hitting the ground only a few feet away. Now only inches.

I dive at the last possible second, and I can almost feel the instrument of my death slicing across my skin.

The bike flies past, unable to react in time.

Zip.

My shot goes straight through the rider's skull. He slumps off his bike as it comes to a stuttering stop a few yards away.

"Nicely done," Teo says in my ear.

I grimace slightly, finally taking note of the seared flesh beneath my ripped suit. Thankfully, nothing seems to be broken, but the friction burn will take an annoying amount of time to heal.

Wincing, I remind myself that it would have been far worse had Teo not warned me. Not for the first time, I thank whatever gods are still out there on my side for bringing Teo Vitale into my life.

"It's not like Alessandro to mess up," I say as I approach the downed Super Duke KTM 1290. I let out an impressed whistle that my enemies would invest so much in taking out little old me.

"Permission to give him an intolerable amount of shit for this, boss?"

"Granted." It would be more effective than whatever punishment I could devise anyway. "I didn't realize Alessandro couldn't count to fucking three."

But despite his failings today, the self-proclaimed "stealth master" had found other ways to ensure he made himself invaluable to the Guild. I'm unsure if I want to know how he secured the intel for this job.

I kick the body of the dead goon away from the bike—Cartel, if the markings on his neck are any indicator. Clearly, the Tunnel Eaters didn't want us getting our hands on their lead informant.

"I'm heading to intercept the target alone," I announce as I mount the bike, not waiting for Teo to try to talk me out of it. It roars to life beneath me within seconds, and I take off toward the rendezvous point.

It's only a few minutes away, but every second that passes only makes the window of opportunity that much smaller. Even as I pull up to the pier, I can see the telltale outline of a speedboat on the horizon, careening toward my target.

The man on the pier watches his incoming escape vessel

fervently. He either doesn't hear my approach, or chooses not to turn around as I close in.

"Apologies. Traffic in Brooklyn is awful this time of the night."

My target whirls around in alarm, and my heart sinks.

Carmine Bellini.

We knew it had to be someone from my father's inner circle, but Bellini had never seemed like the feeding-intel-to-the-enemy type. He was a wallflower at best, and a cowering idiot at worst. But I suppose that's accountants for you.

Perhaps since my father's "retirement", he thought leadership had gone soft enough for him to get away with playing his own games.

"Mister Moretti...Rocco," he stammers.

But I cut him off before he can start feverishly begging for his life. "I'm looking for the man responsible for leaking the Guild's movements to the Cartel. You haven't seen him anywhere, have you?"

"Please," he begs. "It wasn't me."

I step closer, brushing off the debris from my suit as I stalk my prey.

"How was it my father used to deal with traitors like you?" I ponder, noting the ashen look of fear on Bellini's face at the mention of the previous don. "A slit throat in a sleazy motel bathroom three states away?"

"Wrists," Bellini whispers his correction, paling even further.

I don't hide my smirk as I wave at the approaching speedboat. Whoever was driving the thing had at least enough common sense to stop the boat when he noticed the red laser of Alessandro's sniper rifle hovering over their chest.

There's a second of silence before the motor kicks in again, and he begins to turn tail completely.

Bellini watches the boat leave in utter despair, his body shaking with the effort of staying on his feet. "Please, I didn't do this!"

"Ever since assuming my father's title, I've wanted to make a statement," I gesture at him casually. "About how things will be run from now on."

"I…I had nothing to do with this!"

I ignore him. "For that reason, I'm not going to kill you. My father always was a trigger-happy psychopath."

None of what I say seems to ease Bellini's despair.

"The information you sold the Cartel about our last hit was completely off the record. You could not have gotten your hands on it unless you were working with someone else."

Bellini swallows.

"You're going to tell me who your little rat friend is, then I'll let you call back your speedboat, and you can sail off to Timbuk-fucking-tu."

An almighty sob vibrates through Bellini's chest as he shakes his head. "I can't."

I sigh more dramatically than I need to. I'd really hoped I wouldn't need to ship him off to the interrogation room, but it seems nothing is working in my favor today.

"You can," I counter. "My offer leaves the table the second I have to drag you back to the compound. You'll find Alessandro's knife offers you far less vacation time."

"No."

Behind me, I hear the Mercedes pull up, and two sets of

feet hit the deck. Martino must have picked up Teo from the safe house.

Bellini murmurs something as he fumbles with his pocket. Two identical pistols appear next to my shoulders as Martino and Teo train them on the informant.

The safety goes off the second Bellini pulls out his own gun, a tiny, ancient revolver that he awkwardly clings to with both hands.

"Put the gun down," Teo warns at my side.

But Bellini doesn't acknowledge him; he only stares at me. "I'm sorry, Rocco."

"Bellini." It's the only warning I'll give, and we all know it.

"I wanted to see it for myself—what you would do for the Guild," he says as tears stream down his aging face. "You are a hundred times the man your father ever was."

"Boss?" Teo hisses, but I raise a hand to silence him.

He'd noticed at the same time I had, that Bellini's gun wasn't intended for any of us.

"Then help me," I reply evenly. "Tell me who the other rat is. This doesn't have to end in bloodshed."

"You are going to do great things, Rocco."

I cautiously reach out a hand toward him. "Give me the gun, Bellini."

But a cool calm comes over him. His resolve suddenly seems as natural as the waves below us, sweeping up against the shore.

"There is no other rat. It has always been me. You just never wanted to believe an accountant could slip through your defenses."

"Rocco!" Teo cries. But this time, his warning came too late.

Bellini ate the barrel of his gun and pulled the trigger.

2

CASSANDRA

"Bellini, you little bitch!"

I wince as Danny's voice shrieks in my ear. The blonde bombshell in a sparkly bodysuit snatches a chunk of my hair before I can respond, dragging me from my seat at the vanity.

"I knew I should have never let you open for me!"

I gasp as her grip tightens. My scalp burns with pain. "Let go!"

"Why? So you can steal my tips again? You nasty little thief!"

Despite her words, she throws me to the ground. But by the time I recover, it's already too late. Danny snatches up my tip jar from the vanity and rifles through my generous savings.

"Those are mine!" I protest, internally cringing at how juvenile I sound. The tears prickling the corners of my eyes add insult to injury.

Danny merely laughs as she leafs through the bills. "Give me a break. This is twice I'd make in a month." She pauses to shout over her shoulder. "Teresa! I found where our money wandered off to!"

My heart sinks as Teresa appears at the door a moment later. The singer only sneers at me as she waltzes over to Danny.

"Here I was thinking the new girl wouldn't be stupid enough to pull anything in her first week," Teresa says as she takes her half of my money from Danny's outstretched hand. She secures it in her midnight blue bra strap, flicking her jet-black hair over her shoulder.

The two of them together look like night and day—fitting for the *Candelabra*'s two most popular performers. But their charm hadn't lasted long for me. Sharing a dressing room tends to reveal the worst in people quickly.

"I didn't touch your money." I rise, drawing energy from that small kernel of fire inside of me that urged me to defend myself in the first place. "Those are all my tips. You can ask Claudio. There was a stag on table twelve, and they..."

"Here's my problem," Danny cuts me off. "About a week ago, things started to disappear around here. Has that ever happened before, Teresa?"

"You know, I don't think it has, Danny."

"A ring here, a necklace there. I figured I'd let it slide. Let the demure little girl from the sticks borrow a few things. God knows she needs to add a bit of sparkle to her performances."

Teresa giggles at this, and I ignore her.

"I don't need any of your tacky jewelry."

Danny's eyes flash dangerously. "But what I can't turn a blind eye to, is the fact you stole twelve thousand dollars from us. Did you think you could just sleep with the manager and not get caught?"

My gut hollows out at the mention of Claudio. That tiny flame of defiance splutters out into nothingness. He's already warned me about getting along with the other performers. If he finds out about this...

"Danny, please, it wasn't me." I glance at the door nervously. "But if you need the money, take what you need. I just need a few dollars to get a cab home."

But Danny merely scoffs at me. "You should have thought of that before you tried to cross me."

"You don't understand," I try again. "I have nothing else."

"Oh, save us a sob story, will you?" Teresa rolls her eyes.

I step forward, ready to get on my knees to plead with them both. "Please. Just twenty bucks. The rest is yours."

For the briefest moment, something flickers across Danny's face. But before it can manifest into anything more, a shadow falls across the doorway.

"What's going on in here?"

We all turn to see the devastatingly handsome man standing in the doorway. His toned body is clearly visible through his tight black T-shirt as he towers over us, his mouth a grim line beneath his short beard.

I school my face into something more neutral. "Nothing."

But my boyfriend does not acknowledge me. He crosses his arms and stares at Danny, waiting for an explanation.

"We were just doing a little hazing," she chirps innocently. "If Cassandra wants to play with the big girls, she needs to show us she has what it takes."

His eyes glance down at the wad of bills in her hand, then at the empty jar on my vanity. "Are those Cas' tips?"

Finally, he looks at me. Those piercing blue eyes search mine for the answer to his question.

"I..."

Claudio leans against the doorframe. "Daniella, Theresa, kindly return whatever money you took from Cas and go home. Mia just called last orders."

"Narc," Teresa hisses at me as she begrudgingly hands Claudio her bills on the way out.

But Danny lingers to whisper in my ear. "He's not going to be around to protect you forever."

She turns on her heel and stalks away. I don't miss how her fingers linger on Claudio's as she hands over her stack of bills.

Perhaps my blood would boil if I could muster up enough energy to feel anything at all. I slump back down in my chair and close my eyes, taking a breath to anchor myself.

This isn't how I thought moving to Brooklyn would go. Claudio said the girls at the club were lovely, that they'd treat me like a sister. But the bartender was the only person who'd shown me even a shred of kindness.

But did that even count if Mia and I had known each other since we were kids?

"Cas."

My eyes shoot open to see Claudio standing behind me in the mirror. The door to the dressing room closed tightly behind him.

"I'm sorry," I whisper as he places his hands on my shoulders. "I don't know why they hate me."

I try to place a hand over his, but he shakes it off.

"I need you to try harder than this, Cas. They are my

moneymakers. If they ask me to let you go, I won't have a choice."

My shoulders sag. He's right, of course. He's not just my boyfriend now, he's my boss, and I've done nothing but let him down since the moment I arrived.

"I'm sorry," I whisper again.

Something cold and long extinguished rages against my pitiful apology. None of this is my fault. I didn't steal from Danny and Teresa. I didn't ask for him to come to my rescue. I just wanted to sing on an actual stage—the *Candelabra* stage—one of the most notorious clubs in Brooklyn.

I watch him in silence as he gently strokes my cheek. Against my olive skin, his hand looks frighteningly pale, as if I'm being comforted by some kind of ghost.

"I'll get better."

His hand halts its caress, and he leans over my shoulder, holding onto the tops of my arms instead. Eyes meeting mine in the mirror.

"You keep saying that, but I haven't seen any improvements, Cas," he murmurs. "Are you trying to make me look bad?"

All I can do is shake my head as his fingers press firmly into my skin. That extinguished flame inside me rallies to ensure I don't wince.

"It's just girl stuff," I whisper back, more defiant than I'd usually dare. "I'll settle in with them once I've gotten used to this place."

Claudio's expression in the mirror crumbles and the mask he wears in front of everyone else slips away to reveal the boy beneath it. "I thought you loved me."

I swallow down my cry of pain as his fingers press

harder. I whisper as soothingly as I can. "Of course I do, darling."

The pressure eases on my arms, but I don't check to see if he's left a bruise. Breaking eye contact with him would be like somehow admitting I was lying.

"It's just you and me, right?" he breathes in my ear as he stokes my arms up and down, as if reassuring himself that I'm still here.

"I'm with you, Claudio," I reassure him as he moves on to touch my hair. His fingers run through the dark, thick strands, and for a moment, I think he might pull at it like Danny did.

But he sucks in a long breath and finally steps away.

I can't help the way my shoulders sag in relief.

"I just want you to be a star. I knew you were one the moment I set eyes on you." His usual cold mask slowly slips back onto his face. "That's why I brought you here. I saw your potential and knew I had to be the one to guide you to your destiny."

"I know, baby, and you will," I say as earnestly as possible.

"You wouldn't be here if I hadn't found you in Ohio, drowning alongside mediocre talent."

I turn to look at him, eyes snagging on the bills bulging out of the pocket of his jeans. "I will always be grateful that you did."

But it's clear he's stopped listening to me, the facade of the *Candelabra's* talent manager taking over once more. As he stalks back to the door, a sinking feeling settles into my stomach.

"I need you to go out there and close the show better

than ever. The Italians are here, and they're going to be pissed that they missed Daniela's performance."

"Right." I nod absently but can't tear my eyes from his pocket.

"I mean it, Cas. You need to make this up to me, remember?"

He lingers at the door, and I try to persuade myself that he's just forgotten. That asking my next question isn't unreasonable.

"Before you go, could you give me my tips back?"

Claudio stares at me blankly. "You owe me rent."

It feels like he's just punched the air from my lungs. "Right."

His gaze rakes over me once more before he leaves. The act sends a shiver down my spine that I convince myself must be derived from desire. Because what else could it be? My heart thrums rapidly in my chest at the truth in that stare.

He is gorgeous, passionate, and committed to my success. He's the angel who swept into my boring old life in Ohio and promised me the world was ours for the taking.

It's so easy to convince myself that I love him, because he's already done so much for me. He got me this job, housed me, clothed me.

If that's not love, what is?

"Fuck."

I examine my arms in the mirror with a gnawing sense of dread. Hand-shaped bruises are already forming on the tops of my arms, and my strappy black dress does nothing to conceal them.

The intercom buzzes. "Cas, you're on in five!"

There's nothing else I can do. I don the worn leather

jacket hanging on the back of my chair and allow the familiar musky scent of it soothe my rampant anxiety. Danny will give me so much crap for wearing it on stage, but I don't care.

The woman in the mirror stretches her face into a smile, and we rise as one, ready to take on the world. Seven thousand dollars lighter.

As I walk backstage, my heels click against the floor, providing a beat for my vocal warmups. My throat snags more than I'd like it to, but it's already two a.m., and most of our patrons will have already sailed past sobriety.

I just pray that the "Italians" are firmly on that list.

"And now, ladies and gentlemen," Claudio's voice booms as I wait in the wings. "I present the most darling, most talented thing to come out of Ohio in the last twenty years. Please give a round of applause for Miss Cassandra!"

I breathe before I step out onto the stage to the chorus of applause.

As usual, the lights are far too bright. I can just about see Claudio's outline as I approach the microphone. He reaches for me, squeezing my arms as he goes to kiss me on the cheek.

"Don't fuck this up," he whispers.

I smile as he leaves me, the clapping trickling into expectant silence.

Showtime.

"How are we all doing here tonight?" I say into the freestanding microphone.

The question is met with a generous amount of cheering, but I have to squint to determine where it's coming from.

"Could we turn down the lights a little? I want to see

what kind of motley crew waited all this time to listen to little old me."

Thankfully, the blinding spotlight eases, revealing a surprisingly strong turnout.

But my eyes snag on the VIP table directly below the stage. Dressed in a light gray suit and white shirt, which is unbuttoned to reveal the intricate tattoos decorating his chest, he is the most beautiful man I have ever seen.

And when his icy gray eyes light up as he offers me a crooked smile, my entire world collapses around me.

3

ROCCO

"Mia. Who is that?"

The bartender looks up from her tray of perfectly aged single malt to note the angel currently gracing the main stage at the *Candelabra*.

Mia looks at me with narrowed eyes. "Don't even think about it."

I want to laugh and tell her it's far too late for that. The second the woman had walked onto the stage, I had been utterly captivated. How could someone look so lost and yet perfectly belong in the spotlight?

Her tight black dress reveals a dangerous amount of leg, which already has many of the men around me drooling a bit. Yet the vintage leather jacket advocates for her modesty, only allowing us brief glimpses of her surprisingly curvaceous figure.

But all thoughts of deciphering the enigma before more vanished the second she began to sing.

"I haven't seen her before," I mutter as I take my drink from Mia's outstretched hand.

A glance at the fiery redhead makes me aware she's about two seconds away from throwing it in my face.

"I thought you were here to see Danny," she replies tightly.

I lean in, matching her glare. "Just because your father is a valuable asset to me doesn't mean you can talk to me like that."

"I'm so sorry, Your Royal Highness. Would you like me to spell it out for you? Cas is off-limits. End of story."

Cas. My mind turns the name over and over again, trying to imagine what it would sound like on my tongue. *Miss Cassandra*—that's how she'd been introduced. I wonder if that is her real name, or just a stage name.

"You must be close if you're already on a nickname basis," I muse.

"We were childhood friends."

I raise my eyebrows in surprise. The Italian mafia doesn't run in particularly large circles. "A family I know?"

Something flickers across Mia's stony expression, but it's gone before I can pull it apart.

"She moved to Ohio when she was eight. She doesn't know about the Guild."

Cas begins her next song, and it's all I can do to hum non-committally in response to Mia's words as my entire attention is captivated once more.

She must be some kind of siren. The way everything else seems to fade around me has my instincts raging for me to stay alert. But I'm completely helpless.

She might sound like an angel and look like the gods themselves had crafted her to be the living embodiment of desire, but those lips, forming perfect ohs and ahs around the melody...were as sinful as the devil.

What I wouldn't give to trail my tongue across her bottom lip, and hear the sounds she made when I took it between my teeth. Would she sing for me then? Could I make her gasp out my name between the notes of her pleasure?

Then, all of a sudden, her song ends. Everything around me comes back into sharp focus, and I find myself having to reposition myself in my seat.

I turn to see that Mia is back behind the bar, so I take the opportunity to flag down her assistant manager, Terry.

"Sir?" He practically bows as he approaches the VIP table. I absently wonder if I could persuade him to give Mia a few lessons in grace and decorum.

"Please invite Miss Cassandra to my table after her performance."

"Of course, sir."

The next twenty minutes are complete agony. It takes everything within me to maintain a cool facade to conceal the rampantly salacious thoughts running through my mind.

I tell myself it's Danny's fault. We'd broken up again after the incident with Carmine Bellini over a week ago. Despite her constant nagging and clinginess, she'd always been willing to take the edge off most of my darker desires.

Now they are running rampant, projecting onto this poor woman who'd done nothing but appear before me as temptation incarnate. Perhaps Mia was right after all.

"Sir?"

I turn as casually as I can to see that Terry has returned to my table. The woman who will surely be my undoing is standing nervously behind him.

"Miss Cassandra for you, sir."

Cas steps forward, fingers playing with the cuffs of her jacket. "I hope you enjoyed the show tonight."

Her voice is quieter than I expected. Her confidence from when she was on stage is clearly waning now that she is out of the spotlight. But it doesn't stop the pining ache in my chest.

"Miss Cassandra, please, join me for a drink." I indicate to the seat across from me before turning back to Terry. "She'll have a glass of champagne."

"Make that a whiskey," she corrects as she nods to my own glass. "My father always said it was rude not to drink that same thing as your host."

"Smart man."

Cas finally takes her seat as Terry retreats back to the bar. Now that we are face to face, I find myself captivated by her beauty. Her thick, dark hair matches her olive skin perfectly and it cascades down over her shoulders in effortless waves. But it's her unusually bright hazel eyes that render me speechless.

She shifts awkwardly under my intense gaze. "You wanted to see me?"

"I wanted to congratulate you in person. It's been a while since the *Candelabra* has displayed such talent."

A beautiful flush appears across her cheeks, and the sight goes straight to my cock. If such a small amount of praise had this effect on her...

"I'm not sure my colleagues would agree with you," she counters.

"A diplomatic response."

"Self-preservation is in my best interest. I quite enjoy having my hair attached to my head."

My chuckle seems to surprise us both. "You've met Danny then."

"Hard to miss her."

"I seem to have managed it this evening," I muse. "Although I can't complain. Making your acquaintance seems like a more valuable use of my time."

Cas stares at me for a moment, clearly mulling something over. "You know, she talks a lot about her boyfriend when she is backstage—the staggeringly handsome Italian billionaire who reserves the VIP table almost every night."

"Do you agree with her?"

She frowns. "Agree with what?"

"That her ex-boyfriend is staggeringly handsome?" I lean hard on the word "ex" as I speak.

Her tempting mouth drops open, but she's saved a response by two glasses of whiskey slamming onto the table between us.

"Everything all right here, Cas?" Mia stares at me with murderous intent.

I offer her a shit-eating grin in return. "Miss Cassandra and I were just getting acquainted."

"I called last orders an hour ago," she counters.

To her endless list of credits, I add another mark of approval as Cas places a gentle hand on Mia's arm. "I won't be too long. Claudio was asking if you had next week's itinerary yet."

Finally, Mia looks at her friend. "You call me if you need anything."

Cas nods, and Mia makes her retreat, shooting daggers over her shoulder at me.

"I'm sorry, Mia can be...protective." Cas swirls her whiskey around her glass.

"Evidently."

"She's right, though. Claudio will want me backstage soon. I won't be able to stay long."

I smirk. "I'm sure he'll make an exception for me."

She takes a long sip from her glass, and I try not to stare at her throat as she swallows. "I don't think you understand. He can also be very protective."

I pretend to weigh this up for a moment. "Well, I suppose that's the one benefit of owning this place. Everyone here has to do as I say."

"Mister Moretti?" Her eyes practically bulge from their sockets.

"I see my reputation proceeds me."

She takes another long drink.

In the silence, something she said catches in the back of my mind. "Tell me, is there a reason my talent manager is so possessive of you?"

Cas doesn't look me in the eye as she replies. "He...we're living together." Then, more firmly, like a dagger to my chest, "He's my boyfriend."

Of course, nothing can ever be this easy for someone like me.

I smirk to myself as I circle the rim of my glass with a finger. "He's a fool, then."

"Excuse me?"

"For letting you have a drink with a staggeringly handsome Italian billionaire," I answer simply.

"Mister Moretti..."

"Rocco," I correct her.

Her gaze narrows. "Rocco. I'm sorry if I gave you the wrong impression..."

"Don't do that."

"Don't interrupt me," she snaps, her eyes igniting with something that makes my heart race. "I am only interested in maintaining a professional relationship with you. As my employer, you must understand that."

If I wasn't so in awe of her, I might have been blindsided by her flash of confidence.

But I realize that the fire within her is what makes her so irresistible. I saw it when she was on stage, baring her soul. She has been defiantly holding my gaze during our conversation as well, and I find myself lapping it up.

"Then I will respect your wishes," I concede. "Although it is a shame you'll never know the kind of protection *I* could offer you. It's notoriously unparalleled."

She crosses her arms. "Care to enlighten me?"

I chuckle darkly. "It's not the kind of topic discussed with polite company."

"Luckily, I'm not polite. At all."

My eyes roam her defiant face, hungry to speak up her attention. "Well, first, we'd have to take this conversation somewhere far more private. I wouldn't want an audience for all the things I would do to you. At least, not the first time."

To my delight, her pupils begin to dilate at my words. "You aren't serious."

"Deadly," I take a sip of whiskey. "I could hardly protect you without staking my claim. It wouldn't do for you to have another man's name on those perfect lips of yours."

Something dark takes over her expression. "I suppose you'd be wanting my lips around your cock before you even lifted a finger to protect me."

"On the contrary, I'm sure we could find many ways to occupy my fingers."

I don't miss the way her eyes dart to my hand, my finger still circling the rim of my glass. Slowly, I lift it to my mouth and try not to groan as her dark eyes follow the movement.

My cock begins to strain in my pants as her tongue darts out to moisten her bottom lip.

"Rocco, I..."

"Cas!"

We both jump at the sound of Claudio Lazzaro's drawl. I'm not sure I've ever hated a man more in my life.

"Lazzaro, Miss Cassandra here was just delighting me with her company." I don't bother offering him a smile. "It seems you've been holding out on me."

Something in Lazzaro's jaw jumps in response. "Cas only started a week ago, sir."

"Yet it seems you've both known each other a while?"

Cas clears her throat. "Did you need something, darling?"

I want to vomit as the pet name does wonders to the tension in Lazzaro's shoulders. Most of the club's patrons have disappeared while we were talking, and the staff have packed away most of the bar. I wonder if they'd notice if I punched him in the face?

"I need you around back," he says to Cas. He offers no more explanation.

"Right."

I look back at Cas, immediately noting the way she stares emotionlessly down at her hands. Her entire demeanor seems to have changed in an instant.

Where was the confident woman I was speaking to only a moment before? The woman who could match my flirtations beat for a beat while taking me down a peg in the process?

"It seems I've occupied enough of your time," I announce as we both stand.

Without thinking too hard about it, I reach out to take Cas' hand in mine and bring it to my lips. I'm desperately trying to ignore the way my skin lights up at the touch. "Until next time, *Angioletta*."

Her hazel eyes bore into mine. I can only pray that I'm imagining the longing I find there. For both our sakes.

A firm hand clamps down on her shoulder. "You must be warm, Cas. Let's take that jacket off and get you into some normal clothes."

Before she has time to protest, Claudio pulls at her sleeve and drags her out of her leather jacket.

Something primal roars within me at the sight of Cas' exposed flesh, but then...

Then I stop breathing.

Cas tries to cover her arms, but it's too late. Claudio throws a protective—no, *possessive*—arm over her shoulders.

The bruises match his hands perfectly.

4

CASSANDRA

"What did Rocco Moretti want with you?"

We barely make it backstage before the question bursts from Claudio's lips.

I take a steadying breath.

It wasn't as if I could tell him the truth—that it was clear that Rocco wanted to do *many* things with me. I could tell that the desires he spoke aloud only scratched the surface.

The rest of what he wanted had been implied by the way his frighteningly beautiful gray eyes devoured me whole, promising all the secret, terrible, salacious things he would do to me if I would only give him a chance.

And dear God, did I ever want to give him that chance.

Sitting across from him had been the worst kind of torture. Each word that came out of his mouth picked at my resolve so thoroughly I had been seconds away from giving in entirely.

I had been seconds away from suggesting we fall into the nearest bathroom so he could show me exactly what he intended to do with his fingers.

"He was just introducing himself. He's the boss, after all."

"*I'm* your boss," Claudio counters.

I swallow hard. "Of course you are, darling. He was just being polite."

"Moretti doesn't know the meaning of the word."

I can't help but agree with him there.

Claudio must see it on my face because the next thing he asks is, "Did he try to proposition you?"

"Claudio…"

"I will kill him."

"Claudio!" I grab hold of his sleeve, a pitiful attempt to prevent him from leaving, but one that mercifully stops him in his tracks. "It's you and me, remember? I would never betray you like that."

He searches my eyes for the truth, and I pray to everything that's holy that he finds it there.

What the hell was I thinking, allowing myself to be seduced by someone like Rocco Moretti? Not only is he a self-proclaimed billionaire, he's the person who'll be signing my checks.

It's no wonder Claudio is acting like this. I could have sabotaged my entire career tonight. Our careers. All because my mind turns off whenever Moretti looks at me like I'm some lovesick teenager. I need to get a grip.

"I should never have spoken with him privately. I see that now," I tell him. "Whatever he wanted wasn't worth someone coming between us."

"He's a manipulative bastard. You should have known better. You should have come straight to me."

I bow my head in shame. "I know. I'm sorry."

"You're not strong enough to deal with men like Moretti.

They'll spin whatever pretty lies they want to get you into bed with them."

"I'm sorry."

He takes me by the arms again. "You're *mine,* Cas."

I can't stop the hiss of pain that escapes my teeth. But Claudio doesn't let go.

"Please, Claudio. You're hurting me."

"If that bastard approaches you again, what will you say?"

Traitorous tears begin to prickle in my eyes. "I won't say anything. I'll come straight to you."

He releases me finally, and I sag to the floor, focusing on getting air into my lungs.

"You've really pissed me off today, Cas."

"I know. I'm sorry."

"I'm going out. You can see yourself home."

My eyes snap up to his. "But I thought we'd get a cab and go home together?"

"What did I just say?"

There's nothing gentle or loving in his eyes. All I see is sheer annoyance. I look down at my knees on the dirty floor. I stay in place, pathetically kneeling on the floor and maintain my numb silence until I hear him leave. The door closes behind him with a definitive bang.

When the tears come, I'm not entirely sure who I'm crying for. Or for how long. All I know is that when Mia finds me, I'm still kneeling on the floor.

"Hey, hey, hey!" She kneels in front of me, green eyes wide with alarm.

"S-s-sorry."

"Oh shush." She pulls me in for a hug without any warning, knocking the wind out of me. "I'd ask if you're okay, but it seems like a stupid question."

After savoring a moment of her comforting embrace, I pull away, dabbing my eyes with the back of my hand. "I'm just feeling a little overwhelmed."

Her green eyes linger, as Rocco's had, on the tops of my arms. "Please tell me that isn't what I think it is."

"It's fine, Mia. It was an accident."

"You don't need to defend that scumbag. Not to me."

I get to my feet, using the time to compose myself. "I'm handling it, okay? He's not dangerous. He's just passionate."

"Possessive more like," Mia counters, her hands on her hips. "What would happen, do you think, if you broke up with him?"

Her bluntness never ceases to astound me. "I haven't thought about it."

"You know my door is always open, right? You don't have to live with him."

"You live in a studio, Mia. We'd be living on top of each other."

"It would be like having a sleepover every night."

I smile at the blurry memories from our childhood when we did exactly that. "You wouldn't be able to handle the trashy rom-coms I'd make you watch."

"You got me there." Her lazy, reminiscent smile slowly fades. "But I'm serious. Just say the word, and I will murder that fucker in his sleep."

She'll do it, too, without hesitation. I know, because if our situations were reversed, I'd be saying exactly the same thing. The thought of anyone laying a hand on Mia makes my skin crawl.

But it's easy to think that. It's so much harder to redirect that kind of thinking to your own situation.

"I love him," I say with a shrug as if that somehow makes up for everything else.

Mia gives me a long look before holding up her hands so I can help her up. "As soon as that stops being enough, you tell me. Agreed?"

My heart swells for the fiery woman before me and everything she's grown up to be in those years we spent apart. "Agreed."

"Good. Now that's settled, do me a favor and stay the hell away from Rocco Moretti."

I cross my arms. "You weren't exactly subtle earlier. Why do you hate him so much?"

"It's not that I hate him. He's just…" she trails off, trying to find the word. "Very, very bad for you."

"How ominously vague of you, Mia."

I step away, grabbing my sweats and a T-shirt from the pile of discarded clothes in the corner. Mia makes herself comfortable at my vanity as I change behind the folding screen.

She tries again. "He's dangerous."

"How dangerous can a club owner really be?"

"I'm serious, Cas. You think I'd ever be able to face your mother again if I let you run off with someone who could get you killed?"

I physically reel at this information. "What are you talking about?"

"This place? The *Tiny Ballroom, Electrix, Adelaide Bar,* what do they all have in common?"

I rack my memory for any tidbit of information I can recall. "They're all high-end entertainment establishments?"

"Owned by Rocco Moretti."

"So he's into real estate?"

"Cas," she groans in frustration. "An Italian billionaire with a vested interest in laundering money through clubs in Brooklyn?"

"I feel like you're encouraging me to stereotype."

"He's mafia, Cas."

"And my rocket ship is waiting outside to take me to the moon."

I step back into the dressing room just as Mia throws her hands up into the air. "I'm trying to warn you."

"And I'm telling you I appreciate your concern, but I can handle myself."

But despite my words, my mind begins to spin, grasping at anything from our conversation today that could prove Mia's theory to be true.

"I've known Rocco a long time. I know he seems approachable, charming even. But there are parts of him that he will never share with you. Parts that are too dark for you to ever dream of fixing."

"I'm not trying to fix him."

"Then what are you doing with him?" Mia snaps at me. "Because despite my best efforts, you still have that asshole of a boyfriend breathing down your neck every ten seconds."

Exhaustion washes over me at her words. It's so late, and work will already be hell tomorrow if I have to face Danny and Teresa again. "I'm tired, okay? Can we drop this?"

"I'm just trying to look out for you."

I offer her a small, incredibly grateful smile. "I know."

She returns it, and we both head back out into the club. It's strange to see the space lit up and empty, like some kind of soulless shell, compared to how much life is usually crammed into every corner.

I wait by the door as Mia finishes locking up, and we both step out into the brisk night air.

Bracing myself for the long walk ahead, I shove my hands deep into the pockets of my leather jacket. "I'll see you tomorrow?"

But when I turn back to wave, Mia is staring at me.

"How are you getting home?"

"It's fine, Mia."

"I thought you said you made tips yesterday."

I shrug, not wanting to add more fuel to the fire that is the Cassandra-pity-party.

But Mia sees right through it. "I'm not letting you walk back to Brownsville. It's four a.m.."

"I said it's fine!"

"Quit being stubborn and take this," she says, marching over and shoving a couple of bills into my hand.

I grimace as I look at the three twenties she passed to me. "I don't need your charity."

"Then pay me back later," she insists. "I will not be able to sleep tonight if you don't get home safe. And you don't want to see what happens when I have to run a shift on under eight hours of beauty sleep."

I offer her a weak smile. "I don't deserve you."

"Then keep trying to." She gives me a stern look before turning away. "Text me when you're home, okay?"

I wave at her retreating figure and let out a long breath.

It has been seventeen years since I was last in Brooklyn. In that time, the streets have become nearly unrecognizable. Still, I'm able to find a cab within a few minutes after helping a group of party girls to the nearest fast-food chain.

The cab ride takes thirty minutes, and I have to fight with each passing second not to fall asleep.

Claudio's home is in an apartment complex on the wrong side of Brownsville. Seventh floor, no elevator, and a new type of stench emanating from his neighbor's door every time I pass by.

Still, it's more than I can afford while trying to save up for a place of my own.

When we left Ohio, Claudio told me I was welcome here. All I needed to do was keep the space clean, and what was his was mine. But I think a part of me always knew I needed a backup plan, just in case the worst were to happen.

Like if he were to suddenly decide I owed him seven thousand dollars worth of rent.

I shake off the sense of despair and switch on the lights. Claudio is still out, as he promised, leaving me to assess my life in the cold light of the fluorescents.

My new reality is far from the comforts of my family home in Ohio. Claudio has little interest in creature comforts like a bed frame or a dish rack. Everything lives in piles. Piles of plates, clothes, take-out boxes.

I don't have the energy to deal with any of it, so I wander mindlessly to the bedroom and sink into the mattress.

Closing my eyes, I will sleep to take me quickly.

But something keeps nagging in the back of my mind.

"What would happen, do you think? If you broke up with him?"

Lose my job, probably. It's the one good thing to come out of this mess, besides being able to reunite with Mia after almost two decade's worth of a long-distance friendship.

Claudio's face flashes through my mind—the expression

he wore when he thought something might have happened between Rocco and me. He'd hurt me again, that was for sure.

But what if...

What if there was someone who could protect me from his wrath? Someone who seemed more than willing to put Claudio in his place. Someone with the power to do that and more.

Mia's warning rings in my ears.

It's a stupid, ridiculous idea. I'd likely be giving up one kind of prison for another.

But the thought lingers, and sleep continues to evade me.

And Claudio should definitely be home by now. I check my phone for the hundredth time. Nothing except the "goodnight" message I received from Mia an hour ago.

Six a.m. rolls around, then seven a.m. I sit up in anxious frustration. The sun will be rising soon, and there's only one club that keeps its doors open twenty-four-seven for people like Claudio Lazzaro.

I check my wallet and count up Mia's remaining cash as I make the call.

"One taxi to *Electrix,* please."

5

ROCCO

"Claudio Lazzaro is in the private party room on the second floor," Teo confirms over the phone.

It hadn't taken Teo long to find him. In fact, I half suspected he might have been waiting for me to crack down on this asshole for a while.

"Any company with him?"

"You don't want to know."

I don't miss the way Martino grimaces as he pulls us up to the security gate of the staff parking lot. "Are you sure you want to do this?" he mutters.

With a long, drawn-out sigh, I glance up at the monstrosity that is Brooklyn's *Electrix*.

"Not really," I answer honestly.

The *Electrix* was one of the only successful things to come out of my father's reign as the Guild's don. But only because its vast halls quickly became a playground for some of Brooklyn's most notorious criminals.

He had no qualms about harboring some of the most vile cretins this city has ever endured. In fact, Giuliano

Moretti catered to them specifically. Three floors drenched in the worst kind of sin, all dressed up as the most elite party location this side of the bridge.

If I had my way, I would have burned it down the second my father retired. But there are some parts of his legacy that even I can't touch.

"I can always get some of the boys in to smoke him out," Martino offers. "You don't need to concern yourself with personally upholding our bylaws."

"You know how much I love to make a statement." We step out of the car at the same time. "And Lazzaro is just begging to be made an example of."

"Still, this kind of thing is a little below your pay grade."

If Martino wanted to be pedantic, he might also mention that our by-laws only concern the spouses of Guild members, not angelic little girlfriends. But neither he nor Teo have tried to point that out since I explained what I saw at the *Candelabra*.

"Well, shit," Teo's voice suddenly sounds out on speakerphone.

"Problem?"

"Lazzaro is on the list."

Martino curses loudly at my side. "I'm gonna bury Giuliano six feet under."

My father's retirement had been an act of unprecedented bureaucracy for the Guild. It would have been far easier to have just killed him, as many of my father's lieutenants had advised me to do as soon as I came of age.

But I'd wanted to make a statement, start a new chapter in the Guild's torrential, violent history of succession. So that one day, my son wouldn't have to kill me in order to claim his inheritance.

In the end, forcing Giuliano Moretti out had only taken five years to accomplish, and it had required a long list of demands that included preserving the *Electrix* and, apparently, Claudio fucking Lazzaro's employment.

"There's no way around it?" I'm aware I sound desperate. But that bastard is within arms reach, and I've been itching to make him pay ever since I saw those bruises on Cas' arms.

And, if I'm being honest with myself, that's the real reason I'm here. Statement or not, I couldn't sleep when all I could think about were those hazel eyes begging me not to make a scene.

How could anyone even…I can't even bring myself to think about it without white-hot rage coursing through my veins.

"If you're buying the coffee, I might have something in forty-eight hours," Teo admits. "I'd have to comb through every report he's ever made over his decade of employment….see if he's ever messed up enough for us to make something stick."

"And beating up his girlfriend isn't good enough?" Martino growls.

"Not unless she's willing to come forward."

We stand in sullen silence as the music inside the club seems to taunt us.

"I can't fire him. I can't kill him. I can't beat his sorry ass," I say into my phone. "What can I do?"

"Beyond talking to him? Sweet nothing."

I glance over at Martino, who shrugs right back—his eyes gleaming mischievously.

"Good enough for me."

"Rocco, don't…"

I hang up on him, much to Martino's amusement.

We're at the doors a moment later, pushing past the line of disgruntled partygoers who have likely been standing in line all night.

I waste no time admiring the crush of bodies in the main hall and make my way up to the second floor. As decadent as it appears to be—the building was modeled after ancient Greek temples—the pillars here are hollow, and the stonework is merely manipulated styrofoam.

When we reach the illustrious "party rooms" upstairs, we head toward the staff corridor around the back. Though bare and sterile, it offers a back door into each of the private rooms for discreet package delivery—a hold over from the previous don, who liked to run meetings and handle deliveries here.

"Boss?" Martino calls out when we're halfway down the corridor, gesturing toward the two-way mirror a few doors down.

I approach with no small amount of trepidation.

Lazzaro. Sprawled out on the pleather couch, he watches two girls dance before him. All are in various states of undress—and sobriety if the lines of white powder on the table are any indication.

He fumbles lazily at his crotch as the movements of the girl closest to him become more lurid. His tongue licks up her neck and a manicured hand slips down into her lacy white panties. I notice a lipstick stain over her bare nipple.

They all approach Lazzaro, swaying their hips as they go. Hands immediately stroke over his chest, his arms, his...

I finally see their faces. I don't bother knocking. I just kick down the door.

Danny and Teresa scream in shock.

I straighten my suit. "Martino. Make sure no one disturbs us."

"Rocco! Baby, please. It's not what it looks like," Danny runs up to me as she desperately tries to put her clothes back on.

I recoil when she tries to touch me. "You don't owe me an explanation. You can fuck whomever you like. We're over."

"You don't mean that, come on." She shoves her head through what I assume must be Lazzaro's T-shirt. "Claudio said you came to the *Candelabra* tonight. You came to see me."

Her words reek of desperation. It never mattered how beautiful she was, how perfectly symmetrical her features were, or how beautifully she sang; it always came back to the desperate desire to be more, to have more, to be wanted.

She was always desperate for something I would never be able to give her.

"Let me be very clear." I step further into the room. The blood pounding in my ears intensifies the closer I get to that bastard Lazzaro. "We are done."

"Rocco, please." Her eyes brim with tears.

I tell myself it's for her own good. That I'm saving her further heartache down the line. Because if she was worth my affection, I would be in an unstoppable rage right now. And I'm not.

"I'm not here for you."

My words finally seem to connect. She backs away into the corner to where Teresa seems to be consoling herself with another line of coke.

My vision narrows the second I set my eyes on Lazzaro.

"Moretti!" he slurs, not bothering to sit up. "Come to join the party?"

I can't help myself. I grab him by the shoulders and pin him up against the wall. Glass smashes as his legs wildly kick a table over.

"Lemme...lemme fuckin' go!"

"You know why I'm here, Lazzaro?" I hiss in his ear.

"No."

My first pounds into the wall, mere inches from his head. The plaster cracks, and blood trickles from my knuckles, but I don't care.

"Think very fucking hard."

To my surprise, Lazzaro's hot breath hits me as he utters a low laugh. "Your daddy isn't going to be very happy about this, you know."

I let out a warning growl, but Lazzaro only laughs harder.

"It's all right, ladies," he calls over his shoulder. "He's not going to hurt me. He's not allowed to."

"You think my father will go back on five years of work over your pathetic ass? You're fucking delusional."

Lazzaro squirms so he can look me in the eye. "But you're too proud to be the first one to break that little treaty of yours."

Maintaining my grasp on rational thought takes every ounce of my concentration. Because the truth is somehow even more infuriating than this entire situation.

This cowardly piece of shit is right. My father would do anything to get himself back into power.

I let Lazzaro go, and his body slumps to the floor with a satisfying crash. By the door, Martino looks over his shoulder, shooting me an expression that can only mean, *If you don't fuck him up, I will.*

With a shake of my head, he stands down. There has to be a better solution here. I just need to think clearly for one goddamn minute.

"This is about Danny, isn't it?" Lazzaro grumbles. "She wanted to be here."

"That's not true!"

Surprisingly, it's Teresa who holds her chin up defiantly as she shouts the words. Behind her, Danny seems to have entered some kind of shocked fugue state.

"He said if we wanted to keep our spots on the show, we had to…"

"SHUT UP YOU LITTLE BITCH!"

Claudio launches himself at her, crawling across the floor with surprising speed.

I take no small amount of pleasure in stepping on his outstretched hand. The custom metal heel of my Italian leather shoes breaks bone at an agonizingly slow pace.

Claudio's screams soothe something in my very soul.

"You know that I can't remember the day you swore your loyalties to my family," I muse. "Mustn't have been particularly important to me."

Sweat and tears pour from Claudio's face. "I'm loyal to your father, you bastard!"

"But you must know the bylaws you swore to uphold? About protecting our own? Ringing any bells?"

"Fuck you."

"Perhaps I give you too much credit. From where I'm standing," I press my foot down harder for emphasis, "you don't seem like a particularly literate fellow, so I'll spell it out for you."

Something snaps under my foot again, and Claudio's eyes roll back into his head. I sigh in frustration as I step away to grab a glass from the side and chuck the dark liquid in his face.

He wakes up again with a start. "W-what?!"

"Unfortunately for you, coercion and battery aren't things we tolerate in the Guild."

Claudio blinks away the sticky alcohol and looks up at me. "Battery?"

"You might think you're untouchable, but mark my words: you're a dead man walking if you don't clean up your act." I spit on him for good measure. "Do I make myself clear?"

He wipes at his face as he tries to sit up. "I didn't...coerce her."

"You may want to choose your next words very carefully."

"Danny," he pleads with the woman in the corner, who is still seemingly in a catatonic state. "Danny, tell him."

But Danny doesn't even raise her head from where she's been staring at the floor.

Claudio turns back to me. "We've been together for months. I...thought you knew, man."

Months. The word drops into the endless pit of my stomach like a stone. The entire time we'd been together...

A voice that sounds eerily like my father's echoes through my mind. *A real don wouldn't stand for this.*

It doesn't matter whether I can muster up any kind of jealousy about Danny. Now this was a slight against my name. Against my leadership.

I kick him in the ribs. "I demand satisfaction."

Kill him.

I could. It would be so easy. I'd probably enjoy it, even savor it. But...

But. Five years of torment and negotiations would crumble over something like this.

You spent so long wanting to play this part, but now you're on the world stage, you don't have the balls to do what needs to be done. You're weak, Rocco.

I shake away my father's voice. I can't focus with him in my head like this.

"C-Claudio?"

My heart stops as I turn to see a figure at the door. Somehow, she's even more beautiful than I remembered, despite the fact she's swapped out the devastating black dress for sweats.

I harden my heart as I look away from her. "This does not concern you, Miss Cassandra. Walk away."

"You've hurt him."

I can't bear how startled and disappointed she sounds, as if she might have once thought better of me.

Well, it's better to rip that BandAid off now. I suppose it was only a matter of time before she ran away screaming.

"Wait, wait!" Claudio croaks from the floor. "You...you want satisfaction? Take her. Take her for the night."

6

CASSANDRA

"You offer your girlfriend up to me on your behalf? You spineless fucking coward."

My mind reels at the scene before me. A man the size of a damn house is blocking the back exit. Danny and Teresa are cowering in the corner. Claudio is on the floor, half-undressed, clutching his disfigured hand to his chest.

And Rocco...

Any doubts I had about Mia's claims vanished at the sight of the man before me. Gone was the charming billionaire that I drank whiskey with earlier.

This man was murder incarnate. There is nothing else behind those gray eyes as he looms over Claudio as if he is calculating the most excruciating way for him to meet God.

I know at that moment, I should have taken the opportunity to run. I should have run before my fear had a chance to catch me in a chokehold. I'm frozen with terror, afraid to move or speak.

"You demanded satisfaction. She is my peace offering," Claudio half-grunts.

"You do not speak for her." Rocco's voice is like ice slicing across my skin.

Something must have happened. Claudio must have gotten himself in trouble with the mob, and now Rocco has come to collect what he's due.

I want to scream at Claudio for being such an idiot, for even thinking he was smart enough to outwit someone as dangerous as a powerful man in the Italian mafia. A thousand questions bubble up within me, but sheer terror keeps them all down.

"Ask her then," Claudio cries. "She'll do it, won't you, darling? She loves me."

It takes an embarrassing amount of time for the pieces to come together. *Take her for the night,* he'd said.

He wants me to sleep with Rocco to atone for whatever he's done.

Are you *fucking* kidding me?

That too-long dormant flame of anger within me roars to life, spreading through my body and burning through the numbness that had taken its place. For the first time in what feels like months, years even, I feel true anger.

Deep, wounding, unchecked anger.

And it feels so damn good.

"She won't do shit for you," Rocco growls, taking the words right out of my mouth.

I want to destroy Claudio. Completely and thoroughly, for taking an innocent girl from her hometown, for seducing her with promises of fame and fortune, for belittling her, gaslighting her, and *stealing* from her from the moment she arrived.

My embarrassment is nothing compared to the rage roaring joyously through my veins.

"What would happen, do you think? If you broke up with him?"

Mia's voice of reason grounds me. I need to be smart about this, or else I risk losing everything. Which is a surprising consideration when you have nothing to begin with.

"I'll do it," I say before I can talk myself out of it.

Everyone freezes and turns to me.

"Have some self-respect," Teresa mutters.

But I ignore her, staring only at Rocco, registering the confusion that flashes across his expression as he shakes his head. "No," he says, his voice quiet, almost pleading. I don't take the time to ponder why he sounds like that. I'm too angry.

I put my chin in the air. "I'll do it."

"See? She's fine with it," Claudio says from the floor.

Rocco kicks him, and I try my best to keep my face neutral. But I can't hide from Rocco. His eyebrows raise slightly at the sight of my concealed glee.

Please. I have a plan. Please. Trust me, I try to beg with my eyes.

He doesn't owe me anything, so there's no reason for him to agree to this. I have nothing to offer him beyond my gratitude. We might have flirted earlier, but we don't know each other. And he might well be the most dangerous person I've ever met.

It says something about my current situation that I am eagerly considering someone from the mafia to be my best hope of salvation.

"Are you sure?" he asks me softly.

Relief washes through me as I nod.

Claudio exhales when Rocco steps away from him. Not breaking eye contact with me, Rocco steps forward and holds out his hand.

To pull me out of a mess of my own creation.

When our hands touch, it's like nothing I've ever experienced before. The fire brimming within me cries out to his. Like calling to like.

"You will not lay a hand on another woman. Do you understand me?" He's addressing Claudio, but he holds my stare like it's somehow tethering us together.

"Crystal clear."

Vaguely, I'm aware of Claudio keening in agony as Rocco leads me from the room. But it's hard to concentrate on anything beyond the man before me as we pass the giant man at the back entrance and walk down the sterile corridor.

After a moment, Rocco pushes open another door, and we find ourselves in an identical room to the one we were in before. Only this time, we are entirely alone.

"Despite what I might have implied earlier, I am not in the mood to fuck you tonight, *Angioletta.*"

I snatch my hand from him, moving as far away from him as I can to prove my next words. "I only wanted an audience with you. I swear."

He looks at me incredulously, and I realize just how much he was masking over drinks. There is little kindness in his eyes anymore, and violence seems to simmer under his skin to be called upon at his leisure.

He's a predator through and through, assessing me with sharp instinct to determine the kind of threat I might pose to him.

No, I'm not a threat to him. I'm his prey.

"You have about thirty seconds to explain before I go back in there and toss Lazzaro out the window."

I swallow and take a second to steady my racing heart. "Are you a part of the Italian Mafia?"

He blinks at me in surprise before that crooked grin spreads across his face. It still makes my stomach flip despite the danger so evident in his eyes.

"Oh, Miss Cassandra. I *am* the Italian Mafia."

The terror his words evoke is enough to silence me for another moment.

Mia is going to fucking kill me.

I swallow my pride anyway. "I need your help."

"Didn't your father ever warn you about making deals with the devil?"

His words sting more than he can ever know, and I have to look away so he doesn't see the tears pricking my eyes.

"Please. I don't know what Claudio did to you to deserve all this, but if you want to bring him to justice...I think we can help each other."

Rocco tilts his head with unnerving speed. "You want us to work together?"

"I have nothing to offer you," I explain quickly. "I came to Brooklyn on Claudio's word and live with him at his discretion. I'm under contract to perform at the *Candelabra* until my dying breath, and if I try to leave him, he'll..."

My voice snags at the words, but I can see that Rocco understands, probably already knows by the way he glances down at my arms, concealed once more by my father's leather jacket.

"I need a way out," I declare, sounding more confident than I feel.

Rocco takes a casual step forward. "And you think losing you would be a good enough punishment for everything he's done?"

I meet his eyes with determination. "No. But it's a start."

Something akin to feral delight falls across Rocco's face. "You know, there are some things that fall outside my remit."

"Make an exception for me," I push, but stagger back into the wall as Rocco continues his approach.

"Now, why would I do that?"

The wall at my back feels like the only thing holding me up. "What do you want from me?"

His eyes slowly drop all the way to my feet and rise up again. When they return to my face, they are somehow darker. "Many things. But I am not in the business of coercion, Miss Cassandra. I want my women to want me so I can make them beg for it."

My mouth goes dry.

I had planned for him to demand money, or a favor I would be scared to grant. But his suggestion makes me think there might be something else I'd be more than willing to give.

"And if I did?"

"What?"

"Want you."

One moment, he's standing before me, the next, he's pinning me against the wall by the neck. His long, tattooed fingers grab my chin and force me to look up at him.

"Don't tempt me, *Angioletta*."

We're too close. Breathing hard against each other like this is almost unbearable.

"I'm not going to fuck you," he whispers across my skin, and my eyes almost roll back into my head. "Because you are not a currency that I exchange in, as mouthwatering as you are."

His leg brushes up against mine, his bare forearm rubs against my neck, his damn fingers are so close to my lips.

I should be terrified, sobbing, pleading with this man. This is a man who is more than capable of leaning down on my windpipe and suffocating me right now. I'm completely at his mercy, and yet my traitorous body only aches with desire.

The idea should appall me. I should feel shame as my sex throbs between my legs. But even if fucking him won't win me my freedom, I'm a slave to my carnal impulses. It's almost as if the entire world is fading away around me.

All that matters is the man pressing into me.

"Please," I whisper back. "I just want your help."

His gray eyes dart to my lips and I can feel his heart race in his chest. Is he as affected as I am? Does he feel the electricity buzzing beneath my skin?

"And I'm prepared to give it," his voice rumbles, "but I will not indulge in this little fantasy of yours just because you think you owe me something."

I should be relieved, but I'm not. I should thank him and walk away now. He's agreed to what I wanted. But this isn't some little fantasy; this is pure, unfiltered desperation. I don't just want him to touch me. I *need* him to.

And despite his own words, he doesn't move.

He just stares as if he is transfixed by my lips. A war seems to rage within him. His breathing is jagged as if he's physically trying to hold himself back.

In a small, logical part of my mind, I realize why. He sees me as vulnerable—someone who needs his help. Giving in would be to take advantage of me.

But this has nothing to do with what he can do for me and everything to do with my near-feral need for release.

With a sudden surge of confidence, I drag my tongue across my bottom lip.

"Would you like me to beg?" I whisper as flames seem to erupt in his eyes.

He growls out his restraint, and I realize something with terrifying clarity.

He might be the don of the Italian Mafia. He might hold my life in the balance. But at this exact moment...

I'm the one with the power.

Without looking away from him, I turn my head, taking his finger into my mouth.

Rocco goes deathly still. His eyes watch my every movement as my lips slide up and down, letting his finger glide over my tongue. I savor the taste and show him exactly how much I'm enjoying myself with a groan.

I watch as the sound causes Rocco to unravel before me. Pain, lust, helplessness, wanting, hunger, darkness. His head leans closer, and for a moment, I think he might kiss me.

But he presses it into the wall by my shoulder, closing his eyes. "Cas."

Emboldened, I pry his arm from my neck and take his unoccupied hand in both of mine.

I want to see how far he's willing to go, how far I can push this. There's no other thought in my mind other than thinking about all the ways I can make him lose control.

I need him to see me as I am, not as some scared little girl begging for help, but as a woman completely drowning in my desire.

"Touch me," I whisper as I guide his hand across my

body. His finger snags on my nipple as it passes over my breast.

The sensation is so tantalizing I let out a short gasp.

His eyes snap open. "No."

I don't stop. I take his hand further down my body. If he could just feel the wetness pooling between my thighs...

Suddenly, he pulls his finger from my mouth, and both his hands capture mine, pinning them above my head. "Not like this," he growls in my face.

His lips are so close to mine that I can feel his every breath.

"When I have you, you won't be trying to bargain for your life."

I can barely hear him over the pounding in my ears. He's not negotiating with me; he's telling me.

But whatever future moment he's imagining feels too far away. "I want you anyway."

I feel his wince because we are so close. "I'll take you somewhere far away from this hellhole and worship you properly."

It's as if he's trying to convince himself along with me. Nothing has ever felt more terrifying than the prospect of him walking away right now. I feel like I would do anything, say anything, to make him stay.

"Then take me," I beg. "Worship me now. I'm right here." He shakes his head, and my words become desperate. "I want you so fucking badly."

He hisses. "Cas."

My name on his lips sounds more like a promise than a warning.

"If you don't, I'll have to pleasure myself. Or better yet, I'll go next door and see if..."

I realize a moment too late the impact my words have on his resolve.

His head dips to my neck. The sensation of his lips grazing the sensitive skin there has me arching my back, pressing myself into every inch of his body as lightning seems to shoot through my veins. If I cry out, I don't hear it as I succumb entirely to him.

It's better than anything I could have imagined. My nerves seem to be on fire as my desire ricochets through my body at lightning speed, igniting parts of myself that I never even noticed before.

It's all so wrong. So, so wrong. And yet so unbearably right.

Suddenly, he holds my wrists with one hand as he pushes my stomach back into the wall with the other. The sting of rejection is soothed over by the flick of his tongue against my neck.

"Rocco," I hear myself breathe as I tremble beneath him.

His hand slips further down my stomach, dipping beneath the band of my pants toward the place I had just been longing for him to touch.

Every part of me rejoices—screams to get what it wants.

"Please."

I almost sob in relief as he finally reaches my soaked sex, caressing me with surprising gentleness as my mind begins to transcend to another realm of existence. It simply isn't possible to feel everything I'm experiencing right now.

Teeth bite into my skin as Rocco's finger plunges into me. Once. Twice.

A climax immediately begins to build within me, fuelling itself on every groan that escapes his mouth. I long to taste it, want to feel his lips on mine as he coaxes my orgasm out with his long, sure fingers.

"You're so fucking wet for me," he growls against my neck, and all I can do is moan in response.

A thumb slowly circles my clit, and stars erupt across my vision. I curse loudly as my body responds involuntarily, driving his hand further into me. It's not enough, and yet it's more than I can handle.

I need him to know, need him to understand. "Look what you do to me."

I turn my face, searching for his, desperate for the kiss that will send me over the edge…

Then he's gone.

It's like a bucket of ice-cold water has been chucked onto my flaming body. My legs buckle beneath me as I slide to the floor, panting heavily.

"I don't want anything from you for this," he grunts as he straightens himself out. His gray eyes refuse to meet mine, and the rejection hits me like a bullet train.

"I'm going to help you because it's the right thing to do. Not because you opened your legs."

I swallow back the tears that threaten to spill. How could I be so stupid? He must think I'm just some slut willing to blow him for a favor. I want the floor to swallow me whole.

"I'm sorry," I whisper.

"Don't be," his voice bites out, rough and more forceful than I've heard him. "This is my fault. You have my oath. I will help you leave Lazzaro. I won't touch you again."

"You're…"

"Be ready for my next move and lay low. You likely won't have time to gather any personal possessions."

His eyes linger on my neck for a moment before he turns

away toward the door. An unreadable expression masks his face.

"Wait!" I cry, and he mercifully pauses. There are a thousand things I want to say, but all I can muster in my current state is "Thank you."

He doesn't respond. He merely pushes open the door and disappears into the fray of the *Electrix*.

7

ROCCO

It took Teo forty-eight hours to get the information I needed. Then, another twelve for me to put a plan together.

Every second that passed was its own kind of torture. I tried not to imagine what Claudio might be doing to her, what lies she had to come up with in order to follow my instructions.

Lie low.

I should have sent the entire Guild after her right then and there. I should have stayed myself to make sure she was safe.

But a second longer confined in that room with her would have been my undoing. I wouldn't have been able to stop myself from doing something we would both regret. My own frustration has been the root cause of my torment these last two and a half days as it is.

I keep thinking of the bruise on her neck that *I* gave her.

I've never hated myself more. I'm no better than that

scumbag, Lazzaro, marking my territory like some kind of animal.

"You can still back out," Teo murmurs.

I turn to look at the man by my side. He's a brother in every sense besides blood.

"After all this effort?" I reply lightly. "Why would I do that?"

The VIP table at the *Candelabra* is adorned with additional perks this evening. I reach over for the decanter of whisky we've been slowly sharing all evening and pour us both another glass.

"Because if I have to sit here and watch you torment yourself over it for another second, I'll call it off myself."

I can't help the smirk that twitches the corner of my mouth. Trust Teo to see right through me.

We were children together, friends before we knew the implications of our allyship— just two underbosses taking on the world, side by side, with outrageous plans to join our two families to create the ultimate underworld empire.

I still consider Teo to be my equal, even if the rest of the world does not.

The fire that killed his parents took everything that was left of his birthright. His people scattered to the wind in fear. I still remember the day a shaggy-haired boy appeared on our doorstep, begging for sanctuary.

He's hardly a boy anymore. My eyes run over his long, shaggy brown hair that is now pulled back from his face in a disorderly bun.

"I didn't realize you cared."

"The Guild may have agreed that action must be taken," Teo warns, "but your father is still in the dark. Who knows how he might react."

I hide my grimace by taking a sip of my whiskey. "Remind me how much he owes the Guild?"

It had been the early hours of the morning when Teo had discovered that little tidbit about Lazzaro. Hidden under mountains of bullshit, he learned of a loan taken out from the Guild that should have been paid back a month ago.

"One hundred and twenty thousand dollars," Teo doesn't need to double-check his notes; his memory is more than sufficient. "One installment of twelve thousand dollars was made three days ago. One installment of seven thousand was made two days ago."

I do the math. "Leaving one-hundred-and-one thousand."

"I'd be more comfortable if we knew what he had taken the loan out for," Teo insists for maybe the fifth time. The paper trail of Claudio's transactions had ended with a cash withdrawal of all one hundred and twenty thousand dollars.

"Coke? Hookers? A personality transplant?" I offer humorlessly.

"In cash?"

"We've got him, Teo. That's all that matters."

It was enough to get the lieutenants to agree, at least. They'll have my back if my father tries to use this as an excuse to back out of our treaty.

As if summoned by our discussion, Claudio Lazzaro himself appears on the stage before us, one arm strapped to his chest in a sling.

"Ladies and gentlemen! Please give a round of applause for Miss Cassandra!"

He gestures stage right as Cas appears, head bowed as

she strides toward the mic next to him. I don't miss the way she recoils from his attempt to kiss her cheek.

For a moment, the moron just stands there, baffled by her audacity, before storming off backstage.

"Good evening, everyone."

Behind me, someone drops a tray of glasses. I glance over and see Mia staring at Cas with bulging eyes, completely ignoring the carnage at her feet.

I'm staring, not at the bruise on her neck that has tormented me these last two days, but at the matching one under her left eye.

I don't realize I'm standing up until Teo drags me back down.

"I'm going to end that motherfucker."

"Rocco," Teo hisses.

"Let's keep the lights up tonight, shall we?" Cas simply smiles as she adjusts her mic. If she hears my outburst, she doesn't let on as she launches into her first song.

But when I finally tear my eyes away to look at my friend, it's to find my anger reflected back at me.

Suddenly, someone grabs my collar and pulls me backward with a sharp jerk.

"Listen here, Your Majesty. I don't care what it costs me. You go back there and kill that bastard," Mia hisses in my ear as a kitchen knife presses threateningly against my neck.

Honestly, this woman terrifies me more than my father.

"Stand down, Chiavari," I hiss right back. "We're already working on it."

Mia slowly lets me go.

"Take a seat."

She slips into the chair next to Teo, offering him a curt nod. "Princeling."

"Wench."

He holds out his hand, and she rolls her eyes before resentfully handing over her weapon.

"What's the plan?"

"I need you to clear out the office upstairs," I tell her, although my eyes wander back to the stage.

"Do you want me to lay out the tarp?"

Teo answers for me. "We can't kill him yet. But Rocco has a plan to get her out, at least."

"Give me my knife back, and I'll do it myself!"

"He's on the list, Chiavari," Teo explains. "Our hands are tied."

"I'll make it look like an accident."

"Mia," I tear myself away from Cas' performance to intercept the redhead's warpath, "don't complicate things for me. That's an order."

Her green eyes narrow, but I see the resignation in her eyes. Despite all her bravado, I'm still her don.

"Make sure they're both upstairs at the end of the show. Don't leave her alone with him."

"Never again," she mutters her agreement as the three of us watch in sullen silence as Cas finishes her song.

As the room erupts in applause, Mia takes her leave—only to hesitate at my shoulder. "You mess this up, you hurt her…I will tear both of you a new one."

With that, she saunters back into the crowd.

"Remind me why we put up with her again?" Teo murmurs.

"Her father has single-handedly funded the Guild for decades?"

"I'm starting to think it's not worth it."

We spend the rest of Cas' performance slowly nursing

our drinks and trying not to watch the clock. By the time she announces her final song, I'm already on my feet.

Teo is only two steps behind me as we stride across the room toward the staircase. A nod from Mia is all the confirmation we need—the office is clear, and no one will be disturbing us tonight.

When Mia appears at the door ten minutes later, Cas and Lazzaro are in tow, and her face is set into a grim line of determination.

I've taken the time to make myself comfortable behind my desk, leaning back in the ancient leather seat with practiced ease. Teo lounges on the couch by the fireplace, feigning disinterest as he palms through one of the bookcases' many tomes.

I try not to stare too openly at Cas, but I appraise her anyway. She's still in her performance outfit, so there may still be additional damage hidden under that leather jacket of hers.

"Mister Moretti," Lazzaro greets me tightly, and I tear myself away.

"Lazzaro. Why don't you take a seat?"

He alone walks forward to the single chair in front of my desk. When he realizes Cas hasn't followed, he snaps his fingers at her.

Mia takes a step further into the room.

"Miss Chiavari," I say firmly, "would you mind closing the door on your way out?"

The look she gives me could level a building, but she obeys regardless, shooting her friend one last, desperate look before clicking the door shut behind her.

"I trust our...arrangement the other night was to your

satisfaction?" Lazzaro has the nerve to ask as he makes himself comfortable in the chair.

Cas drifts awkwardly to his side, the bruised side of her face turned away from me.

"Quite," I offer him a tight smile. "You're a lucky man, Lazzaro."

He has to believe I'm doing him a favor. It's the only way to prevent him from taking this straight to my father. My plan only works if Giuliano is kept in the dark for as long as possible.

Even if it means I look like an even bigger asshole, I have to play the part to get Lazzaro to trust me. Which means I have to speak his language.

"I like to think so."

I gesture carelessly in Cas' direction. "Do you find yourself particularly attached to her?"

"What do you mean?"

"Since Danny is no longer of any use to me, I'm in the market for an upgrade. And after her...performance the other night, well. I must say I'm impressed."

Both of them stiffen at my words, and I can't bring myself to look at Cas for fear that my mask will completely crumble.

"You want Cas?"

"On a...trial basis, really." I shrug. "Perhaps I can sweeten the deal for you?"

Lazzaro stares at me as if trying to decipher my next move. "What kind of deal?"

"Claudio," Cas' voice cracks as she tries to protest.

That fucking scum bastard.

"I've recently been informed that you took a loan from the Guild a few months ago."

Claudio's head snaps to where Teo is lounging, and he glares at him.

Teo waves back merrily in return.

"You owe them money?" Cas whispers in horror.

It dawns on me that there is a very real possibility that Cas has no idea that Lazzaro is a part of the mafia. That, on top of everything else, he's lied to her about the nature of his employment.

Would Cas have even followed him to Brooklyn if she'd known? Probably not.

It's an unfairly bitter pill to swallow.

"After your recent payments, you're down to one hundred and one thousand."

"I'm aware," Lazzaro answers through his teeth.

"I'm glad to hear it," I smile again. "Because at this very moment in time, I find myself in a forgiving mood."

Claudio blinks as he begins to understand what I'm getting at.

Still, I keep nudging him along. "Teo, what's the interest rate on loans from the Guild?"

"There isn't one," he replies promptly.

"And why is that?"

"Because there aren't any late payments."

Perhaps the most effective banking system in the world. The threat of death tends to keep prospective borrowers away. Mia's father, Chiavari, makes that abundantly and terrifyingly clear.

The fact that Lazzaro has gone so long without making a repayment is a massive anomaly—one that speaks to a corruption that goes far deeper than the few factions that defected when my father retired.

To have even pulled this off, Lazzaro would have needed an accomplice within my inner circle.

"How interesting."

Despite Carmine Bellini's insistence that he was the only rat trading secrets with the Cartel, information is still getting out from somewhere embarrassingly high up the food chain.

So I don't think it's a coincidence that both these things are happening at the same time. In fact, I'd be willing to bet my life that the second rat and Lazzaro's accomplice are one and the same person.

We just need Lazzaro to slip up and lead us to them.

"You're due to make your final payment next week, aren't you?" I lie.

The date I'm referring to was taken from the forged loan agreement Teo initially dug up. The original expired over a month ago.

"Yes," Claudio plays along gratefully, and it feels a bit like leading a lamb to slaughter.

I pick up the fountain pen at my side and examine its opal exterior with disinterest. "Given my forgiving mood and the fact you have something I desire, I would like to make you an offer, Claudio Lazzaro."

Claudio sits up a little straighter. "All right."

"I will strike off your remaining one hundred and one thousand dollars...in exchange for a hundred and one nights with your darling Miss Cassandra."

8

CASSANDRA

"You've got to be fucking joking."

The words explode from my mouth before I can stop them. Even Teo looks up from his book to stare at me in surprise.

How was this the best idea Rocco could come up with? Trade me for Claudio's debt? It's hard to feel relieved that he kept his word when the solution is somehow far more revolting than the problem.

"Miss Cassandra," Rocco begins, but I don't let him finish.

"I'm not some kind of commodity you can barter for!"

"Cas," Claudio glares at me. "Don't speak to him like that."

But I ignore him, too enraged to mind my tongue.

"What happened to, '*She won't do shit for you*'?" I mock his words from the other night, hoping to strike a nerve. "What happened to condemning coercion?"

Rocco merely watches me, amusement dancing across his stupidly beautiful face as he twirls the opal fountain pen across his fingers. "And here I thought you were willing to beg for it, *Angioletta.*"

That stupid, stupid, stupid nickname sends a pang of longing through my entire body. As it has done every waking second we've been apart.

Even in my dreams, I find myself back in that room, imagining all the things I'd let him do to me if only he hadn't stepped away. I imagined all the desires he would whisper in my ear that I would, oh-so-willingly, beg to fulfill for him.

It might have been the only thing that kept me sane as I fell asleep next to Claudio, who had hit me the second he noticed the bruise on my neck.

I'd endured all of it, the names he threw at me, the pain, to fulfill my side of our bargain. To lay low until Rocco announced his intentions.

But when I look at Rocco now, I see that alluding to what happened in that room serves another purpose than just pissing me off. It reminds me of the oath he made.

Both not to touch me again and to free me from Claudio.

"Or was I mistaken?" He asks with a pointed look. He may as well have said, "This is your last chance to back out".

I might not like his methods, but the fact remains. He's trying to help me.

And I need to play my part.

I let color flush my cheeks as I look back at Claudio. "I never said that."

"You slut," he snipes back.

It's not the first time he's said it these last few days, but it still makes me wince.

From the fireplace, the sound of paper ripping tears through the moment.

"Sorry, am I interrupting?" Teo asks innocently as he discards his book and pockets the page he ripped out.

Out of the corner of my eye, I notice Rocco sweeping something into the trash can by his feet.

"As charming as this little exchange has been," Rocco snatches our attention right back, "I have places to be. Lazzaro, you have my offer. Cassandra, should he accept, can I presume you will be as agreeable as you were the other night?"

I have to bite my tongue while I formulate an appropriate response.

"I only agreed because Claudio was in trouble."

"And he's going to be in a lot more if he doesn't make his payment next week."

I look up at Claudio, pretending to try to discern what he wants me to do. "Will you make the payment, darling?"

Claudio doesn't look me in the eye when he replies. "No."

Though it sickens me to my very core, I reach for his hands. "Claudio, if I need to do this, I will."

He snatches them away before I can touch him.

"She would need to keep working," Claudio declares, all but sealing my fate.

Rocco tuts. "I'm afraid I can't allow that."

"What?" I say, my voice a few octaves higher than usual.

"Cassandra will be joining me on a trip out of town," Rocco announces before examining his nails and refusing to elaborate.

My teeth grind together. What exactly is he playing at?

Claudio, for once, seems to agree with me. "The *Candelabra* will be missing an act."

"Things were operating just fine before Cassandra arrived. I trust you'll be able to manage without her."

"So what, you'll fuck her for three months and then hand her back to me like a used-up plaything?"

Rocco goes deathly still. It's the only telltale sign of his anger. "Are you really willing to lecture me about secondhand goods, Lazzaro? May I remind you that what I'm offering may well be the difference between your miserable life and a miserable death?"

An old kind of fury rears its ugly head within me at their words. It burns bright and hot as I will myself not to interfere, not to protest the way they're talking about me, as if I'm not even here.

I almost break at the look on Claudio's face.

He's not angry, or sad, or even scared. He looks speculative. Hopeful even.

"And you will write off the entire debt."

"On the condition that she stays with me until the hundred and one days are up."

Claudio shakes his head in disbelief. "You really want her that badly?"

Rocco looks over at me carelessly. The way his eyes rake over me feels so dangerous. He's exposing his feelings completely, and displaying his intentions for the world to see. "I think the real question is, do you want her enough to deny me?"

I swallow hard, knowing in my heart what Claudio's answer will be.

"Mister Moretti, I accept your offer."

And the tiny shred of hope that Claudio would even try to fight for me completely dies. I feel foolish for it, for even thinking he was capable of being half the person he pretended to be when we first met.

But that sweet, attentive man who whispered about the wonders of the world in my ear had never even existed.

Hell, I don't have any idea who he is anymore. If he's been running the *Candelabra* on Rocco's behalf, taking sizable loans from this "guild", there is a very real possibility that Claudio has been a part of the mafia himself from the very beginning.

Was everyone at the *Candelabra* somehow involved with this? Danny and Teresa had been there the other night, too.

My blood runs cold.

Mia.

No, she wouldn't have lied to me...would she? Yet she knew about Rocco and warned me to stay away from him.

Which means, at the very least, she knows about all of this. She knows who Criag is, too, and said nothing to me.

How many more lies will I have to endure from people who were supposed to love me back?

A hand gently grabs my neck, and I realize I must have been spiraling for at least a minute.

Claudio hunches over the desk, signing some kind of paperwork, and Rocco...Rocco is standing behind me. His thumb gently strokes at the parting gift he left me the last time we were together.

"Don't be upset, *Angioletta*. You're in safe hands now."

I want to laugh loudly and bitterly. What does safe even look like to a mafia don?

"Come," he says simply as he leads me to his seat behind the desk. "You must be tired of standing."

It's only when I've sat down that I realize my legs are shaking.

All of this is really happening.

"It's done," Claudio announces, slamming the pen on the desk.

"Excellent."

"What shall I do with her things?"

Rocco nods toward Teo. "Someone will swing by to pick them up."

Claudio nods back as he just stands there awkwardly. "So that's it?"

"That's it."

The asshole has the nerve to look relieved.

"So I'll see you in a few months, Cas?"

I gape up at him. The reality of what he's just done is setting in hard and fast. "That's it? That's all you have to say to me?"

"Cas..."

"You just sold me to the fucking mafia, you dick!"

"You wanted this."

"I wanted YOU," I scream. "I wanted YOU to fight for me. To even just pretend that you loved me as much as you claimed to."

I launch myself over the desk at him, only for Rocco to catch me by the waist. "I think that's your cue to leave, Lazzaro."

"I'M NOT FINISHED!"

But Claudio turns his back on me anyway, stepping out the door without even a glance over his shoulder.

"GET BACK HERE YOU COWARD!"

"Cas. It's okay, it's over." Rocco's voice is so gentle that he barely sounds like the same person he was a moment ago.

"He...he just left me."

"I know. I'm sorry."

Heavy tears fall freely down my face as the exhaustion sets in.

"What would happen, do you think? If you broke up with him?"

I didn't think it would feel like this. Like someone had been excavating a hole in my chest, only to remove the debris in one brutal blow. I feel lighter, but I also feel like I've lost something vitally important.

"I have some things to attend to." Rocco falls into the chair in front of me, looking about as tired as I feel. "Teo will take you to the safe house. I trust him like a brother. No harm will come to you."

"Fine." I stare down at my lap, and something pale catches my eye.

"I also feel like I should apologize in advance for this."

"For what?"

The last thing I see before the blindfold covers my eyes, is the two halves of a snapped, opal fountain pen lying at the bottom of the trash can.

I WAKE up somewhere entirely unfamiliar.

Vaguely, I remember how I got here. I remember how Teo had to all but carry me down to the back exit of the *Candelabra,* how I sat silently blindfolded in the back of a car before promptly falling asleep.

Someone must have roused me when we arrived, but they didn't remove the blindfold until I entered this room. The last thing I remember was the welcome sight of a mattress with an actual bed frame before I collapsed.

Slowly, I rouse myself and wince at the headache that's

beginning to form behind my eyes. I almost cry at the sight of a glass of water on the bedside table.

I finish the entire thing before I remember that I'm in a mafia safehouse and that drugging the water would be a very mafia-like thing for someone to do.

I'll have to be more vigilant from now on.

I turn on the bedside light and look around for a clock. When I come up empty, I slowly get to my feet to approach the window, which is hidden by a set of drawn curtains.

The material is thick and heavy in my hands as I pull the layers apart, capable of shielding away the brightest summer's day.

But it's dark when I look outside at the residential street of brownstone homes. I must still be in New York at the very least, but beyond that, I have no idea where I am.

I climb onto the deep windowsill to peer down below. There's pavement a few floors below, but no one seems to move beneath the streetlights.

It must be late then, which makes sense, since my internal body clock has more or less adjusted to the *Candelabra's* nocturnal shift patterns.

Not that it matters anymore.

Knock, knock, knock.

He doesn't wait for me to respond before opening the door.

But Rocco doesn't enter. He simply leans against the doorframe, letting the moonlight wash over his tired features as he watches me cautiously.

Even now, with his suit jacket discarded and his sleeves rolled up to his elbows, he looks unfairly beautiful. The tattoos that climb up his arms tell a hundred stories that I will likely never learn, and his thick hair falls dangerously across his eyes.

"I saw your light was on."

Was he just waiting up for me? Or does he have one of his goons stationed outside my door?

I instinctively go to bury my hands in my jacket, before it registers that I'm now wearing a set of cotton pajamas. I flush at the thought of Rocco undressing me.

As if reading my mind, he says, "My housekeeper, Donatella, thought you might be more comfortable in those. You'll meet her tomorrow."

"Okay." I don't move from my perch as I stare at him expectantly.

He clears his throat. "If you need anything while you're here, she will be able to sort it out."

"Aren't you going to fuck me every night for three months and then hand me back to Claudio like a used-up plaything?"

My bitter words make the Mafia don flinch. "I'm sorry you had to hear all that. This is, unfortunately, a delicate situation, and I needed Lazzaro to give you up without too much protest."

"Well, I'm glad your little secret mobster mission was a huge success."

He stares at me. "You're upset."

"I'm tired. There's a big fucking difference."

"Then rest." He straightens himself up and reaches for the door handle. "I'll be away tomorrow, so you'll have the house to yourself."

"Wait, this is your house?"

The ghost of a smile creeps onto his lips. "I told you,

Miss Cassandra. The protection I offer is notoriously unparalleled."

9

ROCCO

"I take it your little intervention with Claudio Lazzaro went well?"

Marco Chiavari fell into step at my side as I marched through the compound.

As a child, I had been quite afraid of his stern demeanor and unflinching ability to cut to the heart of any conversation.

But over the years, I've come to respect the older man a great deal, and not just for his iron-clad hold of the Guild's finances and generous personal donations to the cause.

Or his fiery-haired daughter, who'd been a pain in my ass since she could speak in complete sentences.

"Transfer the money from my personal account. His debt is settled."

I turn the corner, heading toward the meeting room at the end of the corridor, but Marco grabs my arm to pull me back.

"I had another look at Lazzaro's loan documents," Marco speaks so quietly that his thick mustache barely moves.

"Oh?" I keep my face as neutral as possible.

If anyone could dig up the truth about Lazzaro besides Teo, it would be Marco. But as a member of my inner circle, I couldn't share my plan with him. Not if there was even the slightest possibility he could be the rat.

"Someone forged it. The original expired a month ago."

"Is that so?"

Marco blinks as if suddenly seeing right through me. "You knew about this?"

"If you continue that line of thought to its natural conclusion," I reply softly, "You'd realize I would have to have a very good reason for not telling anyone."

"Claudio Lazzaro has made a mockery of my life's work," he growls back.

He's deadly serious, too. Marco doesn't mess with money.

I take him in for a moment, considering. The thought of Marco willingly bending his rules for someone like Lazzaro is, in fairness, laughable.

So far, only Teo and I know of the plan to flush out the rat. Martino might have picked up a few things on a need-to-know basis, but aside from that, I was up against the entire Guild's lieutenants alone.

Another set of eyes could be a valuable asset.

"I imagine there would only be a few behind that door over there," I point to the meeting room. "With the knowledge to be able to accomplish something like that? It's funny how information seems to be leaking out everywhere these days."

Marco stares at the meeting room door, cogs almost visibly turning beneath that salt-and-pepper hair. "You think it's the rat."

I shrug before pulling away down the corridor. "Let's circle back to this later, shall we?"

He doesn't reply until I reach the meeting room door.

Someone wolf whistles as soon as I walk in.

"Here he is!" Alessandro croons as he balances on the back legs of his chair. "Today is the day to put in your requests, folks."

"You sleep well last night, boss?"

"Hey, could I borrow a hundred? There was this girl I was chatting with at the bar last night..."

I roll my eyes as I approach the seat at the head of the table. "All right. Enough."

"He's in a good mood."

"Glad you're finally getting laid again, man."

"I said, enough!" My voice carries through the room.

The twelve other people around the long, rectangular table fall into an obedient silence.

Everyone except Alessandro, who mock whispers across the table to Marco. "Is it too late for him to get a refund?"

I glance over at Martino, who's taken his usual position standing at my back, and nod.

In one swift movement, the giant man kicks out Alessandro's chair from under him and smashes his head into the table with a satisfying crunch.

"Anyone else?" I survey my inner circle with a bored look.

No one dares meet my eye as I give the order for Martino to let go. Alessandro curses under his breath as blood begins to trickle down his nose.

"You're on thin ice after that little mischief at the docks," I reply to his unasked question. "Try not to piss me off, please."

Alessandro grumbles something about only ever seeing two bikes but thankfully shuts up.

"Since it's already public knowledge, I can confirm the negotiations with Lazzaro were concluded yesterday. Marco is in the process of rectifying the accounts."

Marco merely nods his confirmation.

"I'm sure the *Candelabra* will be very grateful to him for not sending his daughter out to make good on the repayment."

This earns me a few good chuckles, and whatever tension was in the room fizzles out.

I quickly turn to other matters, pleased that many seem to have already moved on from the Lazzaro issue.

Having them believe I would actually do something like pay off a man for his girlfriend doesn't feel good. The fact so many of them had barely battered an eyelash when I'd brought it to them a few days ago was even more concerning.

But strangely, it wasn't my reputation I was worried about.

Claudio's little outburst in the negotiations had me inches away from snapping the fucker's neck. Instead, my nice opal fountain pen had paid the price.

But glancing over at Alessandro and some of the others at this table, it was clear their opinion of Cas was barely worth remarking on.

The words they use to describe her, what they believe she's doing to me behind closed doors, makes me want to beat them all bloody.

The only thing worse is that voice in the back of my head that wants nothing more than for me to go home right now and take her, taste her, consume her, exactly like they're all imagining.

I focus on Marco's financial report to try to calm the boner that is threatening to make its presence known.

"Move forty million into the off-shore," I offer my input. "I'd like to move on the new real estate project this month."

I note the approval in more than a few eyes. My plans to create a new club venue could very well make the *Electrix* obsolete within a few years. Then we can destroy those private rooms for good.

Where I had pinned Cas against a wall and allowed the reins of my restraint to slip. Where those perfect lips had gasped my name as I'd indulged myself, however briefly, between her legs.

That night, I hadn't slept until I had gotten myself off to her lingering lemon and chamomile scent, hating myself in the aftermath.

Because I know, logically, that she is in a very vulnerable position. The way she retreated into herself after Claudio signed that fake contract was a testament to that.

The last thing she needs is a pervert like me trying to take advantage of her just because all logic seems to dive out a fifty-story window whenever I'm around her.

"I got some bad news and some more bad news."

I refocus as Teo, sitting on my right side as usual, takes the proverbial floor.

"The Cartel intercepted our shipment yesterday before we could secure the South African package."

Tobacco. A partial payment for the luxury goods we'd offered them last month. A useful commodity, but a bulky one in large enough quantities. And the South Africans had wanted a lot of handbags.

"All of it?"

Teo nods grimly.

"How did they even pull that off? There must have been at least four shipping containers."

"That's the worst news," Teo replies. "The Cartel pulled off the heist before the ship had even docked."

A disgruntled murmur begins around the table. "Could the South Africans have screwed us over?"

I shake my head. "No. Dante saw the shipment off personally. He's traveling back to the US as we speak."

"Then how the hell did they know it was coming in?"

"One of Rubio's underlings squeaked about something interesting a few days ago," Alessandro speaks up for the first time since he'd managed to get his nose to stop bleeding.

I brace myself for his next words.

Amos Rubio commands an admirable amount of respect from his Cartel. Which unfortunately means the most effective way to get anything out of them is through a more hands-on interrogation.

Though knowing Alessandro's preferred methods of extraction, it might be more appropriate to call it a hands-off approach. Nails and fingers were often the first to go missing.

"Said 'only Rome can topple Rome'."

A silence falls across the room as the implication sets heavy upon our shoulders.

Teo, God bless him, breaks it. "Technically, I think the Germanic forces toppled Rome."

"Save it, Teo."

"I'm just pointing out that the Cartel might not be as clever as they think they are."

"Yet they keep landing their blows time after time."

"Information has to be getting out to them still."

"How is this still happening?"

"I thought Carmine was the informant."

"But what if he wasn't? Or if he wasn't acting alone?"

"Great, so there's another rat."

"Probably in this room."

I stand up, slamming my hand on the table. "I will not let a dead man sow discord among us."

"What did Carmine say to you that night at the docks?"

I turn to look at the woman sitting at the opposite end of the table. So far, she hadn't contributed at all to the meeting, but she had a habit of making people listen when she did speak up.

"Not a lot." I match her icy gaze.

Her silver hair ripples as she shakes her head. "Perhaps you should have prevented him from blowing his brain out."

"I'm glad you feel confident offering this adVitale retrospectively, Esther."

The lines on her weathered face pull into a cruel smile. "Your father would have acted with greater wisdom. Maybe Giuliano would be a valuable consultant on this issue."

"Bold of you to undermine your don at a time like this." I let her see the wrath boiling behind my eyes.

"Who's sowing discord now?"

The challenge in her voice has those around her murmuring nervously.

I only have a second to make a decision.

Esther is an older player with a well-known distaste for the Cartel—rooted in a cruel combination of racism and ignorance. She doesn't fit the profile of our rat, as much as I would like to pin this on her.

And yet, this isn't the first time she's called me out on

this. She'd been one of the last to agree to my father's retirement conditions and she was the oldest member of his previous guard.

She believes herself to be untouchable, and that's a very dangerous thing.

"I'd like to thank you for your years of serVitale here." I bow my head with the little respect I can muster. "But I believe I have become weary of your council."

"You wouldn't dare."

I nod at Martino once more. "Please have your son briefed ahead of our next meeting; I wouldn't want him to fall behind."

Esther takes one look at Martino's approach and begins to screech. "You can't. I'm on your father's list."

"Giuliano Moretti holds no power in this room." I let authority reverberate through my words. "Any suggestion otherwise is an insult to the Guild. Let this be a warning to all."

Martino, ever a better man than I, gives Esther the option to see herself out.

It's almost comical how everyone watches the door slam behind her, then wearily turns back to look at me.

I sigh. "Your concerns about another leak are valid. However, I will not tolerate any finger-pointing or whistleblowing in this room. I offer you all the same courtesy you gave me when I became your don. Trust."

I make sure to look them all in the eye before continuing. "We will continue to interrogate the Cartel for more information. Until then, remain calm and vigilant."

"You might have just solved the problem by kicking the old hag out," Alessandro mutters.

I give the others a moment to register his words. Let them think that they're safe again.

"If there's nothing else, you all have places to be."

10

CASSANDRA

The next time I wake up, the sun is already past its peak.

I blink around my new room, registering all the details now illuminated in the light of day.

Besides the door Rocco entered through last night, there are two others in each corner. The walls are tall, decorated with intricate molding, and the wooden floor is intermittently broken up by thick carpet.

The entire space feels extravagant, and yet its neutral tones are impersonal. A guest room, perhaps?

How often does a Mafia don host polite company?

But my musings are cut short by a rasping on the door.

I have the urge to pull my bedsheets over my chest. "Come in?"

But it's not Rocco who enters.

A tiny woman gently pushes the door open. There's a tray of what appears to be breakfast balancing on her ample hip and a determined look on her surprisingly youthful face.

"It's about time you get up, ma'am." Her British accent catches me off-guard.

"You must be Donatella."

"Charmed, I'm sure." She unceremoniously drops her tray on my bedside table before hurrying to fling the curtains open. "Eat something, please."

Bemused by her curtness, I examine the veritable feast she's laid out before me.

"How long has it been since…" Since my so-called boyfriend signed me away to a mafia don. "Since I arrived here?"

Donatella has to climb onto the windowsill in order to reach the window latch. Her efforts are rewarded with a delightful breeze entering the room.

"Couple of days, give or take."

My stomach rumbles in confirmation.

As if hearing it too, Donatella chastises me, "Eat."

I don't wait to be told again as I help myself to the pastries, jams, and fruit before me. I even enjoy the English Breakfast Tea, despite never having been partial to it before.

I focus on all the textures in my mouth, anything to distract myself from formulating a thought beyond satisfying my seemingly insatiable hunger.

When I finally lean back from my meal, it's to find Donatella examining me.

Feline, I think, is the best way to describe her. I can almost imagine her tail flicking around in discontent. Only, she's shaped more like a chubby little housecat than a panther or a lion.

"I should have woken you yesterday."

I'm not entirely sure how to respond to that, so I just shrug instead.

"I'll run you a bath," she decides a second later, turning on her heel to approach one of the other doors in the room.

It reveals a large en suite. A free-standing bath sits with pride in the middle of the room, seemingly already stocked with more toiletries than I could use in a lifetime.

I slide off the bed to take a closer look. "What is this place?"

"Mister Moretti's brownstone." Donatella raises her voice over the sound of the running water.

"I figured that much out for myself, thanks." I regret the snark in my tone as soon as Donatella shoots me a glare. "I meant, how big is it? Are all the rooms like this?"

"If you behave, I might give you a tour later."

I ignore her and leave the bathroom to examine the final unopened door in my room.

I'm not sure why I'm surprised to find a fully stocked walk-in wardrobe. I think my room alone is bigger than Claudio's entire apartment.

As I explore, my hand reaches out to touch the soft sleeves of the seemingly thousands of coats that hang in the closet.

"Four floors, three bedrooms, five bathrooms, and a gym," Donatella's voice chirping voice says behind me. "One of his more modest homes."

I raise an eyebrow at that. "So this isn't his only place of residence?"

Perhaps Rocco won't be staying here after all. I'm not sure why I suddenly feel so disappointed by this. If anything, he would only make things more complicated for me.

"It's his only home in Brooklyn. His mansion in South

Africa is my personal favorite. But the villa in the Canary Islands is also right up there."

Right. *Billionaire* Italian don. How could I forget?

"Your bath is ready," Donatella announces without missing a beat.

With one last longing look at the unexplored wardrobe, I follow the housekeeper back into the en suite.

The refreshing smell of lilac fills the air as bubbles waft romantically from the free-standing tub. But I hesitate before taking another step forward, giving Donatella a pointed look.

"Nothing I haven't seen before, love," she mutters but turns around anyway.

Still, I feel my cheeks flush as I quickly strip down and step into the near-scalding water. The instant relief I feel as my shoulders slip under the surface almost makes me groan aloud.

Between being bedridden for several days and the stress of the last week, my shoulders were now incredibly grateful for some TLC. I stretch out my toes, content to just close my eyes and soak for a little while.

Except someone dunks their hands in the water and begins scrubbing at my hair.

"Excuse me?" I splutter out just as another wave of water is dunked on my head.

"You need a thorough clean," Donatella replies simply as she selects a bottle of the vast array of products around us.

"I can wash my own hair."

Donatella snorts. "Evidently not if you've not been able to get out of bed for two days."

"This is unnecessary."

"Mister Moretti disagrees."

I cross my hands across my chest self-consciously. "Unbelievable. Where does that fucker get off?"

Water splashes into my eyes. "Not another word about the don. He may be demanding, but his heart is in the right place."

I want to scowl at her petulantly, but I'm too afraid to open my eyes again. "Tell me about him."

"What do you want to know?"

"How long have you worked here?"

"That's not a question about him."

I remain stubbornly silent until she lets out an exasperated sigh. "Over twenty years now."

"How old were you when you started?" I ask in disbelief.

"Probably about the same age as you."

I finally find the bravery to crack open an eyelid and turn toward her to examine her youthful face.

At my expression, she cracks a smile. "Unlike some, I actually bathe every day."

But her smile fades as her eyes drop to the tops of my arms. Something dark crosses her eyes as she looks back up at me. No, at my bruised cheek.

"I have some Arnica cream downstairs. I won't be a moment."

Without another word, she slips out of the room, finally leaving me alone.

With nothing but my thoughts.

I desperately try to organize them into some sense of coherency before they completely overwhelm me again. The truths are the easiest to identify.

Number one, Claudio Lazzaro is the worst thing that ever happened to me.

Number two, I made a deal with the devil in order to get away from him.

Number three, there's a good chance everyone around me is a part of the Italian mafia.

Number four, I have no job and no source of income.

Number five, Rocco Moretti is the most attractive man I've ever met.

Despite everything else, all the chaos of the last few days, it's that final point that snags in my mind the most.

How could a man who didn't even exist to me a few weeks ago become so instrumental in not only my livelihood, but my every waking thought?

From the moment we met, I'd felt that strange allure, been helpless to his flirtations. I'd even considered what it might have been like to give in to him before any of this had even happened.

But where did that leave us now?

Perhaps I was always a piece of a larger plan to him. Maybe he had been orchestrating getting me to leave Claudio from the start. Perhaps that was his way of drawing a line in the sand and pulling me over it to stand next to him.

Maybe that night at *Electrix* had meant nothing to him. Maybe it was just a perk of the job to be seduced by someone so willing to give herself over. Maybe he had his fill when he sank his teeth into my neck and felt my desire between my legs.

My own fingers drift beneath the water at the memory.

The memory of his breath on my neck still sends shivers of pure, animalistic lust down my spine. I imagine his lips trailing over my skin as he reaches up to my ear, biting at my lobe. In my mind, his hand rubs across my chest, and my nipple pebbles under his touch.

"Angioletta."

I touch myself as I imagine his voice whispering in my ear. The warm bathwater is an unnecessary lubricant for my already-soaked core.

His devastating eyes, the way his hair falls across his face. The way his strong, tattooed arms held me in place like they were capable of lifting me entirely off the floor. If he hadn't stopped, would he have fucked me against that wall?

I imagine it now as I work myself harder, the way he would have teased me with his fingers, bringing me to the brink of orgasm but ultimately denying my pleasure.

How I would have waited, desperate and dripping, for him to pull out his cock, thick with his own desire. I would have begged for it, cried for it as he lined himself up to my core.

How I would have screamed when he thrust into me, oh so fucking hard. Again and again. And again. As my pleasure would have built and built and...

How his lips would have finally, finally met mine...

I tremble as my body finds its feeble release. My fingers are a poor imitation of my own imagination, but at least it does something to relieve the pressure that had been building within me since that night.

In the clarity that follows, I step out of my bath and drain away the water, sweeping my sinful thoughts down the drain as well.. A cold shower soothes my flushed skin, so that by the time I walk back into the bedroom in my towel, my heartbeat has returned to normal.

Donatella enters a moment later with an excessively

large first aid kit, blissfully unaware of my transgressions, and levels mea serious look on me.

"Is there anything else, aside from the bruises?" she asks, assessing me head to toe.

I just shake my head as she hands over a tube of cream.

"Apply this as often as you nee.; It will speed up the healing process."

"Thank you," I say as I glance at the large first aid kit as she packs it up. "You know how to use all that?"

"I trained as a nurse before I stepped into housekeeping."

Right. "I guess that's normal for mafia housekeepers."

"It comes in handy from time to time," her clipped tone tells me I shouldn't push it. "Mister Moretti isn't prone to injury, however."

"Just his enemies, right?" I reply bitterly.

Outside the soothing bathwater, the crushing reality of Rocco's true identity is harder to ignore. He might have saved me from Claudio, but he's still a mafia don.

How many people has he killed? How many lives has he ruined? Behind his flirtations lies someone deadly, lethal, and emotionless, capable of an unknown number of atrocities.

He isn't a good person, and I am completely and utterly out of my depth.

"You act as if he could escape this life," Donatella says as if reading every thought in my mind. "As if he wasn't reared from birth to fulfill this exact purpose. You could no sooner ask a tiger to change his stripes."

"Is that supposed to make it all okay, then?"

She looks at me through narrowed eyes. "The underworld will always march on. It's better Mister Moretti is at the helm than anyone else."

I want to laugh at her. "So he's a good employer, huh? Does he steal from the rich and give to the poor? Does he send flowers to the wives and children of the men he murders?"

"You don't know what you're talking about."

"I know that he's a criminal. I know that he trades in human lives," I snap back.

"He saved you from a far worse fate."

"To further his own means."

She gives me a long look that I can't quite decipher. "I wouldn't be so sure of that."

"What are you talking about?"

But Donatella merely shakes her head. "Get dressed. If you want a tour, I'll only wait outside for five minutes."

With that, she marches away, her first aid kit in tow.

For a moment, I just stand there contemplating whether it would be worth getting back into bed. But annoying Donatella won't win me any favors, and if I'm honest with myself, I'm more than a little curious about what the rest of the house looks like.

After a too-short browse of the walk-in closet, I manage to find a matching pair of dark and far too lacy underwear, a comfortable pair of jeans, and a pale blouse that does little to disguise the color of my bra beneath.

As I exit, Donatella's eyebrow quirks up at my appearance.

"Next time, give me a little longer to change," I snap at her.

"Compared to that little dress you arrived in, I was actually thinking you look rather composed." She gestures down the hall. "Shall we?"

Natural light pours in from the windows as we walk the corridor, and I catch a glance of myself in a large ornate mirror hanging from the wall.

Despite my hair still drying down my back, I'm surprised to see that Donatella is at least a little bit right. The dark circles I'd become so used to seeing beneath my eyes have subsided, and my outfit seems surprisingly coordinated against my olive skin.

I follow behind Donatella with a small smile as she shows me through the doors that flank us on both sides.

Everything about this house feels regal, though it rarely breaches gaudy or impractical. The gym is perhaps the most impressive room in the house. I haven't been able to afford a membership since I moved here, so I take in the expensive equipment with interest.

"When I arrived," I say after Donatella finishes showing me around the extensive kitchen, "I had a leather jacket. My phone was in my pocket."

Donatella pushes through another door. "Your jacket is hanging in the closet in your room. I believe Mister Moretti has your phone."

We find ourselves standing on the second level, at the top of a set of princess staircases that lead down to the main foyer.

I turn back to her. "Will I ever get it back?"

"Mr. Moretti will be back soon," she replies, not really answering the question.

My shoulders slump. "Let me guess, he wants to control how and when I use my phone. Like he's done with everything else."

Donatella opens her mouth to speak but seems to freeze up suddenly.

"I'd appreciate it if you wouldn't use that tone with my staff, Miss Cassandra."

I whirl around in alarm to find Rocco standing below us by the front door.

That crooked smile flashes despite the fact that his shirt is covered in blood.

11

ROCCO

I could absolutely get used to coming home to that face, even if her expression is a delightful combination of alarm and disgust.

"Are...are you..." Cas seems to choke on the question as she stares at my chest.

I glance down. Ah.

Rubio's underling had needed a little more convincing than I'd anticipated. A shame, really. I quite liked this shirt. "If it's any consolation, the blood is not mine."

Her face immediately hardens. "Monster."

My carefree expression masks the jolt of pain at her words. In the cold light of day, there is no way I can hide my true nature from her anymore, and it's clear she isn't pleased with what she's found.

Instead of addressing her, I turn to Donatella. "Set the table for two tonight. I would like Cassandra to join me for dinner."

"Absolutely not."

I raise an eyebrow at her. "Perhaps I didn't make myself clear. You *will* join me for dinner."

Something about my tone seems to infuriate her. Fire dances behind her eyes as she dips low into a curtsy, her pale shirt doing nothing to conceal her dark underwear beneath.

"My apologies, sir, I forgot my place! Would you like me to present myself entirely naked, or would you like the honor of unwrapping me yourself?"

Despite the sarcasm leeching through every word, my cock twitches at the thought.

"Donatella, please remind Cassandra that she is my guest, not a commodity?" I shoot Cas a warning look as I ascend the staircase toward them. "Despite what she might be so eager to think."

"It's hard not to think such things when that's all you seemed to care about when you traded me for my boyfriend's debt."

Finally, I reach the top of the stairs and can stare down at the defiant young woman before me. "I'm offering you the opportunity to negotiate your own terms, *Angioletta*. I suggest you take it."

I allow myself one blissful moment to soak in her closeness. The fresh scent of her still-damp hair almost floors me.

"Or what? One day, you'll come home with my blood on your shirt?"

At her side, Donatella tuts under her breath but doesn't intervene.

"I did as you asked, Cassandra. You may not like my methods, but they were effective. Now, you can either spend the next months sulking around this house, resenting me for it, or you can join me for dinner to discuss how you'd like to proceed."

Though she doesn't break eye contact, I watch her swallow. "I want my phone back."

"Then I'll see you at seven."

I hold her gaze a moment longer, transfixed by the way her lips part just so.

But I force myself to turn toward my own room and close the door behind me.

I try not to think about her as I strip off my ruined shirt and step into the shower. Try not to imagine what she's doing, only a few measly walls away, as I don fresh clothing.

After the last few days of fruitless investigations, tensions were beginning to rise again in the Guild. Esther's departure had been an effective distraction, but it hadn't prevented the whispers and conspiracies for as long as I would have liked.

Right now, my best lead is Claudio Lazzaro. But in order to get to him, I now need something from Cas.

Which is perhaps the most terrifying part of this entire operation.

I wander down to the dining hall that evening with a clear strategy in mind. Get Cas to agree. Leave her alone. Simple, effective. It's how I would deal with anyone else.

But as the minutes tick by toward seven p.m. with a brutal disregard for my previous instructions, my confidence falters. Perhaps giving her a choice in all this is the wrong move.

My father wouldn't have hesitated; he would have locked her in the bedroom as soon as she'd stepped into it.

I pour myself a large measure of whiskey as his voice scolds me for being too soft, for allowing myself to care what she thought of me. For the sake of the Guild, I needed to turn off my emotions and do what needed to be done.

"In my defense, I'm late because Donatella forced me to wear this stupid dress."

I look up to find Cas standing awkwardly at the door. And my brain seems to short circuit.

It's just a dress. The one she wears on stage is far shorter. But for some reason, the way the dark green fabric wraps around her body, flowing out at her shoulders and around her shins, makes my mouth water.

It hugs her every curve perfectly, and one pull at the string tied at her waist would have the whole thing unraveling. Unwrapping her.

I need to have a word with Donatella.

"Take a seat." I gesture to the chair at the far end of the table. A precaution in case my lesser instincts get the better of me.

To my dismay, Cas takes one look at the chair and drags it to my side. "I'm not shouting at you across the table all night," she insists stubbornly.

I distract myself by waving to the kitchen staff as her knee brushes against mine. Dinner arrives seconds later, giving me a perfect excuse to position myself as far away from her as possible.

It's a simple carbonara, adorned in truffle and seventy-two-month-aged parmesan. But she barely considers the dish before attacking it with her fork.

I watch her, bemused. "I take it you slept well?"

She glowers back. "Out with it, then."

"With what?"

"Whatever offer you're about to make me. Spare me the rhetoric about not being able to refuse."

I don't let her see my amusement. "I would like you to stay here."

"Aren't I already your prisoner until I've paid off Claudio's debt?"

"The deal was a farce." I place the fake contract on the table between us. "You are free to leave whenever you want. I only ask that you stay as a favor to me."

She gives me a bland look as she pulls the contract toward her. I watch as she notes Claudio's signature at the bottom.

"You can tear it up if it makes you feel better," I offer.

"What could you possibly have to gain from this?"

I have to bite my tongue from answering crudely. Instead, I take a gamble, one that I try not to think too hard about.

"I believe Lazzaro has been working with a senior member of my organization to…undermine me."

"Like a rat?"

I smirk. "Exactly. I need Lazzaro to believe that I'm… distracted so that he contacts the rat again without fearing my attention."

"You want Claudio to lead you to him."

"I hope that in your absence, he finds himself bored and resentful enough to try to undermine me again."

She thinks on this a moment. "Is that why you told him we would be out of the country?"

"If it's easier for you to lie low abroad, I can make that happen."

"But you'll be staying here to watch his movements."

I nod as I take a sip of my whisky, allowing her a moment to process my request.

"So I'd essentially be stuck here until you managed to

find whoever it is who's plotting against you? How long would that take?"

I offer her a small smile. "I promise you I will have it done within one hundred and one days."

"Ninety-eight nights left," she corrects me.

"Fine."

"And if you don't do it?"

I pour myself another glass. "Then our arrangement is over. You can go back to Ohio, and you will never hear from me again. The choice is yours."

She goes quiet for a moment before her chair scrapes against the floor. "I want to think about this."

As she begins to leave, a dull kind of ache spreads across my chest. I'm not sure when I make the decision to follow her, but I reach the door before she does and block her path with one lazy, outstretched arm.

Her infuriated expression is almost too endearing.

"I thought the choice was mine," she snaps.

Wordlessly, I reach into my pocket and pull out her phone. It was a bargaining chip I was prepared to hang on to for as long as I needed.

But it's the only thing I can think of that might make her stay, even for just another moment.

"Can I trust you with this?" I ask softly.

It might have been a risk to tell her about my plan to smoke out the rat. But this is borderline reckless. I can almost hear my father screaming at me to stop.

I don't know why it's so important to me that she trusts me, that she stops looking at me with that apprehension in her eyes. But if this small gesture helps alleviate that just a little bit...I can't help feeling that it might be worth it.

Tentatively, she reaches out with her hand to take it from me. "Yes."

All rational thought is telling me that the first call she'll make will be to the police. That I'm risking my unsteady alliance with the NYPD over this.

But as she matches my unblinking stare, it's not betrayal I find there. It's truth and determination. I could be an absolute fool for believing it, but...

Our fingers gently graze each other as I pass the phone to her. Is it my imagination, or do those beautiful hazel eyes flutter closed for just a moment?

"You are not a prisoner here," I reiterate. "I only ask that you help me as I helped you."

Cas looks away to pocket her phone. "I suppose there are worse vacation homes."

"You'd be welcome to stay in my South African home if you'd prefer," I offer, despite the traitorous part of my mind wanting her to stay close at hand.

Those bright eyes meet mine again. "Are you trying to get rid of me?"

"Quite the opposite." The words leave my mouth before I can stop them. I have to physically restrain myself from reaching out and running my hands through her dark hair. "Although I imagine it would be easier."

"I suppose having a random girl staying in your bachelor pad would ruin your reputation," she snarks back.

I shake my head. Always so fiery. It's been a long time since anyone dared talk to me the way she does. The trouble is that I've already discovered what it's like to draw out far more pleasing sounds from that perfect mouth of hers.

Sounds that only continue to torment me every second we're apart.

"I made an oath to you that night in *Electrix* that I would protect you from Lazzaro," I say slowly. "But I also swore I wouldn't touch you again."

Her breath catches at that. "As noble as that was, may I remind me that you grabbed me when you were trading me for Claudio's debt."

She's goading me; I know she is. But still, I step closer, unable to stop myself from demonstrating my next point. "That's not what I meant, and we both know it."

Finally, I allow my fingers to brush her hair back from her face. The way she absently leans into the touch makes my heart begin to pound in my chest.

"I didn't realize it was in a don's nature to exercise self-restraint," she counters, her voice quieter than before.

"It's not in my nature to take advantage of women in desperate situations."

She chuckles darkly. "You seem to think I'm incapable of making my own decisions."

"You really want to argue with me about protecting the best interests of a woman who was being beaten by her boyfriend and decided that begging the local don for help was her best course of action?"

Her eyes narrow at that. "You think I'm an idiot."

"I think you got dealt a shitty hand and took a calculated, if not reckless, risk," I allow. "But I don't think you're an idiot."

She searches my eyes for the truth, and I allow it to shine there.

Finally, she sighs. "If you want my help on this little operation of yours, you have to start treating me as an equal."

"All right, consider it done."

"I want to be trusted with any new information that you get."

I consider this. "At my discretion."

She takes a step closer to me, so close I can see the tiny glimmers of green in her eyes. "And if I want to get on my knees and put your cock in my mouth, you will get off your high horse and trust that it's a decision I'm making for myself."

I feel like something within me snaps in half at her words, knocking me entirely from my axis. *Angioletta,* I had called her. But perhaps *la ammaliatrice* was more fitting.

It's as if she was conjured with the sole purpose of tormenting me. Every movement, each sway of her hips or flick of her hair, those goddamn perfect lips, all beckon to me and tell me to dive head first off the cliff of my own self-restraint.

From her smirk, I know she can see the effect she has on me.

Well, two can play that game.

"Is that an offer, Cassandra?"

Her eyes narrow. "That depends."

"On what?"

"My discretion."

With that, she ducks around me and walks away.

12

CASSANDRA

"Cassy, I was so worried!"

My mom's familiar voice washes over me like a soft blanket, so far removed from everything else I've had to deal with this evening. It's almost jarring to hear it bouncing around the guest room.

"I'm sorry," I murmur into my newly-charged phone.

It had taken a while to convince Donatella to bring me the power cord, and even longer to scroll through the hundreds of messages Mia had left me. But finally, curled up in the safety of my bed, I'd hit the call button to talk to my mom.

"Mia said you just disappeared, and Claudio won't pick up the phone!"

I cringe a little at the sound of his name. "It's...we broke up, Mom. I'm staying with a friend for a bit."

The lie isn't an easy one, but there is no other logical way to explain myself. I suppose we had broken up; it wasn't as if our relationship could ever recover from him selling me to the mafia and me calling him out for being a coward.

Even if the words hadn't technically been said out loud.

"Which friend?"

Describing Rocco Moretti as a "friend" felt completely ridiculous. "Captor" might have been better, but I suppose after what I agreed to at dinner, "colleague" might be more appropriate.

Although aligning myself with the Italian Mafia was a surefire way to get my mother on the next plane to Brooklyn.

"I don't think you know them," I scramble for a name. "Donatella?"

"Is she looking after you?"

My mind flashes back to the near-screaming match we had over the dress I'd had to wear for dinner. "In her own way."

"I never liked that man. I told you that from the very start." Mom sighs. "You should come home. I can send you the money for the flight."

How different my life might have been if I'd only listened to her adVitale back then, instead of acting like a lovesick fool. "It's okay, honestly. Work is going well. I'm finally starting to get noticed."

By the Italian don wanting revenge on my boyfriend. I don't add that part.

"Cassy..."

It's the pitying note to her voice that gets to me. My eyes prickle with tears. I know what she's going to say next, even if I don't want to hear it.

"I know how much you wanted to meet your father."

I blink hard. "He doesn't have anything to do with this."

"Cas."

It had been the world's cruelest prank. I'd boarded that

plane to Brooklyn after seventeen years of wondering if I would ever know my father, only to arrive in his city, days away from meeting him again, and then to receive the news.

Carmine Bellini, died by suicide.

I couldn't mourn a man I didn't know. And yet, the news had been heavier than I had expected it to be. Perhaps that was because I'd been so close to finding out everything I had ever wondered.

Why had he let my mother go? Why had he never tried to contact me? Did he care about us? Did he think about us at all?

Was it his guilt that had killed him?

Was it somehow my fault?

It was part of why I'd been so quick to agree to Claudio's offer to come out here. But even that had backfired in my face.

"It sucked," I admit quietly to the only woman who could possibly understand the kind of grief I'm dealing with, "but he's just the man who gave me a bit of genetic material. You're my mom. That's all I need."

My memories of Carmine are spliced with photos my mom kept lying around. There's nothing solid or concrete to them at all. It's all just a haze of ideas and projections that I can barely grasp onto.

"I know, baby." My mother sighs again. "I'm just sorry that nothing is how you expected it to be."

She could say that again. "Listen, it's getting late. I just wanted you to know that I'm okay. I'll call you again in a few days, all right?"

"You just say the word, baby, and I'll fly out there."

"I know." I smile fondly at my phone. It's nice that some things haven't changed. "I love you."

"Love you too, Cassy."

An eerie silence falls over the room when I hang up. No sirens, no drunken revelers walking the streets, no tourists squealing outside my window. We may as well be a thousand miles away from Brooklyn.

Where the hell is this house?

I lie back in bed and try to settle into the quiet, desperate to ignore the demanding thoughts coursing through my brain.

I'd flirted with him. He'd asked for my help, and I'd offered to suck his cock.

What the hell was I thinking? I'd meant it as a joke...but...

Lying low to help out a criminal organization was one thing, but to make those demands had been a moment of sheer insanity.

Yes, I'd been worried about money. Yes, I'd been sick of everyone lying to me all the time. But all rational thought had apparently evaporated the moment he looked at me like...

Like I was something too precious for him to touch. As if my situation made me vulnerable and scared. As if he was somehow too honorable to besmirch my dignity.

The man who'd come home with another man's blood on his shirt. And made a *joke* about it.

The hypocrisy is almost baffling.

Every time I think about it, I come back to the question: where the hell does Rocco Moretti's morality lie? Because he simply can't be both the savior of broken women *and* the breaker of men.

Can he?

I groan as I toss over to my other side. Maybe I'm just

overcomplicating everything. Maybe he just wants me to play along with his little schemes without a fuss. Would he have really let me leave if I'd said no?

Where would I even go?

He had said Ohio. My mother wants me to go home. But do I want that? I've been here for two weeks, and it's already been two weeks full of more chaos than I've ever endured. Is it worth sticking around in the hope that one day I'll sing on that stage again?

That one day, I might know what happened to my father?

I shake the the thought from my mind and toss over again.

I got dealt a shitty hand, that's what Rocco had said. I played my cards, and this is the result. I got myself here, and now I won't be able to leave for the foreseeable future. That was my choice.

Maybe that could be a good thing. Maybe I should start trying to live with that.

Maybe I could stop pretending that Rocco isn't sleeping three doors down from me.

I'm not sure he has any idea what he does to me. I'm not sure I feel anything more for him than pure, carnal attraction. To my dismay, none of those feelings had changed as I watched him at dinner, despite everything I know now.

But if I have to sleep just down the hall from him for the next three months, it's going to take everything within me not to kick down his door impulsively and demand he make good on his threats to fuck me.

As if I don't have enough to deal with, trying to curb my rampant arousal whenever he's around is quickly turning into a full-time occupation. It's infuriating and so fucking frustrating.

My thighs squeeze together in the hopes of that pounding lust subsiding. But it feels so impossible.

Because he's right there. Right outside my door, down the corridor fourteen paces, the first door on the left.

Maybe I could just go and see if he's still awake.

Maybe I could just…

Fuck it.

I get out of bed and fly toward the door.

It's late, he's asleep. Nothing will happen. I just want to see if…

I stop dead.

There, standing in the hall, staring at my door, is Rocco.

The darkness masks his face, but I can see by the way his shoulders rise and fall that he's breathing deeply.

"Cas," his voice is low, almost gravely. "Get back in your room."

"Why?"

The tension between us thickens. That unspoken thing between us lashes out, hungry, predatory.

He steps closer, and a strip of moonlight illuminates his face. I almost gasp.

"Because I'm about three seconds away from pushing you through those doors and fucking you until you scream."

That look, that darkness in his eyes, spells only one thing. Everything seems to click in place. It's not just me. He feels it, too, is being driven mad by it.

It would take nothing at all, and the release that had been building within me for days would finally subside. I could finally think straight. I could finally…

"Then why are your clothes still on?"

The invitation is out of my mouth before I can talk myself out of it.

Rocco wastes no time. He stalks forward, arms encapsulating me as he picks me straight off the floor.

I gasp, not at the firmness of his touch or the electricity that seems to bounce off his skin, but at how hard his crotch is as it presses into mine. It feels so fucking good. My legs instantly wrap around his waist, pulling him in closer.

He hisses in my ear as he carries us back into my room, back onto the bed. He throws me down carelessly, and I whimper at the lack of contact with his body.

In the darkness of the room, I can barely make out his silhouette.

"You think you could just sit there in that fucking dress," his voice vibrates across my skin as his hands spread open my legs, "and torment me like that?"

I can't answer as his deft hands hoist up the skirt of my dress and begin to massage my inner thighs. I squirm under his touch, nudging him further toward the place I want him to be.

"Were you trying to lure me here, *Angioletta?* Is this at your *discretion?*"

His hands disappear, and I look for him frantically. A dark shadow looms over me as if he is contemplating exactly how he wants to take me.

I'd been too brash at dinner, antagonizing him like that. Now he's making me wait as some kind of cruel revenge.

"Please, Rocco," I beg the shadow before me. "Don't you want to feel how wet I am?"

I begin to rub at the thin material of my panties to prove my point, gasping at the delightful friction I can create with little effort.

Rocco slaps my hand away. It's a sharp movement that I barely have time to register before he's lying between my legs.

"Were you this wet at dinner?"

I can't think as his breath tickles along my thigh.

"If I'd dipped below the table, would you have welcomed me then and there?"

He nips at my upper thigh, and I yelp in pleasure.

"Would you have spread your legs like this for me?"

His teeth nip along my skin, closer and closer to...

"Fuck!" I gasp as he reaches my panties.

I shamelessly push myself into his face, quivering as his nose presses into me, as his hands reach around me to firmly grasp my ass, keeping me there.

I feel more than see his jaw move as he licks all the way up the soaked panties.

Nothing has ever tormented me like this before.

"Take them off," I gasp out once the stars have subsided from my vision.

"As you wish."

It's a fluid, well-practiced movement. I hear a tearing sound, and then suddenly, I'm lying before him entirely exposed.

"Your dress." his voice is low and smooth as honey as a hand reaches out to pull at the measly tie at my waist. It instantly falls off my shoulders and pools at my waist.

Revealing my bare chest.

I don't know if he pauses to admire me, because the next thing I feel is his mouth enclosing my hardened nipple. Never could I have imagined something like that feeling so good.

"You're so fucking beautiful," he hisses between tugging

at the sensitive peak with his teeth. I cry out at the delightful twinge of pain, and in response, he soothes it over with a careless lash of his tongue.

It's almost enough to make me come undone right then and there.

But the draw of my exposed sex proves too irresistible. I've barely recovered before he ducks further down, planting lurid kisses on every piece of skin he encounters. It's all teeth and tongue and sucking and fuck!

He reaches my clit with unceremonious enthusiasm. Like a man starved of food, he relentlessly lathers me in his spit before sucking greedily at my core. As if I wasn't wet enough.

The sensation courses through me like a freight train. Every molecule in my body feels like it's on fire, and he licks and licks and sucks and sucks.

The pleasure within me builds and builds with every filthy lap of his tongue. It's almost too much, but then it's suddenly not. I squirm in desperation as my pleasure begins to plateau.

"More," I cry out as I try to chase my pleasure. "I need you."

"You mean here?"

That cruel, spiteful tongue licks the entire length of my sex before plunging into me.

I must scream because a hand clasps around my mouth. I take his fingers between my lips without thinking as I rock up and down his tongue, riding the newfound wave of pleasure coursing through me.

"Yes, yes!"

Suddenly, his hand disappears from my mouth. His two

spit-soaked fingers encircle my entrance, and within seconds, he buries them inside me.

The pressure building within me finds its release, my orgasm bursting from my lips as his fingers work me harder and harder. That cruel, cruel tongue never gives my clit a moment of respite as he coaxes my pleasure on and on until I'm completely and utterly spent.

By the time I come to my senses again, I can barely breathe. With shaking hands, I prop myself up on the bed to survey the damage.

Just as the bedroom door closes behind Rocco's retreating figure.

13

ROCCO

I would be lying if I said I wasn't avoiding Cassandra.

True, my duties to my work prevent me from staying longer than a few hours at my brownstone. But I remain locked in my room and have Donatella deliver my meals.

I had been a fool to think that taking Cas that night would somehow satiate my hunger for her. That had been a good enough excuse in my near-possessed state of lust.

But if anything, that desire seems to have expanded tenfold. And the creature I will surely become in her presence is not one I care to inflict on anyone.

Especially her. She did not ask for my affections, willing as she was to accept them. And God, did she accept them...

But that does not condemn her to a life trapped in my bedchamber for me to pursue her body at my pleasure... as delightful as that might be to my baser instincts. I am still very much a coward when it comes to them

"Are you sure you don't want me to accompany you?" Teo says at my side.

From the way Martino glances at me in the rearview mirror, I imagine he shares Teo's sentiment.

If anything were to cleanse my mind of Cas' tender breast between my teeth, it would surely be today's meeting.

In the week since the fake contract between Lazzaro and I was concluded, he has remained infuriatingly uninteresting.

Sure, he has been spotted in the private rooms of the *Electrix* almost every night, indulging himself in drugs and women, if Alessandro's reports are to be believed. But there is still nothing from his contact with the rat.

"And subject you to Giuliano's torment?" I brush Teo off. "Believe it or not, I know you well enough to surmise that one of you will not leave that conversation alive."

Teo's fists clench, and I have to look away from the man I would happily call brother.

It had been the worst request on my father's list. Being asked to protect the family that had killed Teo's had been torture. Likely, he only included it to torment us both, but it still weighed heavily that I had accepted. Even Teo himself had implored me to do so.

"I'm still not convinced you will gain anything valuable from him." Teo diverts the conversation to safer, more well trodden territory.

"It is in his best interests to protect the Guild, even if it means answering to me," I say, despite my own reservations.

But at this point, any insight into the identity of the rat would be valuable. Even to just to cross my father off the list of potential suspects.

"We're here, boss," Martino says gruffly as we pull up to a stop on the Upper East Side.

The tower of glass that greets us as we exit is familiar,

although I haven't stepped foot inside since Giuliano's retirement. Teo offers me a curt nod before I go on without him.

The staff can barely raise their eyes to look at me as I approach the elevator, punching in the code to grant me access to the topmost floor.

My father's penthouse is more modest than the home I grew up in. He had sold the Moretti Manor himself in an attempt to pay off the Guild's debts before he had been forced to retire.

It was only one of many reasons the lieutenants petitioned me to seek my inheritance early, but perhaps the most significant. The Moretti name had suffered a great deal under my father's brutal leadership.

But walking into his den now, it was almost hard to imagine him as anything but docile.

"You must think I have become something of a cliche," the graying man says without turning to greet me. His hands are occupied with the tending of an impressive array of greenery.

"That depends," I reply as I approach his makeshift greenhouse. The floor-to-ceiling windows that lead out to the balcony beyond seem to be the perfect climate for his cultivations. "How many of those plants are legal to grow in the US?"

Giuliano smirks to himself. "I'm sure there are some around here somewhere."

Indeed, my father's garden is no mere retirement playground. I note several notable drugs and poisons residing within his carefully pruned collection.

"What is it you want, boy?"

I cross my arms as he slowly removes his gardening gloves. "Does a man need an excuse to visit his father?"

"Perhaps if hell has frozen over," Giuliano muses. "But I'm sure young Teo would be quick to remind me that Dante himself proclaimed the most hellish regions to be made of ice. How *is* my favorite orphan? I note he doesn't deign to visit."

I keep my expression regulated with indifference. "I believe he had a blade made with your name carved along the hilt."

Giuliano chuckles. "Such impertinence. And here I thought you condoned forgiveness."

"Carmine Bellini," I announce to get us back on track.

"What of him."

"You knew him better than I."

"He served me for twenty years," Giuliano allows. "Does his ghost haunt you?"

I ignore him. "Who were his closest acquaintances?"

Giuliano tilts his head as if trying to decipher the meaning behind my question. "He was an accountant. The only person who could tolerate such dire conversation was Chiavari."

I knew as much already. In fact, someone in Bellini's position could have easily forged a loan like the one Lazzaro had obtained, which could completely discredit my theory about there being a second rat linked to Lazzaro.

But why would Bellini do such a thing for Lazzaro? It just didn't add up.

"Your silence is disconcerting, boy. Why do you ask such questions?"

I shake my head. "Were there others he was close to?"

"He divorced his wife some time ago..." Giuliano narrows his eyes. "You believe he had a co-conspirator."

"Information continues to leak to the Cartel. I'm simply eliminating the possibility."

For a moment, Giuliano stares at me in silence. Then, a cruel grin stretches across his lips. "My, my. It must be dire indeed if you've come to me for help."

"I merely wanted to confirm a few details."

"Then it would be an honor to serve the new don with whatever details he might need!" Giuliano sneers.

I take a step back, recognizing the menace in his eyes instantly. "This was a mistake."

"Have you spoken to Chiavari? Considering how close their families were and how insolent that daughter of his is, you would do well to be rid of him. He was always such a bore, whining on and on about my spending."

"You disgraced the family name with your frivolity."

"I will do with *my* family name however I see fit, boy."

I chuckle darkly. "That name holds no power for you anymore. You agreed as such upon your retirement."

"My hands were tied," he bites back.

"May I remind you that if you do not cooperate, I could so very easily take the title the old way. That you live here, tending to your crops, at my discretion."

My father appraises me disapprovingly. "You will not, or else you would have done so already these last five years."

"You are right in that regard. But I could so easily inform my contacts at the NYPD of your garden here and leave you in their more than capable hands."

"And betray one of your own? You will be blacklisted."

"Which is why I am grateful for your cooperation on this matter," I snap back.

For a moment, there's a tense beat between us. So far, everything about this conversation is so reminiscent of our previous negotiations, I may as well have taken a time machine back five years and spared myself the trouble.

Then Giuliano sighs. "All this for a son you are yet to possess," Giuliano looks at me with vague interest. "Although I do hear that you've purchased a mistress."

I try not to reveal the anger that stirs within me at the mention of Cas.

But Giuliano seems to notice my reaction anyway and chuckles to himself. "I suppose a grandchild is a grandchild, even if it is a bastard."

"You would feel an affinity to bastards, wouldn't you? Considering you are one." It's too easy for me to kick at an old wound. "But unlike you, my children will not have to kill each other in order to take their due inheritance."

A darkness clouds over Giuliano's expression, and I force myself to remain steadfast. "My half-brother was unworthy of the Mafioso. When the time comes, the precedent you set won't matter. Your children will kill for that power, too."

"I will not allow it," I declare.

"It won't matter." Giuliano's cruel expression only deepens as he approaches. "You presume to control something you cannot."

"I will raise my sons with honor."

Giuliano laughs. "As I raised *my* son to scorn such idealistic weakness. And look how that turned out."

I can't help but flinch at his words.

Scorched would be a better word to describe what he had done to me. The evidence of which had long been concealed by the tattoos that now spread across my skin.

Giuliano Moretti is a monster, intent on nothing more than taking out his displeasure on all those who disappoint him. My mere existence is the greatest disappointment of all.

Perhaps I should wear his disapproval as a badge of honor.

"I am done here." I turn away from my father and head back toward the door.

But Giuliano stops me in my tracks. "You dismissed Esther Romario from your inner circle. How long will it be until you revoke the other promises you made me?"

"Esther was tired. Old. There was no other motivation for the dismissal."

"She didn't suggest you reinstate me then?"

I turn back to level him with a glare. "I ask you not to interfere with my governance of the Guild. I will not ask again."

Giuliano just smiles back at me. "There are still those that will support my claim as the rightful don. You should be careful not to break any more of the sanctions on my list, or else who knows the wrath you may invoke."

"I have little fear of Claudio Lazzaro's wrath if that's what you refer to."

Something ignites behind Giuliano's expression. "You don't know what you're talking about."

"Don't I?" I turn back to him, daring a step forward. "Why should such a lowlife appear on your list at all, then?"

"He is instrumental in our operations."

"He grooms women to perform at the *Candelabra*. He is in no way vital." I step closer. "In fact, it seems the only person to believe so is you. Why would that be?"

"He has exhibited great loyalty to me."

I feign a pitying look. "But not to me, his actual don. Perhaps I will kill him after all."

"He remains on my list."

"And on mine for Bellini's conspirators," I reveal, watching the former don't face intently. "I would be careful how much you defend him, or else some might think you were actively campaigning against the Guild."

Something in Giuliano's temple twitches, and I instinctively brace myself for a blow that never comes.

"You dare accuse me of such a thing?" Giuliano stalks forward to me.

"Just eliminating the possibility."

"You listen here, boy." He almost spits the word in my face, and I can smell the telltale scent of liquor on his breath. "The Guild is my legacy, you hear me? You think me capable of selling information to the fucking Cartel?"

My face remains entirely neutral. "I believe you capable of sowing ruin whenever you put your mind to it."

This time, he does go to strike me.

Only, I'm not a boy anymore.

Wham.

No sooner does his hands grasp my collar than I pivot and slam him into the ground.

"I am done here," I say as I see myself out.

From the floor, Giuliano wheezes after me. "You're a disgrace."

"I get that from you."

There's no remorse in my words, only my cool demeanor disguising the rapidly beating heart of a child.

Teo and Martino still wait by the car, whispering to each other in low voices.

"Time to go," I announce.

Teo gives me a once over, clearly noting the childish panic behind my schooled expression. But he doesn't comment.

"You think he's in on it?" Teo asks instead as he opens the car door for me.

I glance up at the glass skyscraper one last time. "If he is, he's enraged enough to make his next move as soon as possible."

14

CASSANDRA

I almost don't believe my eyes when I find Rocco sitting on the couch in the brownstone lounge.

After a week of nothing but closed doors, I was beginning to think the Mafia don was a figment of my imagination.

Surely I had only dreamed of our night together. I've never encountered a man who knew how to eat me out so masterfully. Every touch a tease, every movement of his tongue, a calculated step toward the greatest climax of my life.

Disappearing afterward had been one thing, but being ignored in the days that followed had been torture. I felt like an idiot, looking up from my book at the smallest sound, pestering Donatella about his dinner plans.

It took an embarrassing amount of time for the truth to sink in: my obsession was entirely one-sided.

Now, he sits there with his whiskey, staring out of the window and looking more miserable than anyone I've ever seen. A vicious part of me tells me I should leave him alone to let him stew in his own displeasure.

But my feet have a mind of their own.

He looks up at my approach, dazed as if I'd jerked him away from whatever he was thinking about.

It's unfair how breathtaking he is. His dark hair falls over his gray eyes with such effortless style that my heart already begins to throb in my chest.

I'm remembering the way he looked up at me through those bangs as his tongue plunged inside of me.

"Cassandra. I didn't realize you were still awake."

I glance at the clock. It is well past midnight, but my body is still struggling to adjust to a normal schedule.

He looks at me expectantly, so I just shrug. "I was thinking about taking you up on your offer."

"Which one?"

"Donatella tells me your home in South Africa is gorgeous. If you're going to avoid me for the entirety of my stay here, I think I'd prefer to be somewhere warmer."

"You want to leave." He gives me a blank, unreadable look.

"I want to uphold my end of the bargain without boring myself to death in the process."

That part was, at the very least, true. Beyond reading and working out in the albeit very well-equipped gym, there had been very little to occupy my time.

"Is the house not to your liking?"

"It's more an issue with the host, actually," I bite back.

He starts at that, then smiles into his drink. "Ah."

"I thought we might have come to an understanding the other day."

"While I lay between your legs, you mean?"

I flush at the memory. "When I asked to be involved in your scheme against Claudio."

"If memory serves, I agreed to involve you at *my* discretion."

I narrow my eyes. "I see, so is hiding in your bedroom part of this scheme that I'm not allowed to know about?"

He says nothing to this, seemingly intent on ignoring me despite the fact I'm now looming over him.

Fine. If he's going to act like a child, so will I. I reach over and snatch the glass from his hand. He watches me intently as I take a sip, then another, to settle my nerves. I don't stop until it's empty, and I slam it back down on the table before him.

He doesn't flinch. He just stares at my mouth.

How can this man be so hot and cold with me? I thought he wanted to ignore me, to pretend what happened never did. But it's so hard to tell what he's thinking when he looks at me like that.

"Look." I try to hold myself with as much dignity as I can. "I don't care if you're not...you know..."

"What?"

Fuck, he was really going to make me say it. "If you're not looking for a relationship, that's fine. I'd just rather know, either way."

He blinks back at me. "You think this is casual for me?"

His words send a cold shiver across my skin. For a moment, I can almost pretend that he cares.

"You are the one who left. You are the one who avoided me all week. What else am I supposed to think?"

"Is that what you want? To be in a relationship with me?"

Under his icy gray eyes, I suddenly become aware of

every insignificant movement I make—the rise and fall of my chest, my shuddering breaths.

I can't discern a single thing he is thinking, and yet my body reacts almost instinctively to the intensity of that gaze.

"I..." I find speech escapes me when he looks at me like this. "I don't know."

"I recommend you don't think on it." He finally releases me with a small, flippant smile. "My line of work does not allow me the time required to fulfill such...duties."

Right. Murderous billionaire Mafia don.

There is absolutely no reason for me to feel so disappointed. Hadn't I just gotten myself out of a very toxic relationship? Why on earth would I feel like anything beyond sex with this man would lead anywhere good?

"However, should you request me to your room again, I wouldn't deny you." His eyes seem to darken with his words. "Kissing is off the table, but I'm sure I'd be able to make time for whatever else you might desire."

It shouldn't matter what he thinks. But his words strike an irksome chord. "Is that how you proposition all your women? I might be able to squeeze in a quick fuck between selling drugs and murdering traitors?"

"Is that what you think I do?" He gives me a humorous look.

"You've not given me any reason to think otherwise."

"You know I own the *Candelabra,* though."

I cross my arms. "Likely as a front for all your illicit activities."

He merely shrugs. "Sometimes I take clients there. The ambiance and spectacle of the performances help me win them over. But in terms of illicit activities, I predominantly deal in luxury goods."

My shock must be clear on my face as he laughs loudly. "It's not what you were expecting?"

"So what, you illegally trade Italian leather shoes?"

"Artwork, mostly," he corrects me. "And not always illegally. In fact, the Museum of Modern Art wouldn't be the institution it is today without us."

I fold my arms. "You expect me to believe that you're like the good guy mafia, then?"

"No, you are also right." He looks away from me as he stands to approach the drink cabinet beside us. "Murder is a useful tool to create fear."

I watch in nervous silence as he reaches for the whiskey decanter and pours. He then picks up his glass and takes a long drink. "Plus, we do also sell drugs on the side. But that's mainly to annoy the Cartel."

I take a heavy seat on the now unoccupied couch. A cool sense of dread falls on my shoulders. "Oh my God."

"What?"

"You're going to kill me, aren't you?"

He lets out an inelegant snort as he turns back to me. "For what?"

"You just told me all your trade secrets." My palms begin to sweat. "I could go to the police. I could tell them everything."

Rocco, however, doesn't seem concerned. "Cas, you've been here a week already. If you were going to do such a thing, I'm fairly certain you would have done so by now."

"You really trust me that much?"

He considers me a moment. "I don't know. But my gut is telling me I can enjoy a drink with you without the fear of you revealing my darkest deeds to the authorities."

With that, he pushes a second glass of whiskey into my hand and sits down beside me.

For a moment, we sit in companionable silence as we drink. It feels so surreal, and yet bizarrely like the most normal thing in the world.

"What is your father like?" he asks suddenly.

I cringe at the question, but there's no way he could know how his words would affect me. So, instead, I just shrug. "I didn't know him well."

He immediately clocks my shift in tense. "When did he pass?"

"A few weeks ago, actually." I try to speak as casually as I can.

But Rocco becomes very serious. "I've been insensitive. I'm so sorry for your loss. Has the funeral passed already? I can organize for you to leave if you need to."

"It's fine, really." I offer him a small smile at his kindness. "I didn't know him. It was more of a shock than anything else."

"I can imagine."

I have to look away from the pity in his eyes. "I lived with my mother for almost two decades. She's the only parent I've ever needed and the only one I really recognize. Sure, it might have been nice to reconnect with him, but..."

"But it's hard to grieve someone you don't know," Rocco finishes for me.

We sit in silence for a moment as the truth of his words wash over me.

"Besides, I don't think his friends even knew to invite us to the funeral." I sigh. "So, to answer your original question, disappointing. I think."

Rocco smirks at that. "Perhaps we do have something in common, then."

I suddenly recall the look on his face when I entered the lounge. How miserable he'd seemed drinking alone in here.

I hesitate before daring my next question. "Was...was your father also...a mafia don?"

"Oh yes. I only took the position from him a year ago."

I blink at that. A *year?* From his money and demeanor, I had assumed he'd been doing this his whole life.

"Is he...still alive?" The question escapes me before I have a chance to consider it fully.

Thankfully, Rocco seems to find the humor in it. "Yes. He decided to take an early retirement."

"Is that normal?"

"No."

"What's he like?"

A thousand answers seem to stir behind those gray eyes. "He's taken to gardening. He's excited at the prospect of grandchildren. He's still determined to prove he knows better than me."

"And that's disappointing?"

He smirks. "Because it's so very unfairly normal of him."

"Is that a bad thing?" As I ask, I bring my legs up under me, curious about the sadness behind his smirk.

"You have very few opportunities to be normal as a mafioso."

"So surely you should allow him such pleasures in his retirement?"

He finishes his drink quickly. "Can we talk about something else?" he snaps.

I cringe a little at his sharpness. "I've upset you."

"You've...it's not your fault. I think I'm just in a foul mood after seeing him."

"Parents can't always be as we hope them to be." I sigh, thinking of the picture of my parents my mother had kept in the back of the drawer.

I let the silence stretch, content with just sitting in his company. It's a strange feeling, especially considering that I entered this room wanting nothing better than to chew him out and threaten to leave.

"He was an asshole, my father. Ever since I was young," Rocco finally admits. "Too absorbed in drinking and gambling away my inheritance to pay me much mind. But when he did..."

He trails off as if realizing himself. "Sorry, you didn't ask to hear this."

"I'm happy to," I reply quickly. "You seem different today." I flush at the way his eyebrow raises. "What I mean is, maybe it will help to talk about it."

"In truth? It may explain some of my actions regarding you. My father...I preferred it when he didn't notice me. His attention often came with more violent tendencies, and I quickly learned how to endure his wrath."

"Rocco..."

"I swore I would never hurt an innocent the way he hurt me." he looks away. "When I saw you that first night at the *Candelabra*...those bruises...I couldn't comprehend why anyone would lay a hand on you."

I breathe in and out slowly. "You said in *Electrix* that you would help me because it was the right thing to do."

It hadn't made any sense. How could a mafia Don be so willing to do something without anything in return?

But now...

"I'm not a good man, Cas. But any innocent on the receiving end of such abuse will always find shelter here."

I feel my heart swelling in my chest. So much of my opinion of the man before me was based on assumption.

"Rocco..."

"I don't want your pity," he states firmly, staring down at his hands. "I just wanted you to know why. I hope it gives you some reassurance about my intentions."

But I'm already shaking my head. Because there's nothing I want more than to kiss him right now.

So I do.

15

ROCCO

My mind goes blank as her lips touch mine.

All I feel is an almost holy sense of calm. All that matters is that she's there in front of me, willingly kissing me.

Those lips...her sinful mouth pressed against mine. How many times had I imagined this? How often had I forced myself to deny the urge to kiss her?

It wasn't something I ever let myself do. Kissing always felt too personal and emotional. Even with Danny, I wouldn't let her kiss me for fear she would get too attached.

But after so long...od, does it feel good.

My hand reaches to press into the back of her head. Her lips part willingly for my tongue. I want...I want...I want...

I need to stop.

I pull away abruptly.

"What?" Her eyes are wide with alarm and rejection.

"We shouldn't."

Something scorching hot crosses her face. "You had no trouble fucking me with your tongue the other day."

She tries to pull away, but I hold fast. "I mean. We shouldn't kiss."

"Why not?"

"Because it's too..." I glance down, suddenly distracted by her swollen lips.

She snorts. "You think I'm going to fall in love with you over a kiss?"

I chuckle to myself. "It's not you I'm worried about."

Her dark brow shoots up. But she doesn't say anything. She doesn't protest as I pull her back to me, resting my forehead against hers.

"I can't let anything serious happen between us. You'll only be disappointed," I reiterate softly.

To my surprise, she tilts her head toward mine again.

"Cas..."

But she kisses my cheek, then after a moment, kisses the other.

"Is this okay?" she whispers against my skin, sending pure desire trembling through my body.

"It's the principle of

She kisses the corner of my mouth. "What about this?"

"Cas," I groan. "Enough."

"You want me to stop?" She pulls me away, but my hand doesn't let her move too far.

"I want you..."

That's all I can get out. I bury my head in her shoulder, my senses rejoicing in her scent, her touch.

"I'm so intoxicated by you," I whisper. "If I start...I don't think I can stop."

A hand tangles itself in my hair, pulling gently, soothingly. At the touch, I can feel every muscle in my body relaxing.

"Why not?"

I scrunch my eyes closed. "This isn't a life you want, Cas."

She's silent for a moment. Her fingers continue combing through my hair. "Then what do we do?"

We. The word reverberates through my body like a siren's song.

"Because I can't sleep in that room knowing you're just down the hall. I can't pretend there's nothing going on here. I've been going insane all week wondering if I dreamed this whole thing up."

I pull away, looking straight into those deep hazel eyes.

But all I see is my own fear reflecting back at me.

Just because *this* could so easily turn out to be the worst mistake of my life, it doesn't mean it has to be hers.

I look away, pulling on a mask of an easy smirk. "It's just physical, *Angioletta*. It will pass."

"Will it?" she whispers back defiantly.

She glances at my lips again. All it would take would be for me to lean forward and close those few inches.

But a kiss from her will surely unravel every last inch of my resolve to protect her. Not from herself this time, but from *me*.

I offer her a crooked smile. "Would you like me to prove it?"

My cock hardens at her dilated pupils.

It's nothing personal. I scream at myself like a mantra over and over again. *It's just physical.*

My fingers tighten in the back of her hair, and I pull her away.

"Ah!" she cries as her head tilts back. Revealing the perfect expanse of her neck to my mouth.

I waste no time devouring it, planting kisses and teeth and tongue along every inch. I'm doing everything I would have done to that sinful mouth of hers.

But this will do. It will have to do.

"Rocco."

I look up at her through hooded eyes. "Physical, see?"

I tug her hair again, earning me the most delightful sound. With a satisfied smirk, I pair my next assault with a bite at the base of her neck. The combination causes her to curl her body toward me, submitting herself entirely.

Just how I like it.

"Do that again," she demands, her voice thick with lust. "I want your mark on me."

My next bite at her neck is one that I fully relish in, my tongue dancing around the mark and sucking. Hard. The possessive brute within me encourages me to claim what is rightfully mine.

And her gasps in return are so devastatingly rewarding I have to palm at my crotch to ease some of the tension.

Suddenly, her hands are there as well, as if sensing my desperation. She's fumbling with my belt in her eagerness.

"Careful now," I say as I lick the entire length of her neck. "I won't stop."

"Then don't."

It's all the permission my depraved brain needs.

My hands are on her chest next, tearing away at her blouse in one swift movement as she desperately tries to rid me of my pants.

The bra beneath is scandalously small, accentuating the generous curves of her breasts with thin lines of black lace.

I preferred it when she didn't wear a bra at all.

"No." Her hand slaps against mine as I attempt to pry

the slip of material away. "You've ruined enough of my underwear."

I growl at the memory of her panties giving way to my teeth. Her palm at my crotch only prolongs the noise.

There's nothing in this moment besides her. All I can smell, all I can think of is *Cassandra. Cassandra.* Every move she makes, every sound that escapes those sweet lips only draws me further into this trance.

She squeezes at my crotch again, and I realize she's managed to remove my pants entirely. Her fingers wrap themselves around my shaft.

Fuck. I need her. Now.

"Rocco!" she half squeals as I suddenly stand, dragging her up with me.

It feels almost practiced the way she immediately wraps her legs around me. I stride out of the room, trying to remember through the fog of lust where my fucking room is.

But then her lips are there again. On my cheeks, in my hair. Everywhere on my face besides my mouth.

"Angioletta. Mi ucciderai."

This woman will be my end.

I move faster than I ever have in my life, pushing through doors with reckless abandon as I try to dislodge her.

But God. Those kisses. Those lips. That tenderness. I am lost entirely to it.

It's no use.

She has already taken my heart.

The only thing I can do is try to prevent her from ever knowing it.

With one final surge of resolve, I push her from me. It

feels like I'm detaching my own limb as she falls away directly onto my own bed.

Thankfully, her giggles reach me moment later, unconcerned by my inner turmoil. She's delectable, enticing, overwhelming.

I stalk across the bed to her on my hands and knees. "No more kisses," I scold her.

Daringly, she leans forward and plants one on my nose. "Or what?"

It's exactly the wrong question, and we both know it.

It takes nothing for me to lift her, to turn her over so that she leans back against my chest. "Or," I bite at her ear, "I will have to punish you."

She gasps as one hand grabs her neck, the other finally freeing my throbbing cock from my boxers. I press into her back, letting her feel the entirety of my want and desire.

"Bend over," I demand as I push her forward by the neck.

Her amble rear raises willinging in the air, and I smack it affectionately.

Her responding whimper is like music to my ears. "You like that?"

I take a cheek in my hand and squeeze down hard enough to bruise.

"Mmmhmmm," she whines in response.

Greedily, I rid her of her pants and indulge her again. This time the pink mark against her slapped skin has my hand grasping at my cock.

The other goes to seek out her sex. I almost cum in my own hand at the feeling of wetness I find there. Her little gasps at my touch are even more exciting.

"Please, Rocco," she begs me, bending down further into

the bed. The call of her dripping core is more intoxicating than any substance in existence.

I can't deny her. Not when I can barely deny myself.

I line myself up at her entrance and reach forward, finding purchase in her hair and her breast.

"Please."

I slam into her, and my world explodes around me.

Our joint cries harmonize as I withdraw and enter again. Both of us are in desperate need of friction. I want to feel the tightening of her around me again and again.

I pull her hair back, and she moans so lavishly I almost come undone.

"Rocco."

My name on her lips is like a lightning bolt directly to my own fervent desires. I need to move. Need to work us both into the frenzy that we are both teetering on the edge of.

So, I let myself loose. I'm massaging her breast, pulling her hair, drawing every gorgeous, illicit sound from her mouth and every moment begging myself to turn her around, to capture those lips with mine and dive head-first into oblivion.

But I can't, I won't.

The pressure of my climax builds and builds with every thrust deeper and deeper. Her taut ass slaps against me with every feverish movement.

"More," she chokes out.

Instinctively, I let my hand drop down from her breast to encircle her clit, massaging there in time with every thrust I make.

But her moans aren't nearly enough.

More.

My other hand peels itself from her hair and encircles her neck. The purchase I find there allows me to drive in deeper and further than before.

Cas seems to revel in the constraint.

She pushes herself down ever further, so much so her groans are partially muffled by the bed itself.

I circle her clit once more with my finger.

"Fuck, Rocco..."

I can feel her then, tightening around me. She's going to reach her climax before me.

My fingers tighten around her neck. I pick up the pace. Each thrust pushes her further and further into the mattress.

"Rocco!"

Her scent, her *desire,* engulfs me.

I rub at her sensitive clit relentlessly as I feel my cock pulsing with its own release.

Her hand reaches back, grabbing my wrist. It's forceful yet gentle. Controlling, yet careless.

She screams my name, and I let myself go at the sound.

All we can do is cling to each other as I pound into her again. Then again. Then, one last time.

I have to grab her hips to keep myself steady as a dazzling brightness overcomes my vision, as I completely succumb to my own climax.

Vaguely, I'm aware of her own panting beneath me as I ride the wave of ecstasy.

It's a release like nothing I've ever experienced before.

As I come to, there's nothing I can do except curl myself around her, pulling her closer to my chest.

And as we both lie there, breathing in the insanity of our own ecstasy, I try not to imagine how it would feel to do this for the rest of my miserable existence.

16

CASSANDRA

"You're going to leave, aren't you," I whisper across Rocco's chest in the aftermath.

His lack of response is an answer in and of itself.

I trace over the lines of his tattoos, wondering if I should commit them to memory. How many more times will he let me lay next to him like this? How many women have wondered the same thing?

He said it himself: nothing serious could ever happen between us. Yet that foolish hope that maybe I could be the exception lingers.

I don't even know if that's what *I* want, yet the distance between us already feels painful even though he's right there.

He gets up slowly, untangling me from his side as he does.

"I must return to work."

"Right." I try not to sound bitter.

"I'll be back tomorrow."

"Okay."

"Cas."

"What?"

"Look at me."

Begrudgingly, I do. The soft expression on his handsome face is almost unbearable. "This doesn't need to happen again."

But God, do I want it to, though. I don't want to stop, ever. And that's perhaps the most terrifying truth of it all.

"It's just physical, right?" I repeat his words back to him.

"Right."

Still, we lay in silence for another moment before he leaves.

I try to fall back to sleep, but it cruelly evades me. Instead, I shift myself up and glance around his room which is illuminated by the gray of early morning light.

I am a little surprised by how little there is to examine, though. His bed is larger than mine, and the empty space where he was lying is almost cavernous. But aside from the bed, there's nothing much in the room.

Two doors lead off into what I assume must be the same matching en-suite and walk-in closet as my room. The only real thing of note is the huge painting that looms on the wall opposite me.

Curious, I rise to take a closer look. I don't know a lot about paintings, but after our discussion last night, it wouldn't surprise me if Rocco had kept back something insanely rare for himself.

It seems to be made from some kind of oil-based paint, that much I can decipher, at least. Although there's no real structure represented at all on the canvas, the abstract merging of line and color is intriguing.

In fact, the longer I stare at it, the more I think I might see figures hidden within the brush strokes. But as I blink, they seem to disappear once more.

The signature at the bottom is not one I recognize. Nor does it come up when I search for it on my phone.

With a sigh, I move on. Begrudgingly, I take myself back to my bedroom.

If Donatella noticed anything last night, she doesn't comment on it when she knocks on my door several hours later.

"Shall I run you a bath?" she asks in that clipped English accent.

I groan a little in confirmation. Finally dozing off back in my own bed, I've woken up to find my body stiff all over. There's no mystery as to why: Rocco's methods in the bedroom leave no room for fragility.

It's not something I ever thought I would enjoy, but when he pulled at my hair and squeezed at my neck, something feral came over me. It's almost as if I subconsciously wanted to reclaim such sensations as purely pleasurable.

An interesting turn of events, but not one I care to think about too hard. Claudio barely lasted long enough to remember my own satisfaction, so it's equally likely these tastes have always been a part of me.

"Do you have any plans for today?" Donatella drags me from my thoughts.

It's become something of a routine since I've been staying here. Donatella will wake me with the offer of a bath, and we'll make small talk until she's bored enough to leave me to stew in the warm water alone. She always claims another errand needs her attention.

"I was thinking about staying in today, actually," I reply sarcastically.

She doesn't rise to the bait. "There is a great deal to watch on the television. Or else you could assist me in the kitchen if you wanted to do something more practical."

"I think I'll use the gym."

"And then what?"

"I don't know!" I turn to her, somewhat annoyed by her pestering when I've had so little sleep.

She matches my glare with her own. "I am at your disposal. You can do anything you want while you're here."

"If you're at my disposal, why don't you leave me alone?" I snap back.

Donatella looks me over once. "Fine. I need to prepare breakfast."

With that, she takes her leave.

I can't help but feel like she's judging me. Honestly, since coming here, I've found little motivation to do anything other than wallow in my own self-pity.

It's pathetic, but after everything that happened with my father, then Claudio, and now Rocco, I've needed the time to collect myself. To figure out where this all leaves me.

I step out of the bath and immediately go to the closet to retrieve my gym wear. Exploring the contents of the walk-in closet had taken me an entire afternoon.

To my surprise, it is equipped with a fairly even split of both men's and women's designs in a variety of different sizes. This makes a lot of sense, but I'm close to trying on everything it has to offer and it hasn't even been a week.

Not that it really matters, as Donatella brings me back freshly washed and ironed clothing every morning.

The day passes dangerously slowly. My boredom peaks

enough to feel the temptation to answer one of the thousands of messages Mia left on my phone.

But I ignore them. Claudio's betrayal had been enough to shake my entire world to its core. If Mia is somehow in on this, if she knew about the mafia or is somehow even a part of it, I'm not sure what I will do.

What would I even say to her? "Oh yeah, remember that guy you told me to stay away from? We're living together while he baits my ex into exposing someone in his elite mafia billionaire circle. Also, we're fucking now, apparently."

It's just physical, he said. I tell myself that's enough, that he's right. That anything more would not only be very, very complicated, but likely incredibly dangerous, considering his line of work.

When I see him again the next day, it's when I catch him walking down the corridor to his bedroom.

He looks at me for a moment, then jerks his head toward his bedroom door in invitation.

And it's stupid and careless and only going to end in pain, but...I follow him inside.

When he touches me, it feels worth it. It feels like I'm finally able to escape this goddamn place. I feel alive and wanted, Worshiped by that tongue as he explores every part of me except my lips.

It becomes our own secret game. I meet him in his bedroom, or he approaches mine. I casually straddle him on the couch, or he bends me over the kitchen counter.

We don't talk, we don't need to. Our bodies respond to each other almost instantly, already frustrated and in need of release. It's pure, mindless physical abandon.

The high of it is otherworldly. It's addictive, and I can't

help the way I'm drawn to him, how I seek him out again and again like a moth to a damn flame. But in the aftermath, I always return to that empty feeling.

I crave his kiss.

Even as he ties my hands to his bedframe and takes me so hard and so fucking fast that I see goddamn stars. There's always a part of me that remembers what it was like to place my lips on his.

I want his hand to hold the back of my head and not let go.

"Cas?" he asks when we lie back on the soft rug of his bedroom floor. Breathless. Completely and utterly spent.

"Mmm?"

"I'm going to be away for a few days."

Something sinks in my stomach. "Right."

"Will you be okay here?"

I sit up, hugging my knees to my chest. "I think I can manage to get myself off without you."

He growls, tugging me back down to him and making me giggle in the process. He pinches my sides, only making me howl louder.

I squirm away from him, but his arms entirely envelop me, pressing me back into his chest and holding me tight.

I let my eyes flutter closed at the feeling of his closeness.

"Don't you dare." He teases my ear with his teeth.

Dear God, this man.

I push him away, more for my own sanity than anything else. "I'll be fine. Does this have anything to do with the rat?"

"Actually, no. I need to settle a few things in South Africa," he admits, a careless hand running through his hair.

"I'd invite you, but you'd likely be stuck on a plane the whole time."

"A private one?" I give him a conspiratorial look.

"That we would share with many of my men," he says as he shoots me down. "Unless you like a few spectators?"

I grimace. "Pass. Any update on Claudio?"

He shakes his head tiredly. "Nothing. It's becoming…an issue. I'll let you know if anything changes when I get back."

I give him a disbelieving look. Despite our previous discussions, he hasn't told me anything about his plans so far.

"I mean it," he reiterates, seemingly reading my expression.

"Whatever you say."

I go to stand up, but Rocco reaches for my hand.

"I will see you in a few days."

To my surprise, he lifts my knuckles to his lips and kisses them softly.

It's such a tender gesture I can almost feel myself melt at the touch.

"Try not to miss me too much," I manage to reply before turning on my heel and walking away before I do something stupid like beg him to take me anyway.

Or kiss him.

The next day starts the same as any other. However, knowing that Rocco won't return that evening already sets a sour tone.

It's not until I leave the bathroom that I decide to check my phone.

As usual, there are about a hundred notifications from Mia. But something else catches my eye.

One New Message. Claudio Lazzaro.

My heart begins to thump wildly in my chest. It must be almost a month since the day he signed me away to Rocco. This entire time, I haven't heard a thing from him. No message of remorse, no goading email calling me a slut.

Not even the pile of personal items he'd promised to send over.

With a shaking hand, I unlock my phone and read it.

"This is shit, Cas. I want to see you."

A glance at the timestamp tells me everything I need to know about how sober he was when he messaged.

I think about ignoring it, letting him stew in the realization that he'd fucked up for as long as possible. He deserves it, after all.

But...

But Rocco doesn't have any other leads. He hasn't been able to get anything out of him so far, and we're already a third of the way through our time together.

What would any of this be for if the hundred and one days pass without anything happening? I would go back to Ohio, closing this weird chapter as a fever dream.

I might not be a super-rich mafioso, but there is one thing I know how to do better than anyone else.

I can make Claudio talk endlessly about himself.

A plan begins to take root as I type back my response.

Donatella knocks on my door a moment later. "Breakfast!"

"I'm not feeling good today," I call back, forcing my voice to sound gravelly. "I think I'm going to stay in bed and sleep it off."

"You should still eat something."

"I'll eat later," I insist.

I can almost hear her rolling her eyes through the door. "Call me if you need any medication."

As soon as I hear her footsteps disappear, I spring into action.

In my first few days here, I'd contemplated how difficult it would be to escape out the window. I even fashioned a rope out of some of the men's shirts from the closet. I retrieve it now, stashed in one of the drawers Donatella never bothers to look in.

Within seconds, I'm crouched on the damp ground outside. The years of sneaking out to perform at bars were finally working in my favor. And with one quick vault over the fence, I make it into the yard of the neighboring brownstone.

After so many weeks of being cooped up, I try not to spend much time reveling in the fresh air.

I don't know where the brownstone is in Brooklyn. But as long as I can find a main road, I'll be able to summon a cab. The jingle of too few coins in my purse reminds me to pray I'm not too far away.

There, only a few blocks away, seems to be a busier road.

I stride toward it, focused on my goal.

So much so that I don't hear anyone approaching behind me.

"What the *hell* are you doing?"

17

ROCCO

I storm into the house, throwing my jacket to the floor as I kick open the door to the lounge.

"What. The. Fuck."

Before me, Cas sits curled up on the couch. Teo stands over her, monitoring her every move.

"I thought you said I was free to leave as I pleased." She meets my anger with her own. "You set this asshole on guard dog duty?"

I don't need to look at Teo to know he's rolling his eyes.

The plane had been on the fucking runway when his message came through, saying hat Cas had climbed out the goddamn *window*.

I couldn't get home fast enough.

He showed me the messages he'd been tracking on Lazzaro's phone.

"This is shit, Cas. I want to see you."

I miss you too, baby. So much. If we meet, will you get in trouble?

"Come to the Candelabra. I can keep you safe here."
You promise?
"I need you. Now."
Fuck, baby. I'll try...I'll be there soon.

Every word made me want to gouge out my eyeballs.

There were so many layers to my anger. But jealousy raged wilder and hotter than any other.

Some deep part of my logical brain registers that I have no right to be mad. *I* was the one who initiated the casual nature of our relationship. *I* was the one who wanted her to leave at the end of all this and have a normal life.

But with Claudio *fucking* Lazzaro? The guy she begged me to save her from?

One text and she was already willing to defy our agreement, to escape my home and fuck him instead.

"I was gone for less than four goddamn hours," I spit out.

"He manhandled me!"

"If we're pointing fingers," Teo butts in. "She kicked me quite a bit too."

She turns her rage at him. "You jumped me out of nowhere! What did you expect?"

"Teo," I say through my teeth. "Leave us."

My most trusted friend studies me closely for a moment before silently making his exit.

Cas bristles in the eerie silence that follows.

She was going to him. She let me touch her last night, but she was going to *him*.

"I'm not going to apologize," she states stubbornly. "I didn't break our agreement."

"You didn't have the opportunity to."

"Because you had Teo drag me back to this *prison!*"

Her words enrage me so fiercely that I can barely see beyond the red in my vision.

"Because you were running back to *him* the second my back was turned."

Every defiant expression of her body flickers out like a candle.

"What?" she whispers, suddenly looking horrified.

"You think I was going to stand by and let you jeopardize everything I've done because you were that desperate to fuck him again?"

Her eyes bulge. "You've been tracking my phone."

"We've been tracking *his*."

"Rocco..."

"Not another word out of your damn mouth, Cassandra."

I want to hit something. I want to feel something be crushed beneath my fists.

How could I have deluded myself so badly?

I was helpless around her, forced to keep her at arm's length to protect her from myself, but too weak not to touch her. Be close to her. Dream of her. Taste her.

But that didn't mean she felt the same way.

Even though I thought I'd felt it. Even though she melted every time I held her, even though she sought me out just as much as I did her.

Had any of it been real? Was it all so that I would relax enough for her to plan her great escape?

"Rocco!"

She's suddenly there, right in front of me. Those stunning hazel eyes pierce through my anger like a shot to the heart.

Gently she touches my clenched fists, slowly unfurling them to reveal the bloody marks my nails have made in my palms.

"You really think I would go back to him?" She whispers, and I can hear the pain in her voice. "After everything he did? After everything *I* did to get away."

I snatch my hands away. "You tell me. Because from where I'm standing, that's exactly what you were doing."

"I told you I wanted to be part of this. I told you I could help." Her eyes flood with tears. "I was going to him to help *you,* and you dare accuse me of betraying you?"

She backs away a step. "I hadn't heard from him in weeks. You think it's a coincidence he messaged me the second you were heading out of town?"

My entire body goes entirely still. "You were walking into a trap."

"Willingly," she hisses back, moving further away. "For *you.*"

"You damn idiot."

She flinches at my harshness. "Maybe. But at least I was doing something to ensure all this isn't for fucking nothing."

I don't call out after her when she storms away. I just fall, exhausted, onto the couch, my mind racing.

She had no proof of her intentions, but she was right. Why would anyone willingly run back to the arms of their abuser unless they needed something in return?

Hell, it was the only reason I ever sought out my own father.

And I'd come in here accusing her of something unthinkable.

I groan into my hands. What a fucking mess.

In the days that follow, Cas does not come out of her room.

Donatella tries to coax her out with food, but she refuses to even crack open the door to receive it.

"She hasn't eaten anything in almost three days," my housekeeper announces as she enters my office.

I rarely work from home, but with my men tying up loose ends in South Africa without me, it was easy to make my excuses instead of working at the compound.

"What do you expect me to do?"

Donatella levels me with an exasperated look. "You asked me to keep an eye on her and alert you to any concerning behavior. This is *very* concerning behavior."

"If she's going to act like a child, she's welcome to. She's not going to die of hunger over this."

"I think you severely underestimate how stubborn she is."

I put my pen down. "I still don't hear you offering a solution."

"You could apologize."

"For what?"

She throws her hands up. "I don't know, for not telling her you'd be stationing Teo here while you were gone? For immediately thinking the worst of her before considering all your options?"

"You overstep, Donatella."

"You asked," she snaps back. "If she doesn't eat anything by this time tomorrow, I'll hand in my resignation."

Great. As if I didn't already have enough on my plate.

Donatella leaves me to wallow in her ultimatum as I slump back into my chair.

The Guild is breathing down my throat to identify the potential rat. My father has remained eerily quiet. Lazzaro is being less than helpful, and I have no other leads right now.

As much as I hate to admit it, Cas' plan was a good idea. If she could get him to slip up, even once…but we need to resolve this little tantrum of hers first.

Three days is too long to go without food; she must be ravenous right now. I still remember the way she attacked her food that first evening we ate together.

Struck by sudden inspiration, I leave my desk and make my way to the kitchen.

It's been a long time since I've used the kitchen to make anything more than a coffee. Unless you counted when I slid Cas behind the counter to take her from behind.

My eyes linger on that particular spot a little too long.

But cooking is like riding a bike. Soon, pots are simmering on the stove as I chop and fry my way through the familiar recipe. I'm just grating the truffle to adorn the carbonara, when I sense someone behind me.

"I thought you were on a hunger strike," I say without turning around.

"Is this some kind of cruel joke? Frying bacon with the doors open?"

I glance over my shoulder.

It's almost startling to see her looking so small and thin again. It's so similar to how she'd looked when she'd first arrived.

I had barely noticed the change over these last few weeks, but I realize it now. A month of steady food, regular exercise, and without the stress of an abusive asshole lingering over her had done wonders for her appearance.

But in the span of three short days, that progress seems to have faded. Her skin is grayer, her cheeks more taunt. Even her hair lies dully across her shoulders.

"It worked, didn't it?" I say as I serve up two plates. The larger I push toward her. "Eat."

I think she might deny me for a moment, but suddenly, she picks up the fork and begins eating ferociously.

At least Donatella will stick around now. I tuck into my own meal slowly—content to watch her consume every mouthful.

I can almost see the color returning to her cheeks as she sits back from her empty plate.

"I owe you an apology," I begin cautiously. "I jumped to a conclusion I had no right to make."

She points her nose in the air and looks away.

"And I'm sorry for making you feel like you were a prisoner here." I take a deep breath. "But..."

She sighs. "But?"

"But what you did was reckless, despite your intentions. You should have told me what you were planning. I would have helped you."

"And you would have just let me go? Willingly?" She challenges me with a hard glare. "Your sense of male pride wouldn't have tried to stop me."

I bite the inside of my cheek. "We could have come up with a more sensible plan."

"We didn't have time for that," she counters. "You don't know him as I do. His moods are...fleeting. If I'd waited until you'd returned, he would have sobered up enough to think twice about meeting me."

I consider this a moment. "Teo tells me he's messaged you since."

She pulls out her phone and slides it over for me to see.

An irrational pang of jealousy overcomes me when I re-read the old message thread:

"I need you. Now."

Fuck, baby. I'll try...I'll be there soon.

Then, the new messages from Lazzaro:

"I'm waiting backstage."

"Cas, where are you?"

"Are you seriously giving me blue-balls right now?"

"Fuck you. I can't believe this."

"Ungrateful slut."

I try not to crush the phone in my hand.

"I had an opening, and I missed it," Cas says, seemingly entirely unbothered by the content of the messages.

I give myself a moment to calm down. "Perhaps. But perhaps not." I gesture to the phone in my hand. "May I?"

She simply shrugs as I begin typing out a reply. I hit send and slide the phone back for her to read for herself.

I'm sorry, baby. He found out and wouldn't let me leave.

Please, I'll come tonight. I promise you, I'll get away this time.

Cas looks at me curiously. "Appealing to his sense of male pride."

"Works both ways."

"Does this mean you'll let me go?"

"It means I see the value in this confrontation and that I trust you will share any relevant information with me afterward."

Cas' phone pings with a response. We both look down at the same time.

"Bastard. Come home to me, baby. I'll be backstage again tonight."

"Looks like we have some work to do," I announce, standing up and offering her a hand. "Do you think you're up for it?"

She swallows tightly as she takes it. "I need to see him again. I need to put an end to it."

The realization that hits me as she says this threatens to topple me.

Her hunger strike hadn't been just about the way I had acted. I had also robbed her of a chance to get closure on the bastard, to put that piece of her life behind her.

All I can do is squeeze her hand gently. My own silent apology. "You will."

Her answering smile makes my heart flutter. "I'm sorry for not telling you. I admit, I might have acted a little…rashly."

I feel myself laughing for the first time in what feels like a lifetime.

"Friends?" she asks with those big, hazel eyes gazing at me so unfairly.

Who am I to deny her anything?

I pull her to me, wrapping my arms around her. And God, have I missed this closeness these last few days. I've missed the feeling of her pressed against my chest, of her hands grasping my shirt to pull me impossibly closer.

"Friends," I agree, completely unable to stop myself from kissing the top of her head that she tucks under my chin.

We stand there a moment too long before I force myself to step back. "Come on, we need to make a quit pitstop."

"Where?"

"Fifth Avenue."

She stares at me blankly. "Why?"

"We're going shopping."

"Again, *why?*"

"Because if you're going to confront Lazzaro tonight at the *Candelabra*, I will have to insist on going with you."

Her eyes bulge at this. "W-what?"

"And you should know by now that no woman of mine would be caught dead in anything but the best."

18

CASSANDRA

I don't recognize myself in the mirror.

I've done intense shopping trips before. Hell, my mom and I even visited the Mall of America when I was a kid.

But nothing compared to what Rocco just made me do. Somehow, they measured me for this dress *while* a gentleman named Hugo descended on my hair with foils. The soft highlights now frame my face, amplifying my new layers.

I'm still unsure how and when someone got to my nails, but their dark maroon color perfectly matches my near-black outfit.

The material hugs every one of my curves as it falls in sleek waves to my heeled feet. The long slit down the side comes scandalously close to my upper thigh. But that has nothing on the deep plunge of my neckline.

It's almost as if the fabric has been stitched into my skin —it leaves nothing to the imagination.

My appearance would be distracting if Rocco wasn't standing behind me.

His own suit is tailored to perfection, as always. But it's his shirt, a dark red match to my dress, that's unbuttoned far enough to reveal the tattoos beneath that makes my mouth water.

"You're perfect," he whispers in my ear. His eyes rove over my body hungrily.

I'm about two seconds away from demanding we stay home and entertain ourselves another way.

But...our newfound alliance still feels somewhat tentative. It's the same as before, except somehow it isn't. I don't think I realized the implications of calling Rocco my " friend" before he returned the sentiment.

I shake my head to try and clear it of distractions. I have a job to do.

The plan is simple. Go into the *Candelabra,* pretend to be Rocco's doting mistress, and slip away to confront Claudio.

"Remember, get him to talk about how he acquired the loan," Rocco reiterates as he tucks a hidden mic into the strap of my dress. "Anything else is a bonus. But leave at the first sign of trouble."

He goes over this at least five more times on our way over to the club.

There's something almost heartbreakingly familiar about standing in front of the *Candelabra* once more. Everything in my world has been flipped upside down, but there it is, standing tall and proud, exactly the same as the day I left it.

"Shall we?"

I turn to see Rocco offering me his arm. I reach out and

take it, finding no small amount of reassurance from his touch.

"Remember," he whispers in my ear as he reaches out to push open the door. "Tonight, you're *my* trophy. Act like it."

We step through those doors together, only to be greeted with resolute silence.

As my eyes adjust to the mood lighting, I wonder if it's because the place is entirely empty. But to my dismay, I find instead that every one of the club's patrons has turned to look at us.

Even Danny, standing on the stage, has faltered in her song. She coughs quickly and tries to recover.

"Rocco," I hiss nervously, glancing wildly around us.

His arm wraps around my waist as he turns to nuzzle my ear. "Relax. Now, giggle as if I've said something funny."

The sound I make doesn't feel entirely natural, but it seems to satisfy his request. He leads us both toward the VIP table at the very end of the stage.

I almost wish we could sit at the back of the room. At least that way, Danny wouldn't be able to glare down at me so much.

Rocco pulls a seat out for me. "*Angioletta.*"

I sit down awkwardly. "Remind me why this is all necessary?"

Rocco chuckles as he pulls his own chair next to mine, draping a protective, arrogant arm over my shoulder.

Again, he nuzzles into my ear. "My men are under the assumption that I bought you from Lazzaro for a particular purpose," he purrs. "I'd like to keep up that appearance as much as possible."

His mouth grazes on my jaw, and my eyes flutter closed.

"You really think they'd care that much? You didn't need to dress me up like this."

His tongue darts out along my neck. "But where is the fun in that?"

Fuck. I can already feel myself getting damp. And this dress is far too revealing for that to lead anywhere good.

"CAS!"

We leap apart like startled teenagers at the sound of Mia's voice.

The woman I consider to be my oldest friend marches towards us on the warpath—her fiery red hair streaming behind her like a banner.

But she stops just short of our table, eyes practically bulging at the sight of us so close together.

I cross my legs in annoyance. "Mia."

"You," she tries, then starts again. "I was so worried about you."

"I'm fine."

My words come out far colder than I intend them to. But that old ache in my chest flares up at the sight of her.

She knew who Rocco was and that Claudio had been a mafia man when we were dating. Yet she kept the mafia and the Guild and all the Italian bullshit from me, even though she *knew* I was involved.

She lied to me for almost twenty years. And I don't think I'm ready to deal with that yet.

Her expression shifts to defensiveness at my tone. "I sent you like a million messages."

"I know."

Mia's eyes shift over to Rocco menacingly. "What have you done to her?"

To his credit, he doesn't wilt under her gaze. "I told her the truth, Chiavari. Now, I must ask you to leave us alone."

The slight waver in her eyes at his order tells me everything I need to know.

"You work for him, don't you?"

She looks back at me in alarm. "It's not what you think, Cas. Please."

"You hid this from me."

"I was trying to protect you!"

Around us, people begin applauding as Danny finishes her set.

"And what an excellent job you did of that," I reply bitterly.

Mia seems frozen in place, torn between obeying the orders of her don and trying to reason with me.

I save myself the heartache of watching her choose.

"Excuse me, I need the bathroom." I stand abruptly and march away before she can reply.

I can almost feel Rocco's eyes on me as I walk straight up to the backstage door instead and slip through.

In my heart, I know how I acted toward Mia was cruel. But her deceit just raises more and more troubling questions. Do her parents know? Are they somehow involved in all this, too?

My father and hers had been friends from *work*.

Mia may have lied, but my own mother might have known all this too. And that is more heartbreaking than I know how to deal with right now.

Instead, I take a deep breath and force myself to focus on the task at hand. Find Claudio. Get him to talk.

Everything else I can figure out later.

But it turns out I don't have to look very hard.

I hear him as I round the corner to my old dressing room.

Moaning. Loudly.

A shiver of disgust runs across my body. I already hate what I'm about to see before I even open the door.

There, leaning against *my* fucking dressing table, is Claudio. His pants are wrapped around his ankles as fucking Teresa, in her fucking midnight blue body suit, fu his fucking cock in her fucking mouth.

Fuck.

My anger doesn't rage within. It burns everything around me to a crisp.

They both seem to feel it at the same time. Claudio's eyes shoot open just as Teresa lets out a pathetic scream and scampers away.

"Cas!" Claudio chokes on the word as he fully registers who he's staring at and what I'm wearing.

He awkwardly scrambles for his boxers and pants as Teresa all but crawls away. Coward.

"I thought you said you wanted to meet me here."

Awareness seems to flood his expression finally. I can't even begin to imagine how many drugs he's on right now.

"I did, I do, baby!" he slurs slightly as he steps toward me, still fumbling with his belt. "It's so good to see you."

"Did you spend all the money you traded me for on drugs?"

Claudio makes an odd, dismissive sound. "Of course not! You paid off a loan, baby. I'm a free man because of you."

"Clearly."

"Don't be like that," he groans. "Teresa and I are just friends."

"She was literally just in here sucking your cock!"

He gives me a blank look. "Was she really?"

This isn't going anywhere, so I change tactics.

"Look, I came here tonight to see *you*. To see if you could be trusted enough to start over again after everything that happened. But clearly, this was a mistake."

I make to leave and try not to flinch as he grabs my arm. "You can trust me, baby."

"Can I?"

"Of course. I'm gonna make you a star, remember?"

I pretend to consider his grim smile as something I could possibly adore. "Then tell me something."

"Anything."

"Why would you take that money from the mafia? It's so dangerous! What could you possibly have needed it for to be worth the risk?"

He blinks at me for a moment. "You, baby."

For a moment, I think I must have misheard him. "What are you talking about?"

"You think flights to Ohio are cheap? You think I could afford all those fancy meals I took you on?"

I shake my head. Even if he'd taken me to Michelin-star restaurants—which he definitely didn't—there's no way he could have spent one hundred and one thousand dollars over the course of our courtship.

"You took a loan from the Mafia to pay for our dates?" I can feel a laugh bubbling up inside me. "You really think I'm going to believe that?"

He moans loudly as he slumps down in the seat. "You're fucking expensive, Cas! I had to buy a whole new apartment for you, remember?"

Remarkably, something does ring true as he says this.

But he told me he was moving to the apartment in Brownsville because he got a promotion at work.

A promotion...within the mafia.

I laugh him off. "Who in their right mind, mafia or not, would loan anyone money so they can date someone?"

"I don't know, Cas," he slurs. "Ask fucking Bellini."

Now, he's really not making any kind of sense. "*I'm* Bellini, Claudio. Cassandra Bellini, remember?"

"Fucking Bellini!" he shouts suddenly, almost startling himself out of the chair in the process.

There's no point talking to him anymore, not when he's like this.

If I'm being honest with myself, I'd wanted more from this conversation. I wanted him to be sober enough to see me as I am now: happy without him. I wanted that to hurt him. I wanted him to feel even a little bit of my own pain.

But instead, I'm left with this intoxicated mess.

"We're done, Claudio," I say anyway. "You can go to hell."

It's not at all satisfying. In fact, it feels as if I've said those words a thousand times already. There's no need for closure when it comes to something you've already moved on from.

I think he tries to call after me, but I'm already out the door.

At least I got something out of him, even if nothing about it made any sense at all.

Maybe everything he said was an elaborate lie to get me back on side. It was as if he thought claiming that I was the reason he took the loan was some kind of romantic gesture.

All I can do is hope that this wasn't some massive waste of time.

I push through the doors leading me back into the *Candelabra* and plaster on a sultry smile. Now that my part was done, there was no reason for us to head straight back to the brownstone.

But Mia careens around the side of the bar and marches straight toward me. I can tell she's trying to get me to stop and speak with her, so I turn to avoid her.

Only to see...

Words escape me. My entire world spins out from under me.

"Cas! It's not worth it."

Vaguely, I'm aware of Mia's hands holding down my shaking arms.

As I watch Danny straddling Rocco's lap, her lips pressed up against his.

19

ROCCO

Danny slides herself onto my lap far too easily.

"Have you forgiven me yet?" she purrs in my ear.

I glance over at the backstage door, but Cas hasn't emerged yet. "I'll give you about three seconds to get off me before I make a scene."

The last time I saw her was that night at the *Electrix*. I thought she might have finally understood that our little arrangement was over, but considering the stench of alcohol on her breath, it seems she's not making particularly rational decisions right now.

She scowls at me. "Please. You can't seriously think we believe you'd settle down with someone like Bellini."

The name catches me off guard. "What? Who are you talking about?"

Danny laughs. Her golden hair cascades down her back as she throws back her head. "You haven't changed a bit! You've been fucking her all this time, but you still don't know her name?"

She keeps talking, but it becomes background noise to the thoughts racing through my mind.

Danny is talking about Cassandra. Cassandra Bellini. It was a common enough name. Except...

It wasn't a coincidence. It couldn't be.

Carmine *Bellini*. The man who sold Guild intel to the Cartel had a family. At least, he used to before his wife divorced him.

Seventeen years ago.

At the same time, Cassandra moved from Brooklyn to Ohio at the age of eight with only her mother.

Carmine *Bellini*. Whose only friend in my father's inner circle was Marco Chiavari. Whose daughter had been childhood friends with Cassandra.

But perhaps the most damning piece of evidence was that Cassandra's father died a month ago.

When Carmine *Bellini* had shot himself in the head before my very eyes.

"You know it's true," Danny is saying, but I can barely hear her over the ringing in my ear. "Let's just get back to the way things were."

Cassandra can't know. Couldn't know. Could she?

Could she have been playing me this whole time to enact some kind of sick revenge?

I can't believe that. Refuse to. She's been through too much for that to have been an act. I had seen the truth in her eyes when she'd bargained for her protection.

Besides, she's been alone with me in my own home countless times. Countless, very *vulnerable* times, and yet she's done nothing to take advantage of that.

But why is she here? Now? After seventeen years, magically appearing only a week before Carmine's death?

If her mother had taken her to Ohio to get *away* from Carmine and the Guild and all the pressures of the Italian Mafia, why would she suddenly know to come back now? Why not come as soon as she turned eighteen?

Is it all just a tragic coincidence? Carmine finally found the courage to reach out, only to die before he got the chance to meet.

Unless…somehow, he *knew* he was going to die.

But what kind of father would drag their estranged daughter into something like that? He must have known his life was on the line when he betrayed the Guild. Would he really endanger her like that? For the sake of his own closure?

"You are going to do great things, Rocco."

None of this makes any sense. Every question only branches out into five more.

Somehow, this has to be connected to the missing rat. The timing is just too perfect. I just need to figure out *how*.

A pair of lips press against mine, and I'm abruptly torn from my spiral.

For a moment, I remain entirely frozen, stunned that I had let my guard down so thoroughly that I hadn't noticed Danny's very obvious intentions.

The feeling of her tongue attempting to gain access to my mouth jolts me into action.

My hand snatches at her golden hair, and I pull down sharply.

Her gasp elicits nothing but contempt.

"What the fuck are you doing?"

My entire body begins to shake with rage. I am entirely disgusted by every inch of her skin that touches mine.

"Rocco!" She turns those watery blue eyes on me to no effect.

"Get. Off. Me."

I don't know if it's the threat of my tone or the sharpness of my expression, but something akin to fear crosses her face. Good.

She scrambles away, landing straight on the floor, and I release her hair with a flick of my wrist.

"If you dare touch me again," I hiss down at her. "If you touch anyone again without their consent, you will never get up on that stage again."

Danny puts her hand to her mouth to conceal a sob. "I... I thought..."

"You did not think," I correct as I snap my fingers.

Terry is there in an instant. "Sir?"

"Escort Miss Lombardi from the premises."

I sit back in my chair as the bartender tries to pry a sobbing Danny from the floor. So much for not making a scene.

I look around for one of my more able-bodied men to assist, only for my attention to snag on a retreating figure about to push through the main exit—her black dress snags on Mia's persistent feet at her heels.

When Cas' turns so she she can free herself, her face is streaked with tears.

My insides hollow out.

Did she just see that?

I'm on my feet a heartbeat later, pushing through the crowds to chase after her, not caring that everyone around me seems to be staring.

"Boss?" Teo's voice crackles through my earpiece. "You might want to listen to what Lazzaro just said."

"Not now," I bite back.

"Did you know that Cassandra's surname is Bellini?"

"I said, not now!"

I yank the damn thing from my ear and throw it to the ground.

Because it doesn't matter. Even though it absolutely should.

I should be running after her to demand the answers I need, to confront her about being Carmine Bellini's daughter.

Yet the only thing I can think about is how I've hurt her again. That she might think someone like Danny could hold my attention for even a second now that *she* was in my life.

That despite every inch of distance I have tried to put between us, my heart aches at the mere thought of it.

There is nothing rational that spurs my steps toward her.

Only the memory of her tear-stained face and the thunderous voice in my head screaming at me to make this right.

Someone grabs my arm before I can make it to the front doors.

"Haven't you done enough?" Mia hisses at me.

"Remove your hand, or you will lose it."

"I told her to stay away from you."

I turn to look at the redhead. She has the decency to swallow her next words and let go.

Vaguely, I'm aware that she curses as I push through the front doors of the *Candelabra*.

"Cassandra!" I start shouting into the night.

But she's nowhere in sight.

I mindlessly begin to stride forward, taking in every face that passes by.

It's a cool night, and it's nearing the early hours of the

morning. There are enough people around for her to get lost in, but not enough to find anyone sober to ask if they've seen her pass by.

"CASS!" I shout again. I have to think this through logically.

Where would she go?

We'd arrived by car. My dark chrome Bugatti Mistral is currently parked in the secure parking lot beneath the building. Without a keycode, she couldn't go back down there.

If she called a cab, where would she go? Back to the brownstone? Or would she skip town entirely and get on the next flight to Ohio?

Surely, she wouldn't try walking anywhere. It's too late for that to be even remotely safe, even if she hadn't just appeared publicly on my arm.

The lethal part of my brain already thinks about what would happen to the person who tried to harm her.

My eyes snag on a figure huddled under the nearby bus shelter.

"Cass," I breathe out.

She doesn't look at me as I approach, but I can see the tears still rolling down her face. I can't bear it.

I reach out to tilt her head up to look at me, but she snatches it away. My only option is to get on my knees before her.

"Cassandra." Her name on my lips feels like a prayer.

For a moment, she says nothing.

"Claudio was cheating on me."

It's like a stab to the chest. Was I really so conceited to think her tears were for *me?*

I swallow back my pride. "I'm sorry."

"Did you know?"

My memory snags on that night at the *Electrix*. If I hadn't arrived, he'd likely have had Danny and Teresa that night.

All I can do is nod.

She gasps bitterly. "Figures."

"I didn't mean to keep this from you, Cas."

"But you love keeping me at arm's length," she looks down at me. "Cute enough to fuck but not good enough to kiss?"

My blood runs cold. So she had seen Danny and I.

"Please, Cas. Let me explain."

"You don't need to. I get it. She's beautiful and talented, and you clearly have history." she sniffs. "I'm sorry if my staying with you has strained your relationship with her."

I'm already shaking my head. "Our relationship was over before I met you."

"I don't care. You don't owe me anything, Rocco. We never said anything about exclusivity. It's my own fault I'm..." her voice breaks and she takes a second to gather herself again. "This is just physical, right? You said that from the start."

"I said that to keep you safe." I reach for her hands and hold them firm. "You saw how many people were looking at us today. If any of them thought that I was attached to you. Fuck, if they thought they could exploit *you* as my weakness..."

"Yeah. I know."

"You don't," my voice breaks. "Cas, if anything were to happen to you because of your attachment to me, I'd..."

I have to work hard to keep the horrified sob from escaping my lips.

Cas looks at me with those wide, hazel doe eyes. "Rocco?"

"I wouldn't be able to live with myself. If anyone so much as *looks* at you the wrong way…I can't stop it. I would set the world on fire for you and lay the ashes at your feet."

My heart screams at me to stop. Revealing this much will just scare her out of reach. But for one glorious moment, I swear I see hope in her eyes.

Before she crashes into reality and recoils into herself.

"You think you can just run after me and say all this stuff like you actually care?" she says as she pats away her tears. "I knew you were cruel, but Rocco, *this*? It's too far."

"I'm telling you the truth," I offer desperately.

"You're telling me what I want to hear! You're just saying this stuff because you know I'm the fucking moron who fell for you, and this is the only way to keep me in line."

Everything within me goes quiet. "What did you just say?"

"You can take me back to the brownstone. I'll do whatever you want for these last months. I'll stay true to our agreement. Just, please," she takes a long haggard breath. "Stop saying these things. It's not fair."

I reach for her neck and pull her down to me. "Cass."

"Stop it!"

I can't. "Look at me."

Tears well up in her eyes. "Rocco, you kissed her."

"She kissed *me*. She took advantage of a moment of distraction. It shouldn't have happened. I should have never let it happen."

"Because you want to protect her, too?"

I brush her hair from her face. "No. You are the only person I care about."

"I can't take this," she whispers back.

"Then believe me."

I rise to press my lips with hers.

20

CASSANDRA

I can't breathe.

Rocco must think he's kissing a statue.

Because I can't bring myself to even blink in fear that this might all be a dream, that I might suddenly wake up somewhere far away with nothing but his name to remember him by.

"Cas," he whispers, drawing back an inch that feels like a mile. "Cas, kiss me."

It's not an order; it's a plea.

"I only want you."

His words are like honey.

And the way I kiss him back is sickly sweet.

The rational part of my brain is screaming at me to stop. I know that whatever lies down this path with Rocco Moretti will be dangerous, that I might risk more than a broken heart.

But the way his lips yield to mine shoves such thoughts deep down.

This is intoxicating. I can't get enough of it.

Our mouths glide together, our tongues dancing in a passionate frenzy. I just want more and more and more.

We've only shared one kiss before this, and though my thoughts lingered on it every night before I fell asleep, the memory has nothing on the real thing.

"Cas," he whispers against my mouth, and I taste my own name on his lips.

At some point, my hands tangle in his dark hair, tugging him ever closer.

"Get a fuckin' room!"

We break apart in alarm as someone passes by, shaking their head.

Right. We're sitting at a bus stop in the middle of Brooklyn in the early hours of the morning.

As if on cue, a shiver runs down my spine. Rocco had insisted I leave my leather jacket at home.

"Come on," Rocco murmurs, a little breathless, as he sheds his own jacket and wraps it around my shoulders. "Let's get out of here."

I let him stand me up and guide me back to the *Candelabra* with an arm around my shoulders. For one horrible moment, I think he's about to take us back in. Even just the thought of confronting Danny or Claudio again wipes away all the joy of our kiss.

But he diverts to the parking lot. It's an underground bunker-like space that I'd never realized existed below the *Candelabra* until Rocco had driven into it earlier that evening.

No other cars are parked there as we enter. Only the low thrum of bass music from the venue above us keeps us company as we walk over to the fancy convertible sports car we arrived in.

I'm still tucked under his arm as we approach. His heavenly scent overwhelms my senses as I try to concentrate on putting one foot in front of the other.

The headlights flash in welcome as Rocco reaches for the door.

If there was a time to clear the air, to get my head on straight about what the hell we are to each other, it would be now before I have to ride home with him, so agonizingly close.

"Rocco, I..."

But he cuts me off with another kiss, pushing me back against the car and pinning himself against me. His hand snakes around to the back of my neck, holding me in place.

The hardness of his cock presses into my leg, mere inches from where I need him to be. "Fuck," I gasp when he finally releases my mouth.

But his mouth doesn't stop. He frantically explores the expanse of my exposed neck, and I succumb to him easily. The way his tongue explores my skin sends shivers of delight down my spine.

"I don't think I can do it," he hisses across my collarbone. "I don't think I can drive us back without crashing the damn car."

Wanton desire courses through me as my eyes flash open, assessing the situation. The doors to the bunker are closed; there is no one else around.

With a surge of confidence, I reach behind me and drag open the car door.

"Get in," I instruct him with a desperate shove for good measure.

Thankfully, he doesn't argue and sits down in the passenger seat. I glance over my shoulder one more time before I join him, straddling his waist as I pull the door closed behind me.

The feeling of him hard beneath me has me stifling a groan, especially when his hands start to roam across my chest.

The tinted windows offer us at least some privacy, but the lack of a roof means that anyone could hear us. Not to mention that any cameras looking in from above would certainly catch us.

But when Rocco drags me down to meet his lips again, such concerns escape me. Vaguely, I'm aware of him lowering the seat, but I'm too busy sticking my tongue down his throat like a love-lorn teenager to care.

I have no idea how much time passes as I lay across his chest like that. But suddenly, the low, fluorescent lights flicker out.

I gasp against his mouth.

"It's just the timer," Rocco reassures me, half his face now cast in shadow, the other illuminated with a blue tinge by the center console.

In the half-darkness, my senses become heightened. My ears strain harder for any indication that someone might walk in on us.

Then, a hand reaches for my neck. It happens so suddenly that I let out a short shriek.

"Shhh..." Rocco hisses close to my ear. "Did I scare you?"

I let out a shaking breath.

"N...no?"

His hand begins to explore my chest again, rubbing me through my clothes. I feel the tension beginning to seep down to my core.

"Do you trust me?" His voice is suddenly low, his tongue darting out across my exposed cleavage.

All I can do is nod.

Suddenly, I feel a tug on the back of my dress. A second later, the zipper is entirely undone, and the front of my beautiful, bespoke gown is falling to my waist.

"Rocco!" I cry in alarm.

But he presses in closer to me, covering me with those huge, tattooed arms, and begins to stroke at the bare skin of my stomach. It feels like he's everywhere. Every touch is an unexpected delight that sends shivers of desire through me.

I search frantically for his face, missing the presence of his lips. But then they're on my neck, and I melt into the sensation of his tongue working its way back to my mouth.

When he reaches it, the kiss I give him is filthy, all teeth and tongue and lips. I suck on his lips like it's my only source of oxygen.

His fingers slip around my leg, hoisting the skirt material up my thigh...

"Fuck!" he curses when he finally discovers the bareness of my ass, the lack of clothing standing between him and my now throbbing center.

I bite hard on his lip to try and silence him. But I'm rewarded with a stiff groan as he scrambles to unfasten his pants.

"Do you trust me?" he asks again.

His hands dig into my ass, pushing me closer. I can feel the hardness of his cock, now released from its restraints, pressing into my stomach tantalizingly.

"I trust you to delete whatever footage there is of this."

Rocco pushes me back immediately, allowing me to sit up properly, entirely exposed to the elements. But his hands never leave my skin, grabbing at my chest to keep my breasts from view.

There's nothing but pure lust on his face as he looks up at me.

"Do you think I would share you with anyone?"

He massages my breasts in his hand, thumb flicking over my taut nipples. All I can do is desperately rub my soaked sex up and down his thickening cock.

"Do you think I enjoyed letting you see Lazzaro?"

One hand drops down to lift himself up to meet my eager entrance. But he holds me there, just hovering over the release I so desperately need.

"I could have killed every man in that room who looked at you and wondered what this would feel like."

Finally, he lowers me onto his thick cock. The feeling of him inside me sets my entire body alight.

"Does that scare you?"

It should. It really should. This man is a criminal. There is nothing light about that threat.

But Claudio had started fucking the first woman he stumbled across once I left. Hell, it was likely he'd been doing it already.

Rocco would kill for me.

And there was nothing more intoxicating than that.

"No," I gasp as I plunge myself down to the hilt, arching my back in pleasure. "I trust you to protect me."

"Because you're *mine,* Cas," he hisses into the darkness, and my heart shines right back.

So I ride him, letting him claim me, chasing my pleasure and the soft grunts he makes when I take him whole. The sound of our slapping skin fills the space between us as I bounce over and over.

The darkness only makes everything feel closer, more sensual, more private. I lose myself entirely to it, not caring when Rocco's hands drop from my chest to my waist, slamming me down harder.

And when the urge becomes too overwhelming, I lean forward and take his lips with mine. And this. *This* is what I've been missing. The way his lips set a fire within me is so pleasurable that, even though he pounds so deeply inside me, *this* is what begins my climax.

He can feel it, too. He must because our kisses become more frantic, more filthy, as I slam down harder and harder. The car beneath us shakes in time with the movement.

I could bask in this moment forever. But I have to pull away to adjust my angle, to bury him further.

"Don't leave," his voice gasps in the darkness.

Is he saying that because he can no longer reach my kisses? Or is it something more?

We both groan as this new angle sends pleasure coursing into my core. I won't be able to hold on much longer.

"I won't," I pant back.

I'm completely unaware of his creeping thumb until it's circling my clit.

I move harder, quicker. Suddenly, the friction isn't enough. I need more. More of him. I need to be closer.

I lower myself to him. Frantically searching for his mouth.

But he finds me first. Capturing my lips with his.

Our tongues wrestle as our bodies move in synchronization. His thumb plays with me expertly, bringing me closer and closer to the edge.

I tear myself from his lips, throwing my head back in

ecstasy as we slam into each other, unsure where my body ends and his begins.

His cock twitches inside of me, and it becomes my undoing.

I scream his name as we come together.

And for a moment, there is nothing.

There's just the two of us sharing gasping breaths, aching bodies, and a ragged, broken heartbeat.

I lay on top of him, utterly spent and exhausted. His arms wrap around me gently as we just breathe each other in and out.

This isn't like the other times.

Something has shifted.

Even the way he kisses the top of my head feels more intimate, as if by screaming his name while we came together somehow branded him on my very skin.

"I could just stay here," I murmur across his chest.

But my traitorous body begins to ache, and the tight space of the car's interior becomes increasingly uncomfortable.

Beneath me, Rocco sighs. "Let's go home."

Home. The word resonates with surprising accuracy. It might have only been a month, yet that's what the brownstone has become for me.

It's a quiet ride home, so I try to look out to admire the city lights. But his hand does not leave my thigh, rubbing it so very distractingly with his thumb.

I want to call him out for being so possessive, but it feels so *good* to be driven around by a man who can't keep his hands off me. In a city that he has in his pocket.

For the first time in a long time, I feel powerful.

His casual touch doesn't stop when we finally get back to

the brownstone. He opens my car door and helps me out of the passenger seat. A hand snakes its way around my waist as we walk up to the front doors.

I savor every second of it, wondering how much I can get away with. My hand reaches up to brush his hair out of his eyes. My fingers trail down the arm that's around me. There's so much of him that I haven't explored yet.

When we reach the top of the staircase, I hesitate for only a moment, glancing at my bedroom door down the hall.

"You seriously think I'm going to let you out of my sight?" Rocco says, already pulling me toward his own bedroom.

"My bedroom is cozier, though," I tease back.

He huffs a laugh, immediately stripping off his clothing as we enter his room and he drags me toward the bed. "You're welcome to redecorate."

"Seriously?"

I follow his lead, removing my gorgeous dress and sliding into bed next to him. His arms immediately encircle me.

"Cas, I will give you whatever your heart desires."

21

ROCCO

My entire body feels light. It's as if, for the first time in five years, I've actually been able to relax enough to sleep through the night.

I can feel a gentle breeze from the open window, soothing my skin as I stretch. My arms pop in satisfaction.

They reach down to cradle the woman at my side. She's the reason for this sense of peace that seems to have enveloped me, this woman who has submitted entirely to me, as I have to her.

But my hands find nothing but air.

Finally, I crack my eyes open, only discover the bed beside me is empty.

Ruffled white sheets and her scent are the only things that linger.

"Don't leave me."

"I won't."

She wouldn't. Not so soon.

I can feel my heart beginning to pound within my chest as my mind spins into catastrophe.

I knew exhibiting Cassandra on my arm at the *Candelabra* had been a risk. Any woman I associate with has a target on their back. But usually, my preemptive measures were enough to keep them safe.

I would send someone to trail after them for a few weeks to ensure they left the city or else help them drop into obscurity with a handsome paycheck. My reputation had ensured the rest. I didn't care enough about those women for them to warrant my enemy's interest.

Danny was the only one to insist on sticking around, and Alessandro had reported several incidents that had concerned me.

But Danny could look after herself, and my public displays of affection for her could never have been misconstrued as anything but transactional.

Cas, however…

Had I been so transparent? Had someone somehow realized the truth when I held her possessively at my side? If anyone had entered that parking lot last night and seen how utterly ruined I truly was, there would be no doubt.

Cas is my weakness.

And now she had disappeared.

I jump from the bed, scrambling to find a pair of pants as I examine the scene before me.

The window is open. Someone could have approached in the night and taken her. There was no sign of a struggle, but that meant nothing in my line of work. If she'd been asleep, it would have taken nothing to render her unconscious.

BEEP. BEEP. BEEP. BEEP. BEEP.

The sound of the fire alarm has me springing into action.

The gun I keep in my bottom drawer is in my hand, and I'm out the door a millisecond later.

"CAS! Donatella!"

Who would be foolish enough to attack me in my own home? For one, setting fire to the place was so damn cliche I want to punch something. For another, none of my enemies know where this place is.

Its location is a secret kept between Donatella, Teo, and myself. They are the two people I trust most in this damn world. And now, I suppose, Cassandra.

I hadn't bothered to blindfold her when we traveled to and from the *Candelabra*. In truth, it hadn't even crossed my mind.

I shake the thought away as I pound down the hall, shoving open every door and aiming my gun inside as I pass.

"Cassandra!"

But every door reveals nothing, and every step takes me further panic.

BEEP. BEEP. BEEP. BEEP. BEEP.

I take the stairs two at a time, trying to find the source of the fire. If the fucker who set it off is still there, he will take me to Cassandra.

Someone screams. And my blood runs cold.

The sound sends me careening toward the kitchen. I brace myself as I kick down the door.

I'm immediately greeted with billowing black smoke that renders me temporarily blind.

"CAS?"

I blink away the smoke.

To find Donatella standing barefoot on the counter, frantically wafting at the smoke alarm with a towel. A half dozen charred pieces of bacon are strewn across the floor as if flung from the cast iron pan that still hisses with fat on the ground.

And, at the center of it all, is a sheepish-looking Cas hunched over the tap, wincing in agony.

The gun in my hand feels suddenly entirely unwarranted. I quickly holster it in the back of my pants before anyone can notice.

"What the hell?"

"Sorry!" Cas gives me a frantic look as she approaches. "I didn't mean to wake you."

Finally, the beeping of the alarm subsides, and Donatella hops down from the counter. "Clearly, you were trying to burn the entire house down."

"I was just trying to make breakfast." Cas ducks her head in shame.

A startled laugh escapes my lips as I tug her toward me, needing her closeness to reassure my poor, anxious heart that she is okay.

"I think we'll leave the cooking to Donatella in the future."

Cas returns my embrace hesitantly, so I glance down to try and find the cause. But she's buried her head in my chest.

Donatella grabs a towel to wrap around the still-sizzling panhandle. "You scared me half to death. You could have burned your arm off!"

When Cas cringes against me, I gently pry her arms from around my waist and examine her hands. As I suspected, a large welt seems to be forming on her left palm.

"It's fine," she insists.

But I'm already dragging her back over to the sink and

turning on the water. I stand behind her as I hold her burned hand up to the steady stream of cool water.

"I could do this myself," she murmurs but makes no move to shake me away.

Behind me, I hear Donatella sigh. "I have some chores to catch up on."

I make a mental note to ensure Donatella's bonus is doubled this month when the kitchen door bangs shut behind her.

Finally alone, I take the opportunity to pin Cas against the counter with my other hand and rest my head on her shoulder.

"I'm sorry," Cas sighs as she leans against me seemingly content with my closeness.

"For nearly burning down my house?"

"For being a terrible cook."

I slowly rotate her arm so that the water splashes evenly over the burn. "I don't need you to cook for me."

"I was just trying to do something nice."

With a laugh, I plant a soft kiss on the side of her neck. "It's the thought that counts, *Angioletta.*"

There's a pause where we both seem to bask in the moment comfortably.

"Why do you call me that?" she asks suddenly.

"*Angioletta?*"

"Yes."

I smile. "Do you know what it means?"

She cocks her head slightly. "I might have googled it."

"The first time I saw you singing on the stage at the *Candelabra,* I knew you had to be some kind of angel," I explain. "But then I realized that wasn't true."

She pulls away to look at me. "I'm insulted."

My eyes dart hungrily to her mouth. "You were far too tempting for a little angel."

Cas smirks as she leans forward and takes my bottom lip between her teeth.

I growl in response, pressing my hardening crotch against her so that she can feel my growing desire.

"See?" I breathe once she's released me. "Practically sinful."

She hums happily in response, and Jesus Christ, do I want to bend her over and replay our last adventure in this very kitchen scene by mouth watering scene.

But then her stomach rumbles.

A flush immediately rises in her cheeks. "I..."

With a chuckle, I kiss the top of her head and step away. "Keep your hand under the water. I'll make us breakfast."

"*You,*" she scoffs. "Are you sure you don't want to call Donatella?

"I'll have you know, I'm an exceptional cook."

I grab four eggs from the fridge. Their familiar weight fits comfortably in one hand, and as I set up the frying pan on the stove with the other, I immediately feel myself sink into the zone.

It's been a while since I've bothered with doing this, but the routine of it soothes what remains of my anxiety from earlier.

I take a metal spatula out next and wave it at Cas. "Watch," I say as I throw an egg up into the air over the pan. It falls perfectly on top of my spatula, wedging the shell and cracking the contents into the warm surface below.

She lets out a low whistle. "I'd clap, but..." she waves her injured hand at me. "Where did you learn that?"

"I had a big house and a whole lot of downtime as a kid."

I turn away to the stove. "I figured I'd learn from my father's numerous award-winning chefs."

"Ah, so is it a Michelin-star secret technique?"

"The egg toss?" I say as I throw two slices of bread in the toaster.

"Bringing a gun into the kitchen."

Damn it. I forgot about the pistol shoved into the back of my pants. I'd revealed it to her as soon as I turned my back to her.

"You can never be too careful," I joke.

She hums non-committedly. "Is that a mafia thing?"

"It's a...a" the sizzling eggs fill the silence for a moment, "territorial thing."

"You scared someone's gonna come in here and make better eggs than you?"

I take my time plating up the food in order to formulate my response. It's a simple meal, but I garnish it with salt, pepper, and fresh parsley.

"These days, I have a little more to lose, I suppose," I say as I hand her a plate.

She takes it with her good hand and turns off the faucet in order to join me at the breakfast bench.

"This looks lovely," she replies as she stares down at the food before her.

"Thank you..."

"What are we, Rocco?" The words explode out of her so quickly, I think even she's taken aback by her abruptness.

I blink back. "I assume 'hungry' isn't the answer you're looking for?"

"I thought this was just...you said you just wanted something physical." She bites her lip. "But last night...it didn't feel just physical anymore. And I basically confessed to you, then you kissed me even though you said you wouldn't do that and..."

"Cas." I smile at her flustered words. "Are you asking me out?"

My words have their desired effect. Cas immediately covers her red face with her hands. "Not when you say it like that!"

I can't help the booming laugh that escapes me as I try to carefully pry her hands from her face. "Cassandra Bellini, I adore you. I would very much like to be your boyfriend."

She grimaces. "Ugh. That sounds so juvenile."

"Partners then?"

"Pass."

"Lovers."

"How about I just call you Rocco?" she suggests as she tucks into her food.

I pretend to think about it. "I prefer 'boss', but I'll take it."

"Is Teo your lover, too? He's the only one I've ever heard call you that."

"You see? Lover isn't so bad, is it?"

She rolls her eyes at me. "I take it you listened to the audio from last night."

I blink at her in confusion. "What?"

"You used my surname just now. I don't think I ever told you it before," she gives me a funny look. "It was always 'Cassandra' this or '*Angioletta*' that."

Right. Because Danny only told me her name was Bellini last night. But what does that have to do with the audio she took from her confrontation with Lazzaro?

"What do you think?" she asks. "Lazzaro was high as all hell, right?"

"I…"

I'm saved an answer by Teo storming into the room. "Why the hell haven't you been picking up your damn phone?"

He freezes when he spots the two of us, and I become acutely aware that I'm not wearing a shirt.

"Morning, Vitale," I greet him carefully as his eyebrows shoot up.

If he was suffering under any delusion about the nature of Cas and I's relationship, he wasn't any longer.

"Boss."

Cas snickers at my side.

Teo's eyes narrow. "Cassandra."

"Hi, Teo," she replies innocently.

"Do you need something?" I ask.

"I think you better come to the compound," Teo declares. "If Miss *Bellini* can spare you for a moment."

Ah.

Teo has worked it out, too. He surveys me carefully as if to gauge my reaction, but I merely shrug in response. "Duty calls, I'm afraid, *Angioletta.*"

I make a show of holding her neck as I kiss her softly goodbye.

She hums contentedly. "I'll see you later."

Teo doesn't speak to me again until I've dressed and walked out of the brownstone.

"This just got one hell of a lot more complicated. I hope you know what the fuck you're doing, Moretti," he hisses as I reach my Bugatti.

I glance back at the house, where I can just about make out Cas waving down at us from her bedroom window.

"Me too."

22

CASSANDRA

I don't think I could ever get bored of kissing Rocco.

When I'm not doing it, I'm thinking about it. When I am, I do everything I can to prolong it for as long as possible.

I feel starved when he's not around.

And he's not around one hell of a lot.

As the weeks of our second month fly by, I feel like I see him less and less. The time I spend waiting around pining or taking my frustrations out at the gym begins to wear on me.

I must have fucked Rocco in every room in this house, yet I've also sung in every room of this house, napped in every room in this house, and redecorated every room in this house.

To make it even more suffocating, every request I make to Donatella, or on the rare occasion, Teo, about leaving is always met with an awkward denial.

"Rocco?" I ask one morning as I watch Rocco dress for the day from his bed.

"Cassandra."

I check my phone again to be sure. Despite everything, my first paycheck from the *Candelabra* was deposited into my account. "I was wondering if I might go shopping later?"

His fingers freeze as he buttons up his shirt. "I'm er...a bit tied up the next few days. I'll take you this weekend."

"I can take myself," I insist, sitting up and gathering the duvet to my bare chest.

"What did you want to get?"

"Just some sheet music. There's this new mic I've been looking at for, you know, recording stuff at home, but," I shrug. "I think Claudio still has my laptop."

Rocco nods. "I'll look into it."

"Does that mean I can head out later?"

He approaches to kiss my forehead softly. "Just wait until I get back, all right?"

"All right," I resign myself.

"I love what you've done to the room." He diverts my attention to the redecorated bedroom.

I hadn't done much, only added a few decorative items to make the room feel homier. Donatella and I spent an entire day rearranging the furniture, guided by a book on feng shui I'd found in Rocco's office library.

Rocco's office had provided me with the most entertainment so far. At first, the dusty, underused corners of the library had seemed uninviting, but curiosity had finally gotten the better of me.

There weren't just books on Chinese geomancy; beneath had been files upon files of Italian mafia history.

I've made my way through most of the late 1800s and early 1900s. The Guild was formed by an Italian immigrant,

Josef Moretti, who I suppose must be Rocco's great-great-grandfather—a fugitive from the Sicilian authorities.

It's fascinating, more so because the degrees of separation are so few.

"When will you be home?" I ask, shaking the memory of Josef Moretti taking on the don of the Irish mob in hand-to-hand combat.

"Late." He sighs. "The Cartel are wiping the floor with us."

"Damn Tunnel Eaters," I joke back.

He gives me an odd look. "I'll be interrogating this evening. Don't wait up."

I do anyway. But as he promised, he doesn't return. At some point, I must fall asleep because I awaken the next morning to a key being placed in my hand.

Rocco smiles down at me. "I've got something to show you."

Through bleary eyes, I rise to greet him with a kiss before he takes my hand and leads me down the hall. We stop in front of one of the other bedrooms, and he gestures me forward.

The key slots perfectly into the door, and I push it open.

"Is this..." I step inside with wide eyes. "A recording studio?"

The entire room had been transformed overnight. Sound dampeners now cover every wall, and a brand new recording deck sits shining in the corner.

I approach the microphone in the middle of the room and admire the headphones that are already perched on the stand nearby where reams of sheet music are already on display.

"Surprise," Rocco whispers from behind me, wrapping his arms around my waist.

I'm speechless, both at his generosity and...and... "I thought we were going shopping together?"

"I thought I'd save you a trip." He kisses my cheek before pulling away. "I'll be back late tonight again, so enjoy. I'll see you tomorrow."

I don't know when I reach my breaking point.

But it must have been some time before Rocco arrived home early one evening, and after I sank to my knees before him on the living room couch, desperate to taste him after what felt like days of prolonged absence.

"Fuck, Cas!" he growls as I take his cock to the back of my throat, relishing the way his hands tangle in my hair, pulling at the roots.

I feel his release shuddering through him before he cries out again, and I brace myself for his load.

The groan he makes is so intoxicating I have to force myself not to let my hand dip beneath my pants to take the edge off my own desire.

I swallow him down before releasing him breathlessly, leaning my head against his thigh.

"Rocco?"

"Cassandra."

I look up at him. "I wanted to ask you something."

"Jesus, Cas. Not like that."

"Not like what?" I reply innocently before licking my lips to catch any lingering taste of him.

Rocco tugs me upward to join him on the couch. "You

could look up at me with those eyes, and I'd burn down the damn planet if you asked."

"Would you really?" I tease, bringing my feet up and snuggling into his side.

"Would it excite you if I said yes?"

I kiss the skin of his chest. "Maybe."

"What did you want to say?"

I pause a moment, gathering my nerve. "I was wondering if I might go back to work."

The arm around me tightens slightly. "Why do you want that?"

"I think I miss singing."

"You have the recording studio."

I look up at him, at the tight, irritated line of his jaw. "It's not the same, Rocco. I think you know that."

There's a pause. "Do you…want to see him again?"

It's my turn to feel irritated. We hadn't talked about that night beyond my displeasure at Claudio's lack of sobriety and choice of company.

I thought Rocco had dropped it because it had been a complete waste of time. But the reek of jealousy in his voice gives way to a whole new explanation.

After everything we've been through, had I not made my choice in men crystal clear?

With a huff, I shuffle up on my knees and throw one around his waist, straddling him. He doesn't meet my eye, even when I lower my chest closer to his face.

"Rocco."

"Cassandra."

"I don't want to see him," I say firmly.

Finally, he glances over at me. "You're looking at me like that again. It's distracting from your point."

"Do you want me to close my eyes?"

"I want you to stay here and be safe."

My body sags back on my heels. "Rocco, if I have to stay here for another month, I think I'm going to go insane."

"Then let me take you to South Africa. You'll love it there."

"Sure. If you come with me," I counter.

Rocco's frown deepens. "You know I wouldn't be able to stay."

"Because the Cartel is giving you such a headache? The Tunnel Snakes are acting up again, aren't they?" I cross my arms. "Honestly, I'd prefer to take my chances with Amos Rubio than hide away here."

He raises an eyebrow at me, and I shrug. "You're not as discreet as you think you are."

"You mean you've been snooping in my office."

"Because there is nothing else for me to do here!" I try again. "Please, Rocco. I came to Brooklyn to sing. I haven't been on a stage in almost two months."

"Cas,if anyone with fucking eyes sees us both at the *Candelabra,* they're going to know we're together."

I scoff. "Is that really so awful?"

"I'm trying to keep you alive, Cas." Rocco's hands squeeze my thighs. "If anyone realizes how much you mean to me, you'll have a target on your back for the rest of your life."

I swallow my disappointment. "So that's it? We can be together, but only if you keep me as your dirty little secret."

He growls beneath me. "That is not what I want."

"Then how the hell is *this* supposed to work?"

The question hangs between us like a knife, the edge of

which we've both been dancing along for weeks, begging for either one of us to acknowledge it.

"Cas..." But Rocco fails to come up with an answer.

Can I blame him? When every night, I fall asleep wondering the same thing and come up completely empty.

After a moment, I brave another question. "How does this usually work?"

"Dating?"

"In the Mafia," I clarify. "Surely someone else has been through this before."

Rocco scratches the back of his neck. "My parents had an arranged marriage. My mother was from another prominent family. She had her own bodyguards that ensured her protection, though I don't think she needed it."

I tilt my head slightly. This is the first time I've heard Rocco talk about his mother.

"She was mafioso in her own right," he continues, the ghost of a smile on his lips. "And only put up with my father's bullshit long enough to have me."

"She left him?" I ask before I can stop myself.

Rocco's eyes darken. "No one leaves the Guild."

The threat of his words sits uncomfortably in my stomach.

In the past weeks, I couldn't bring myself to take any of Mia's or my mother's calls. The depths of their potential deceit could be world-shattering, and if I'm being honest with myself, I'm too scared to face them.

But if my theory is true, that my parents were somehow involved in the Mafia too, then how the hell had my mother been allowed to leave?

I shake off that particular rabbit hole. "But you're the don, aren't you?"

"I am now," he corrects. "But the oath we take when we join is an old one. Even if I pardoned someone, it could set an uneasy precedent for those who've spent a lifetime in reluctant servitude."

"But surely it's better to let them go? If they don't want to be there, they can't be of much use to you."

Rocco shrugs. "Even if they did leave, my father would call a hit somehow. He's a miserable bastard like that."

So casually he talks about his father's destruction. Would he really kill someone for breaking their oath? It's not something I'd ever want to find out.

"Remind me never to sign anything when your father's around."

I meant it as a joke, but Rocco's face grows serious. "I wouldn't let you take the Guild's oath."

"Why? Would you get sick of me?" I tease him, trying to bring some lightness to the situation.

"It would be a life sentence." He stares at a point over my shoulder. "And apparently, two months is already grating on you."

I bite the inside of my cheek. "At least then I'd actually be able to do something instead of sitting around the house all day."

He shoots me a warning look. "Trust me. It's not a life you would want."

There's a part of me that wants to argue for the sake of it. But really, what qualifications did I have that would make me an effective mafioso? My one attempt to help had been a complete disaster.

So, instead, I change the subject. "I just want to sing again. Is that really so bad?"

"It's dangerous, Cas," Rocco sighs.

"What if I had bodyguards?" I press. "Your mother had them, right?"

His hand weaves through my hair and gently combs through the loose, brown waves. "It would take some time to make preparations."

A glimmer of hope ignites within me. "I wouldn't need an entire entourage, just someone to make sure I got home okay."

"You will have whoever I say you need to have. I won't negotiate on that."

I grit my teeth, imagining how humiliating it would be to arrive anywhere surrounded by Rocco's mafioso guards. "I don't want to put you out. It's just one performance, so there's really no need. I'll be back home before you know it."

His eyebrow quirks up. "You assume I'll be waiting for you at home."

"I only meant…you're away half the time, and I know you're busy…so."

"My favorite singer will be performing at the *Candelabra*. I wouldn't miss that for the world."

23

ROCCO

"Martino says she'll be on stage soon," Teo announces as he takes a seat next to me at the *Candelabra's* VIP table.

I nod at this, taking in the familiar atmosphere of the packed club.

Alessandro is in the corner with a few of his men, feigning a drunken stag party. Dante has positioned himself on the other side of the room, his own team posing as South African tourists.

Not to mention the handful of lieutenants that had come along for kicks. Each of them had approached the VIP table to offer their sly smiles and transparent intentions: to see what all the fuss was about.

Even Mia is off work tonight, drinking with Marco by the bar. Her fiery gaze narrows on me every few moments, but so far, she has kept her distance. As far as I'm aware, Cas hasn't been in contact with her since the last time we were here.

How many of them I can trust, I don't know. But so far,

Teo and I have been able to keep her surname from becoming public knowledge.

"No sign of him?" I ask. I'd given Claudio Lazzaro very specific orders to make himself scarce tonight.

Thankfully, Teo shakes his head. "Martino hasn't let her out of his sight."

I'm paranoid; I know I am. But you don't make it far in this business if you're not.

"Good."

"Boss...Rocco..." Teo sighs.

I cut him off. "I don't want to talk about it tonight, Vitale."

"You can't ignore it forever," he tries to rationalize. "You have to consider the possibility that she might be working against you."

"I have," I reply firmly, turning myself away to end the conversation.

But Teo has never been one to break under the pressure.

"Carmine hired Lazzaro to bring his daughter to Brooklyn with money he stole from the Guild. He's one of the only people who could have pulled off a loan like that right under Chiavari's nose. You said it yourself."

"I'm not disputing that."

"So it can't be a coincidence that Cassandra Bellini now resides in *your* home with access to your personal files."

I drink to cover my grimace. Finding out that Cas had been rooting through my office was a shock and definitely didn't aid her case. But if she intended to use that information against me, she wouldn't have boasted about knowing it in the first place.

"What are you saying, Vitale? You really think she's the rat?"

He glances over his shoulder before leaning in closer. "I think you'd be a fucking idiot not to consider the possibility."

"Leaks were happening before Cas even came into the picture."

"So she took over from her father after he ate lead."

I shake my head. "She doesn't know anything."

"Right, so she told you that when? While she was sucking your cock?"

A part of me registers the regret in Teo's eyes the second the words leave his mouth. But it's vastly overshadowed by the roar of anger that threatens to consume me.

I dig my fingernails into my palms to steady my breathing.

"You are my brother in everything but blood," I growl out. "But if you don't leave in the next ten seconds, I will kill you."

But Teo only holds my glare with his unnervingly dark eyes. "You are blinded to the truth, Rocco. I'm not going to stop because you wouldn't let me do something this stupid, either."

"You have no idea what you're talking about."

"How's that?" Teo huffs a laugh. "I know you better than anyone. I've seen firsthand how you built the Guild up from nothing, how you fought against your father for five years and emerged victorious. This isn't what you want. The job always comes first."

The job always comes first.

A truth I have lived by my entire life. It's the foundation of everything I have ever done, everything I have become, the song that wakes me up every morning and sends me to sleep every night.

Only...

"Ladies and gentlemen, please welcome to the stage, Miss Cassandra!"

Only Cassandra Bellini has sung another song—one with a pull far stronger than my call to the Guild.

The realization hits me like a ton of fucking bricks.

I'm helpless as I watch Cass take the stage. That tiny black dress and leather jacket are all the more enticing now that I know what they look like on my bedroom floor.

"How are you all doing tonight?" She smiles out to the crowd, that quiet confidence emanating from her very soul.

Only I know she's not quiet. She's boisterous and loud and challenges me at every turn. She's smart, too smart, and far too witty for her own good. I have to work to keep up with her sometimes, but she never lets me lag behind.

"Could we lower the lights a little bit? I want to see who came all the way out here to see little old me," she continues as her spotlight dims around her. "Oh, hi!" she laughs.

And the room laughs with her.

And it's insane that I'm jealous of that laugh. That something else managed to make her smile like that. Her laugh is like a drug to me, and drawing one out of her is the sweetest thing I could ever achieve.

Yet when she begins to sing, the jealousy melts away. It's just pure pride that lingers.

I'm proud of the woman before me for taking on every hardship and coming out the other end. For even being able to get up on that stage—despite the fact her abusive boyfriend put her there to begin with.

I'm proud to call her mine and that she, in turn, did not run at the very thought.

"Teo," I finally gasp out.

"Boss?"

"I love her."

"Fuck."

SHHHHHHHHH.

The power cuts out with an ominous, draining noise, and the *Candelabra* is flooded in darkness.

I'm on my feet in an instant.

"Get to the generator," I hiss to Teo at my side as I blindly check over my pistol and immediately begin to climb onto the stage.

If this is an ambush, I need to get Cas out of here now.

BANG, BANG, BANG.

"Rocco!"

I vaguely hear the sound of Teo screaming my name.

But all I can concentrate on is the rib-breaking impact of three shots to my chest, wedging themselves into my concealed bullet-proof vest.

The force pushes me straight off the stage and sends me crashing into the table below. Glass and alcohol shatter around me, but I can barely breathe, barely get enough oxygen to form a coherent thought.

Slowly, too slowly, the ringing in my ears subsides long enough for me to make out the screaming and chaos around me.

"Rocco!" Teo shouts again. He's so close to me, yet his voice sounds like a whisper.

"Cas," I tug at his arm. "Where's Cas?"

"You've been fucking shot!"

"WHERE IS CAS?"

The shock either wears off, or the adrenaline kicks in a split second later. I scramble to my feet just as an all-too-familiar scream reaches my ears.

"Rocco!"

To his credit, Teo moves as I do, without thinking, toward Cas screams.

We scramble onto the stage in unison, ready to greet whatever we might face.

Only we can't see a thing.

It's pure instinct that has me dodging out of the way of the knife that swings my way. I don't think as I grab my assailant's arm and twist hard. I hear them drop the weapon, but I have no idea where it falls.

"Ugh!" they grunt, giving me a helpful reference point for their face.

The next blow I land hits skin with a sickening crunch.

"Cassandra!" Teo shouts out next to me as I hear him stomping down on another assailant.

But it's another female voice that shouts back. "Princeling?"

"Mia?!"

I aim a kick at my assailant's chest, sending them falling back off the stage, and run toward her voice.

"What the fuck is happening, Mia?" I shout toward her.

"Someone's taken...agh!" She shouts in pain, then lets out an angry growl. A second later, an unknown voice groans in sickening agony, and Mia's gray figure emerges from the darkness. "Someone's taken Cas backstage."

I take off, praying to every god that might listen that it's Martino, that he had the sense to take her somewhere safe.

Two sets of feet pound behind me, and a shaking phone torch appears to guide my path.

Around us is more gunfire, more screams, more unknown horrors that I couldn't have prepared for. But if my paranoia was warranted, then where the hell was my backup?

"Do you have a gun?" I yell at Teo.

"I'm not firing blind. There are civilians in here!"

A shriek sounds behind us as the room is temporarily illuminated by more gunfire, just as another assailant steps into our path.

Under Mia's phone light, I get a better picture of what we're dealing with.

Dark clothes, concealed face. Nearly identical to the goons we took out that night at the dock.

BANG.

The man drops as Teo absorbs the impact of his shot. "Fucking Cartel."

I waste no time leaping over the body to ram open the doors that lay just behind him.

The sterile corridors of the *Candelabra's* backstage are lit in the eerie green of the illuminated exit sign above the back door. And the sliver of light that quickly narrows as it closes.

"Someone's just left," Mia breathes in my right ear before careening forward. Only to stumble on something that grunts on impact.

"Martino!" I yell at the sight of the giant man curled up on the floor.

Martino groans again. "T-they took her."

"WHERE."

"B-behind you."

Thump.

Mia gasps as her eyes roll back into her head, her body crumbling to the floor.

Teo and I turn just in time to see a beast of a man lunge toward us next.

We scatter, causing his fist to pound into the wall behind where my head had just been moments before. The brickwork cracks on impact.

"Who the fuck are you, ugly?" Teo jeers as he tries to split his attention.

He isn't wrong—the man's arms are abnormally large for the size of his body, which already rivals Martino's stature. And the dark balaclava over his face does nothing to hide the gruesome scars that run all over his skin.

I crack my neck. The beast is blocking the hallway to the back exit.

Every second I'm delayed is just opening the window for Cas' abductors.

I launch myself at him, feigning a left hook, but kicking out at his knees at the last second. I'm betting that someone with such impressive upper body strength might have missed leg day.

To my dismay, the beast only wobbles. But Teo coordinates his own attack, slamming his foot into the beast's chest and toppling him over.

"Let's go!" I yell as I try to leap over his body.

But an arm snatches at my leg at the last second.

I grunt as I fall to my knees, trying to shake off the beast's grip. But shy of dislocating my own leg, there's no way out.

I change tactics, flipping over and kicking out with my free leg, planting my heel directly in his face.

He grunts in pain, but his grip doesn't waver.

"Vitale! Find her!" I yell out as my foot smashes through his teeth.

Teo doesn't need to be told twice. He leaps over where we're scrambling on the floor and flies out the door.

I curse with the effort of my next kick to the beast's skull. Finally, finally, his grip loosens and I don't waste the opportunity to free myself.

I throw myself on top of him, pinning his arms down with my knees.

"WHERE ARE THEY TAKING HER?"

The first blow dislocates his jaw. His legs kick up in an attempt to push me off, but I hold fast.

"WHERE ARE THEY TAKING HER?"

The second blow breaks his nose, perhaps his skull. His legs stop moving.

"WHERE ARE THEY TAKING HER?"

The third blow lands with a sickening squelch.

All resistance in his body dies.

Panting, I regard my bloodied hands with indifference. The only remorse I can muster is that I didn't get an answer from him.

I stand, half-staggering toward the exit because that fucker really did a number on my leg.

But when I open the door, it's to be met with a cool midnight breeze.

And Teo, holding Cas' leather jacket with tears in his eyes.

24

CASSANDRA

Thump thump, thump thump.

My eyelids feel like lead as I try to pry them open. Panic was already setting into my bones before the memories emerged from my too-foggy brain.

I was singing. The lights went out. There were gunshots. Then Mia was there. She was trying to get me to safety.

And then...

And then the pain had overwhelmed me, and everything had gone dark.

Thump thump, thump thump.

My body jostles against the unforgiving floor, elbows bashing awkwardly into my side. I try to move them to alleviate the growing ache in my shoulders, only to discover that they've been tied behind my back.

Something had gone wrong. Something terrible. My heart shied away from it, wanting to protect me.

Because I remember the gunshots and Teo's scream. I remember when someone flew into my arms, and it wasn't Rocco's protective embrace but Mia's frantic consolation.

"You're okay. You're okay. You're okay." It was as if trying to reassure herself as much as me.

She had come for me first. The club was filled with danger, but she had come for me. Despite how I'd yelled, accused her of lying to me, ghosted her. When it mattered the most, my friend had my back.

I'm such a fucking asshole. If I hadn't been such a coward, I could have called her back and apologized a thousand times. I would have put this behind us before...

Thump thump, thump thump.

It takes me a while to figure out that my eyes are open. It's not until the sound of the engine finally registers that I realize I'm in the trunk of a car.

I try not to panic. But the claustrophobia and darkness seem to press down harder.

I need to think. Come on, Cassandra.

Taillights. I need to kick out the tail lights. I should be able to flag down anyone on our tail so Rocco can...

My heart lurches. My chest tightens so hard I think I might puke.

No. Not now. I need to concentrate. Damn it.

But the sound of those gunshots fills my ears. Teo screaming his name, a mournful, desperate sound from a man who'd known him his whole life.

Rocco had been shot.

Rocco had been shot three times.

I just about have the wherewithal to turn on my side before I hurl my guts up.

The emptiness is overwhelming. Tears slide down my face, my throat burning, heart-shattering. He can't be...he can't be...he can't be...

Then the stench hits me like a slap to the face.

A voice in my head that sounds almost like Rocco's screams at me to pull myself together. I'm the one in danger right now. If I don't get out of here, I will never know for sure. I will never be able to say goodbye.

Determined, I wriggle down the trunk, inch by painstaking inch, and try to ignore the foul wetness seeping into my clothes. Finally, my foot can reach where I think the taillight must be, so I kick out.

Nothing happens.

I growl in frustration as I kick it again, harder, shoving my heel directly into the plastic casing. But still, nothing seems to move.

"Fuck!" I scream as I start kicking with reckless abandon.

Without any warning, something gives, and my ankle twists at a sickening angle as it pushes all the way through.

I gasp as fresh air immediately fills the small space. I ignore the pain that grips my foot as I scramble around toward the hole I created.

I push my arm through it, and the jagged plastic bites into my arm as I begin to wave frantically.

Maybe someone will see. Maybe someone will call the cops. I don't stop until I feel the car lurch to one side and the engine growl to a stop.

All I can do is wait and listen as the car doors open and two sets of feet approach the back of the car. I'm bracing myself for whatever comes next.

Well, fuck them if they think I'm going anywhere without a fight.

I don't recognize the men that open the trunk. Not that I gave myself much time to examine their faces before I began kicking and screaming with everything I have. My injured ankle throbs with every blow.

"*Mierda,*" one of the men buckles as my attack hits his low-hanging fruit.

But my satisfaction is short-lived when the other manhandles me out of the trunk and throws me over his shoulder.

"You're fucking DEAD!" I scream, unable to do anything else as he carries me through what appears to be some kind of abandoned warehouse.

"*Cállate,*" the man holding me snaps.

But I don't care. "He will fucking kill you for this!"

He shouts something to the man still on his knees by the car that's barely audible over my shouting, before taking me through another set of doors.

The room we enter is two stories tall, entirely bare, save for a few decommissioned pieces of industrial machinery that are covered in dust and cobwebs—fishing, I realize, with a start. We must be near the docks.

The second captor appears behind us, dragging a collapsible chair from the wall to the middle of the room.

"Put me down!" I shout loud enough to burst eardrums.

My captor twitches, and with a grunt, he dumps me on the floor. I wince as I fall heavily onto my bad ankle.

I turn to run, but two sets of arms wrestle me into the chair, tying up my bound hands and feet.

When they step back, wearing a matching pair of smug expressions, I'm entirely motionless.

"You think this will hold me forever?" My voice sounds hoarse from all the screaming. "I'll fucking kill you before he even gets here."

But they both turn away, seemingly content with a job well done.

"Now, now, Cas. There's no need to be like that."

My blood runs cold.

A figure emerges from the shadows. His hair is unkept, stubble overgrown, and his eyes bloodshot and wild as he snorts something from the back of his thumb.

"You bastard."

Claudio shakes his head too rapidly. "Now, now. You can't speak to me like that."

He walks directly over to me, steps clicking against the stark, concrete floor. Every inch closer feels like a hand tightening around my throat.

"Stay the fuck away from me."

But he ignores me. "After everything I've done for you, you still don't treat me with any respect."

I spit at his feet.

Slap.

My vision blurs as I try to breathe through the pain of my throbbing cheek. Claudio has the audacity to shake his hand as if somehow I'd hurt *him*.

"That ends today."

Two fingers gently tilt my chin up. I shake them away with a thrash of my head. But Claudio grabs my chin instead, forcing me to look at him.

"You should be thanking me, baby. I'm saving you." His breath reeks, and I try not to choke.

"You shoved me into the trunk of a fucking car."

His eyes darken. "A necessary precaution. After our last encounter, I was sure that Moretti had turned you against me. But you don't have to worry about him anymore."

The gunshots echo through my mind once again.

No. Claudio wasn't smart enough for this. He couldn't have pulled something like that off.

And yet he's there, standing before me with that smug little smile that makes my heart ice-cold with fear.

"What have you done?" My voice wobbles as I speak.

"You think I was going to let that *bastard* take you away from me? After all the trouble I went to just to bring you here?" His laugh is low and cruel. "You're *mine,* Cassandra Bellini."

"You handed me over to him! You signed that contract!"

Claudio's growl is the only warning I get before he slaps me again.

"I did what I had to. Let him think that he could control me. But none of that matters anymore, baby. He's gone, and we can be together again."

I take my time to recover, letting my hair fall over my face as I try to manage the grief boiling up inside me.

Claudio snarls in disgust. "I knew it. I knew he'd use you up and spit you back out like this. But you'll fall in love with me again in time. For now, you only need to know your place and do exactly as I say."

"Fuck you."

"They will come for you, whoever remains loyal to that bastard, so I'm going to need you to wait right here until they come knocking."

I yank at my restraints desperately, but it's no use. I'm nothing more than bait. Mia…Teo…Martino…they were going to wander right into Claudio's trap.

But…If Claudio only wanted me, then why should he care about the others? Why act against the entire Guild if this was just a personal vendetta against Rocco?

"Why, so you can kill them all and become don yourself?"

It's a shot in the dark, and judging by the way Claudio laughs in response, I missed it by a mile. "Could you imagine? Me?"

He hunches over with merriment, and I cringe slightly at his overreactive display.

Irritated, I bite back. "Then why bother with them? Just take me and leave them behind."

"Oh, I plan on it, but all in good time." He reaches for me again, dragging his fingers through my tangled hair. "It's just a shame he's turned you against me. But that deal was just too good for me to pass up."

All I can do is hope my stare conveys all the loathing and venom that I feel for him.

"I should thank you, really. When your father asked me to pick you up, he took the loan out in my name to incentivize me to bring you back. You know, so the Guild wouldn't track me down and murder me for stealing from them."

My words get stuck in my throat. My father...employed Claudio.

My father was in the Italian mafia.

Claudio grins down at the shock on my face.

"But the fucker went and died on me before he could pay the loan back. If it weren't for that deal with Moretti..." he shakes his head. "It's kinda poetic, though. You paid the price for your father's incompetence."

I think I'm going to vomit again.

Had any of it been real? That first night Claudio had watched me perform in Ohio, he'd asked me for my ID...was it to check that I was the person he was looking for?

"You...stole me from my home," my words tremble in

disbelief. "You seduced me and brought me here on purpose."

"We fell in love!" Claudio's voice booms in my ear. "It wasn't part of the plan, but it happened, didn't it? Don't act like I'm some kind of monster."

"That is exactly what you are."

I can see the rage building behind his eyes and know instinctively that he's about to hit me again. I flinch away the best I can, closing my eyes.

"Touch her, and you're dead."

Time freezes. My heart pounds rapidly. My breaths come out in rapid, short bursts.

When I look up again, there's another figure standing there behind Claudio. His hand is wrapped around the arm about to strike me

He's tall, dark, and menacing. His hair falls over his deathly gray eyes. His shirt is ripped across his chest, revealing the dented bullet-proof vest beneath.

His scent hits me a second later, and I sob at the familiar comfort it brings me.

Alive. Rocco's alive.

Claudio startles. "How the fuck?"

Crunch.

Rocco punches him square in the jaw, sending him crashing to the floor.

"Rocco," I breathe through my tears.

He's alive, he's alive, he's alive.

His gaze softens the second he lays eyes on me. "*Angioletta.*" Relief, pain, and worry lace his tone.

He's by my side a second later, knife in hand. He plants a gentle kiss on my cheek as he reaches around to cut away my bindings. "I thought I'd lost you."

A cruel, near-hysterical laugh booms from behind us, and we both tense in unison as Claudio rights himself from the floor.

"You think *I'm* the monster?" Claudio's manic eyes glance between the two of us. "I guess he didn't tell you, then."

"You're dead, Lazzaro," Rocco snarls.

"Ask him, Cas. Ask him what happened the night your father died."

Something numbingly cold begins to fester around my heart. Nothing Claudio said about my father could be true because that would mean Rocco would have lied to me.

And Rocco had never lied to me.

Yet…Rocco is shaking, visibly angered by Claudio's words.

The numbness only grows.

"Rocco?" I whisper.

But Rocco just cuts away my last binding and stands, looming over Claudio with his knife now pointing at his throat.

"Consider your next words carefully."

Claudio steps back, but that manic grin doesn't fade. "He's been lying to you, Cas."

"Rocco," my voice is desperate. I'm teetering on the edge of my own mania.

"He's the one who killed your father."

25

ROCCO

"*I wanted to see it for myself.—that you would do for the Guild.*"

"*You are a hundred times the man your father ever was.*"

"*You are going to do great things, Rocco.*"

Carmine Bellini's final words echo through me as I watch his daughter collapse in on herself.

The grief is insurmountable. Regret laces my every emotion, every fiber of my being, as Cas looks up at me.

She's finally seeing me for what I truly am: a monster.

"Please," she begs, but I already know it's too late. The truth is out now, and there's nothing I can do to take it back.

I should have done more to save Carmine. I should have torn the gun from his hand the second he drew it. I should have said something, anything, to stop him from pulling that trigger.

But I failed, and I will have to live with those consequences for the rest of my life. Even if that means losing Cas in the process, I know in my heart that I deserve it.

"Not your knight in shining armor anymore, is he?" Lazzaro drones on. He's like a fly buzzing around this shit show with unbridled joy. "I told you I was saving you."

"You killed him," she whispers.

Her words fall upon me like their own kind of death sentence. It takes everything within me to stop my legs from buckling in shame.

The only thing I can manage to gasp is, "I'm sorry."

"Too little, too late, amigo," Lazzaro observes. Vaguely, I'm aware that more people have entered the room. "Shall I kill him for you, Cas?"

She just continues to stare at me, those perfect lips agape in despair.

For one terrible moment, I think she might nod to offer her affirmation to Lazzaro's question—the final nail in the coffin of whatever relationship we once had.

I wouldn't be able to blame her, either. I couldn't resent her for it. It was my fault her father was dead, and she was well within her rights to demand my death in payment.

Instead, something perhaps more terrifying happens.

An eerie calmness seems to wash over her. Her tears stop flowing, her mouth becomes a hard, unreadable line, and her eyes...there's nothing behind them anymore.

When she looks at me, there's nothing of the person I once knew when she speaks again. Her voice is like pure ice being injected into my veins.

"He's dead to me."

Lazzaro starts laughing again, and when I turn back to him, I realize why.

Five men have arrived, dressed head to toe in Cartel black. None of them seem particularly inclined to let us leave without a fight.

I can take them. I know I can, but...I will have to unleash a side of me intended only for my enemies. It's the kind of violence necessary for our survival, for Cas' survival, but it will only reinforce the fact that I'm a monster.

A glance back at her unfeeling face is my only hesitation.

I was supposed to be her protector.

But I can't run from the truth forever. The job has to come first; when all is said and done, I'm no better than Lazzaro.

I hear Lazzaro's frustration before I see it. His clumsy feet pelt against the ground as he runs toward me, tired of waiting to enact his revenge.

But I savor my final look at Cas, taking in her perfect face, those soft features I had peppered with kisses only a few short hours ago. She's the woman I had begun to imagine my life with, the woman I'd only just realized I loved.

My hand snaps up to grab Lazzaro's neck, a mere arm's length away.

But still, I hold Cas' gaze.

"I'm sorry."

For your father.

For who I am.

For what you're about to see.

My other hand reaches for Teo's pistol, and I turn away.

I regret leaving him behind to search for leads on Cas' location. He'd intercepted a police report on a busted-out taillight and suspected kidnapping, and I hadn't not thought twice.

At least I had the wherewithal to take his gun, so I wasn't completely unarmed.

Lazzaro claws at my arm as I walk us forward, using his body to shield me from the Cartel, who are now drawing their own guns.

BANG.

The goon on my right goes down, the shot piercing through the middle of his temple.

I cross my arms to aim at the goon on my left.

BANG.

The second man goes down before the remaining three can begin their own firearm assault. I dart to the side to ensure Cas isn't in their line of fire as gunshots begin to rain around me.

"Don't fucking shoot me!" Lazzaro screeches at them as I keep us weaving through the onslaught toward my next victim.

When they don't listen, he switches to a new tactic. He bites down on my arm hard enough to draw blood.

I curse, throwing him into one of the other attackers, toppling them both over while I round on another.

The man before me has no time to point his gun before I disarm him. My elbow snaps his forearm as my free hand snatches the knife from my belt. The pistol drops to the floor, and I kick it away.

BANG, BANG.

The third assailant opens fire, and I barely have enough time to maneuver my disarmed friend into the spray of bullets before they pound into his back. Blood dribbles from his mouth, his eyes wide with shock.

I wait to reload until I have dropped my cover and thrown my knife at the third assailant.

He reaches up to bash it away, but he's too late. The blade buries itself in his neck, and he falls to his knees, spluttering out the blood now gurgling in his throat.

I turn back just in time to find Lazzaro and his final goon getting to their feet. Lazzaro is seemingly unarmed, but the goon is scrambling for his gun again.

I draw mine once more, but the hollow *click* that sounds as I pull the trigger has me throwing it to one side.

Claudio rushes me as I approach in an attempt to tackle me. But a knee to the chest and a blow to the head have him dropping to the floor a second later.

But a second is all the goon needs.

BANG.

Cas screams.

That same bruising pain winds me as the bullet lodges itself in my vest once more. I can almost hear my ribs cracking on impact as I stagger back a few paces.

I can't take another shot. This knowledge launches me forward faster than I've ever moved before.

The goon steps backward as his gun clicks to indicate that it's empty. His shaking fingers attempt to reload before I launch myself at him. But it's no use.

I'm on him in an instant, arms wrapping themselves around his neck as I squeeze, ignoring the way his body thrashes against mine. I take in a breath and then twist.

SNAP.

His body slumps in my arms.

My chest heaves as I try to rally my strength to take down my final opponent.

Click.

Cold metal presses into my temple.

"Easy there, big boy," Lazzaro sneers as he jams the barrel of his gun into my head.

I stay entirely still. I'm half kneeling as I cradle the final goon in my arms.

"Drop him."

The body hits the floor with an unceremonious thump, and I raise my hands in a display of surrender, eyes staring resolutely on the floor.

"You have no idea how good this feels." Lazzaro laughs cruelly in my ear. "After you stole Cas from me and flaunted how you were fucking her in front of everyone."

I cringe at his words. I had done nothing to dispel the rumors, all of them aiding my subterfuge to get to the very man now pointing a gun at my head.

But there was no way of explaining this to Cas. Not when she'd never believe another word out of my mouth.

"The Cartel was supposed to kill you, but I prefer this one hell of a lot more." He raises his voice for Cas to hear, "Fate works in mysterious ways."

"Let me do it."

My eyes snap up to find Cas approaching. That haunted expression on her face barely acknowledges my existence.

Never before had I noticed how she resembled her father. But when she looks at Lazzaro, I'm struck by how similar she looks to Carmine.

She looks the way he did when the calm claimed him in his final moment.

My heart races in my chest. No. She wouldn't.

"Cas. Please," I beg, but not for my own life.

"He killed my father," she continues, ignoring me. "He lied to me. He kept me from ever meeting him. He stole me from you, and he...he made me fall in love with him."

My breath catches. No. Not like this.

"His life is mine to take."

Lazzaro regards her apprehensive. "You don't have it in you."

"Neither do you."

We both regard her in confusion.

"It's why you hired the Cartel, right?" she continues. "So you wouldn't have the blood of the don on your hands. So you could blame his death on someone else."

"You don't know what you're talking about," Lazzaro laughs, but we can all see the truth in his eyes.

Cas nods to his gun. "You kill him, and half the Guild will be on your tail for the rest of your life. Let me do it."

Lazzaro wipes his face with his free hand.

"You can blame it on me, a scorned lover getting revenge for her dead father. Giving me the credit will go down a hell of a lot better for whoever you're working for."

"You wouldn't do it," Lazzaro says, more to convince himself than anyone else.

"I would do it for you, baby," Cas whispers softly. "An apology. For everything that's happened between us, for getting lured in by a monster. I should have known you were only trying to do what was best for our future together."

It's almost comical how quickly Lazzaro's resolve seems to crumble.

"You want me too, right?" Her voice is as smooth as honey. "You let me do this, and I will do anything you want, go anywhere you want to go. I just want to honor my father."

It's almost as if time itself slows down as Lazzaro gestures her closer.

The barrel never leaves my forehead as she takes it from him.

"Cas," I tremble again. "Don't do this."

She allows herself one steadying breath.

Never before have I been so terrified, terrified that one of us is about to die and that she will have to bear that burden for the rest of her life.

I'd rather kill myself than put that on her shoulders.

I glance around. My knife sticks out of the neck of a goon nearby. Cas' reflexes aren't as good as mine if I can just reach over and grab it...

"You are the worst thing that ever happened to me."

BANG.

The sound rings in my ears as I watch Lazzaro stagger back in shock, blood oozing from his chest over his heart.

He gapes a couple of times as if trying to comprehend what's happening. But as his lifeblood spills onto the floor, his body soon follows.

Claudio Lazzaro falls on his back, his vacant eyes staring open-mouthed at the ceiling as blood pools around him.

Cas killed him.

Cas shot him through the heart and killed him.

I'm panting hard when the ringing in my ears fades enough for me to hear again.

"Cas," I whisper in disbelief.

There's a clatter, the sound of her throwing the gun away.

I stand, whirling around to look at her. Her tiny frame holds the weight of what she's just done, but her face remains unmoved.

"We're even."

Stunned, I watch as she reaches down the neckline of her dress and pulls out a stack of bills. She steps forward, pressing them into my chest. "This should cover the rest of the debt."

I ignore the money and grab her hand instead.

Hundred-dollar bills flutter to the ground, turning red as they land at our feet. "Please, let me explain. Let me take you back to the brownstone. I'll tell you everything you want to know."

"You're dead to me," she repeats. Her words somehow cut even deeper than before.

I cling to her hand as I fall to my knees, not caring that I'm kneeling in a dead man's blood. "I'm sorry. I'm so fucking sorry."

She pulls her arm from my grasp, and I fall onto my hands before her. It feels like my heart has been carved from my chest.

"Don't try to find me."

"Please," I beg. The word spills out over and over again. The tightness in my chest suffocates me as I hyperventilate.

I can't lose her. I can't. How can I live with myself? How can I breath without her? I'd do anything. Anything. Please. Don't go. Please.

But when I finally gather my courage to look up at her again, Cassandra Bellini is nowhere to be found.

26

CASSANDRA

Everything is numb.

Everything I've ever felt seems like something distant and intangible. Like I'm somehow suspended underwater while life continues above me, entirely unreachable.

All I can focus on is putting one foot in front of the other. The city streets are cast in gray light as the early hours of the morning creep in.

I'm freezing. I know this because everything is shaking. Because I'm still only wearing this stupid black dress, walking around in the cold.

But none of the bleary-eyed morning commuters seem to bat an eyelid. Nor do they seem to care about the blood splattered across my legs and arms.

Claudio's blood.

It had been like unlocking a door to the darkest part of me. A part that I'd sealed shut my entire life for fear of what it might mean.

But knowing who my father was, what my family had been…

I am a daughter of the mafia. And in that moment, between aiming and pulling the trigger, I dug deep into that part of myself, barely flinching at the recoil as the bullet had found its home in Claudio's chest.

I want to feel remorse for it. I want to feel anything at all for it. But from the moment I saw Claudio pulling a gun on Rocco, everything had shut down. It was as if my body instinctively knew it needed to put me in this numb, self-preservation mode.

Someone bumps into my shoulder as I navigate across the next block of unfamiliar houses. The jerk causes my ankle to flash in pain.

Where the hell even am I?

I've been on autopilot since Rocco got down on his knees and begged me to stay.

I slow at the next intersection to read the street sign. Brighton.

I've been here before—my second day in Brooklyn. It seems so long ago now, but I still remember the address.

It's the same address I've been writing to these last few years, ever since she moved out of her parents' place.

It takes me twenty minutes to orient myself and find it, counting the doors until I reach the small apartment complex.

"Mia? It's me." My voice is hoarse as I speak into the intercom.

I don't even know if she's here. But a second later, the front door buzzes open.

I step into the familiar foyer and make my way up to the second floor.

Mandy is already halfway down the corridor when I get there; her apartment door flung open further down the hall.

For a second, we just stand there, frozen as we take each other in.

Dark circles have blossomed under her eyes; from lack of sleep or the darkening bruise over her cheek, I can't be sure.

"You look like shit," I say.

She throws herself at me, arms pulling me in so tightly I can barely breathe. But God, do I need this. The numbness burns away under human contact, leaving me with nothing but raw, uncontrollable grief.

"Shhhhh," Mia strokes my hair as the sobs begin to rack my body. "Come on."

She takes my hand, leading me into her tiny studio apartment and gently sitting me down on her bed.

Wordlessly, she climbs over to lie next to me and opens her arms to me once more.

I'm not sure how much time passes while we lie there as everything pours out of me in one messy stream of grief.

Grief for my father, a man I never knew. A man who thought it wise to bring me to this godforsaken place. For him dying before I had a chance to damn him to hell.

Grief for my mother, who had lied to me my whole life. Who had somehow managed to leave the Italian mafia and would have never wanted this for me.

Grief for Claudio Lazzaro, who I had so earnestly and naively loved. Who had so completely and utterly ruined me. Who was now dead by my own hand.

Grief for the girl I once was, the person I would never be again.

I can't process anything else more. Can't even think *his*

name without becoming overwhelmed by the immensity of my own emotions.

The humiliation, the anger, the pain, the longing are all vying for my attention all at once.

My tears finally, finally begin to subside and Mia, the constant rock tethering me to reality with her soothing words the entire time, begins to stretch out a little stiffly.

"Let me get us some water," she says gently as she pries me off of her.

I roll over so I can bury my face in her pillow.

"Unless you'd like anything stronger?"

A sudden craving overwhelms me. "Do you have any breakfast tea?"

Mia gives me a bemused look. "I'm sorry, when did you turn into the Queen of England?"

The thought of Donatella twangs my already sensitive heart strings. My face immediately crumples into a new wave of tears.

"Shit," Mia says in alarm. "I'm sorry, I'll go get some tea, okay? Just wait here."

Absently, I'm aware of the front door opening and closing as I try to get myself under control again. By the time she returns, I've managed to sit myself up, although I'm still clutching the pillow.

Mia appears a moment later, a steaming mug in her hand. "All they had was decaf, but..."

I take it from her gratefully, warming my hands on the porcelain.

"How are you feeling?" Mia says as she rejoins me on the bed.

"Like crap."

"You have a bruise," she says, pointing to my cheek.

I snort darkly. "I guess we match."

"Who..."

"Claudio."

Mia goes deathly still. "I will kill him."

"I might have beaten you to it."

She blinks at me, taking me in. No doubt she's already noticed the blood splattered over my body.

"Explain."

So I do. I tell her everything. About coming to Brooklyn, realizing that Claudio was an abusive asshole, how I had gone to *him* for help. The words keep pouring out as I tell her about the brownstone and how I'd been trying to help the Guild unearth the rat.

By the time I reach the events of the night before, Mia is clutching her own pillow. Her eyes are wide, but she refuses to interrupt as I tell her about being thrown in a trunk. I tell her about what Claudio had revealed about my father and how I shot him.

When I finish, I'm met with her silence. The light of the afternoon slowly fades in the window behind her.

It's a tiny apartment. The bed faces the only window and the TV stand. Behind the headboard is a compact kitchen without a freezer, and next to the front door is a small, half-concealed bathroom that somehow crams in both a shower and toilet.

But despite the size, it's the only place in Brooklyn I want to be right now.

"I'm so sorry, Cas."

I look over at my friend and shake my head. "It's not your fault. You tried to warn me, for God's sake."

"I should have told you the truth from the very beginning."

The sadness and pity in her eyes make me swallow down any biting response. Instead I merely ask, "Could you tell me the truth now?"

She sighs, repositioning herself so she can lean back against the wall. "My dad...your dad...they were part of Giuliano Moretti's inner circle. They were accountants, really. Carmine had a way with numbers, and my father appreciates that kind of thing."

You could hear a pin drop as Mia draws her next breath.

"I didn't know about it officially until I was sixteen. But by that point, I'd already guessed. I thought about writing to you about it a hundred times over, but..." she pauses before continuing. "They told me what your mom went through to get you out, and I just couldn't."

"No one leaves," I whisper back.

Mia nods. "Your mom went to Giuliano herself a week after Teo Vitale's family was murdered. I didn't know until much later how dark things were at that point. That my own father had considered leaving as well."

"Someone killed Teo's parents?"

"And his sister." Mia stares out the window. "She was our age, Cas. She used to play with us sometimes."

I literally shudder at the hazy memory that resurfaces. I suddenly remember a dark-haired girl with a bright smile running around the park with us tailing behind her. Squeals of delight escaped her lips as Mia tackled her to the floor in my mind's eye.

"I don't know how your mom convinced him," Mia continues. "But with the Vitale family gone, Giuliano told her if she wanted to leave, she had to disappear for good. Neither of you were ever meant to come back to Brooklyn again."

Then why did my father have me brought back? The question bubbles to the surface, but I choke it back down.

"But you and your family stayed?" I ask instead.

"Things started to change when Roccowhen Giuliano started losing power. I was eighteen and ready to prove myself, so I started helping my dad out here and there." Her cheeks flush a little, and she looks away.

I narrow my eyes at her. "What else?"

"I tend the bar."

"Mia."

"Cassandra."

"Tell me."

She sighs. "On occasion, I've been known to help my father collect his debts."

To my jaw-dropping surprise, she pulls out a knife that was somehow concealed within her jeans and begins to twirl it around her fingers with expert precision.

I watch as the tiny blade catches the light every few seconds, utterly transfixed.

"I'm not entirely proud of it, but I am good at what I do. Good enough that people tend to leave me alone, at least," she admits, "I try not to get involved with Guild politics, anyhow."

A familiar numbness begins to grip my heart once more. "But you knew what really happened to my father, didn't you?"

Sadness immediately slumps Mia's shoulders. "Teo and Martino were there that night, too. They said that... Rocco...he did everything he could to get Carmine to stop."

I blink at her in confusion. "Claudio said...*he* killed him."

"I'm sure Rocco feels that way too," Mia sighs. "But your father's suicide wasn't his fault."

Her words hover between us, but I refuse to let them sink in. "No."

But Mia persists anyway. "They'd discovered your father was selling information to the Cartel and was trying to make a run for it. Rocco was only bringing him in for questioning because there was no way in hell Carmine was working alone."

"I'm done with this."

"Cas, Carmine took his own life instead of giving up his co-conspirator. Rocco offered him a peaceful way out."

I stand up. "Can I take a shower?" The words come out harsher than I intended, but finally, Mia seems to drop it.

"I'll make us some dinner. Lasagne good for you?"

I nod, trying to focus on anything other than the ringing in my ears. As soon as the bathroom door closes behind me, I strip down and all but run into the shower, allowing the scorching water to burn on my skin as I regain control of my breathing.

It's complicated. All so fucking complicated. Because my father is dead. And *he* might not have pulled the trigger, but that didn't stop *him* from being the reason my father is now dead.

I let the numbness take over my body once more, relishing the escape from the turmoil of my emotions. I'm soothed by the scorching water that washes away the sins of the night before.

My mind only snags on one tiny thing.

I killed a man. And I still can't bring myself to care.

I shudder when I turn off the shower and step back into the real world. Wrapping a towel around myself, I head back into the apartment to see if Mia has any spare clothes I can borrow.

"Hey, Mia?" I say as I open the door.

The smell of freshly baked lasagne hits me like a ton of bricks.

"Cas?"

Nausea rises within me so fast that I stagger back into the bathroom, searching desperately for the toilet bowl.

I make it just in time.

Mia is there a second later, pulling back my hair with dutiful care as I heave whatever was left in my stomach into the toilet bowl.

"Fuck," I gasp as I finally rest my head against the porcelain. "I must have a virus or something."

I'm too exhausted to notice how still Mia has become. "Why?"

"I threw up in that trunk earlier, too."

I lean back on my heels and go to wash myself off, but Mia's arm holds me steady.

"What?"

She bites her lip. "It was the lasagne, wasn't it?"

"What? No." I try to brush her off. She's been so kind to me today. I don't want to insult her food on top of everything else.

"Cassandra. When was your last period?"

27

ROCCO

I can see the blood leaking through the wrap on my hand. But I don't care. The light leather of the punching bag is already stained.

Each blow only adds to a tapestry of a million other smears.

Heavy metal music thrums through the room as I hold the bag steady, preparing for my next set of at least ten more.

I'm exercising until my body is too exhausted even to think.

I'm about to throw another punch, when someone touches my shoulder.

If it were anyone else, the blow I redirect toward the person who approached would have knocked them out completely. But clearly, Teo was expecting my reaction and he ducks cleanly out of my way.

"The fuck, man," I grumble as I pull my earphones out.

"I called your name like five times."

At the entrance to the gym, Donatella leans against the

doorframe. Her pitying expression is the same one that has haunted me these last two days.

Now Teo has one to match.

For fuck's sake.

"What do you want?" I snap as I return my attention to the punching bag.

"The Guild thinks you killed Claudio Lazzaro."

I expected as much. The incident at the *Candelabra* had been a public one. Those who hadn't been in attendance had still found out all the gory details within hours.

"Then, remind them that Lazzaro conspired with the Cartel to kidnap Bellini."

There had been numerous accounts of the Cartel's presence as they wreaked havoc, so there was no debating that much. Not to mention, Alessandro had them squealing the truth in less than twenty-four hours.

Lazzaro had recently become very involved in the Cartel. Though he wasn't high up enough in the Guild to account for all the information breaches, he certainly played a part in leaking some of the information.

Teo and Donatella shared a glance. "Some are...still sympathetic toward Lazzaro's intentions."

My next punch slams into the bag with enough force to unhook the thing entirely from the ceiling. We all watch as it slams into the far wall and slowly begins to roll back to us.

"What do you mean?" I say as pleasantly as I can.

Teo levels me with a firm look. "Some of the old guard are anxious that you killed someone from your father's list over a woman—a woman that you conspired to obtain and humiliate Lazzaro with."

"Don't fucking sugarcoat it," I reply sarcastically.

"It might be best if you showed your face," Teo continues, unperturbed. "To alleviate these concerns."

I turn on him in irritation. "And say what? That was actually Bellini who shot him in the back of the head?"

"I meant maybe double down on the 'he was working with the Cartel and also probably the rat' thing, but sure, I guess."

I don't bother replying as I pick up the bag and hang it back up.

"We need to do damage control here. You know what they're like. One sniff of blood and those sharks will descend on you."

I keep throwing out my punches, keeping a steady rhythm.

"Marco is here. So is Martino and Dante. They want to discuss the attack in more detail."

One, two, three. One, two, three. One, two, three.

"They're worried about you, Rocco. I'm worried about you."

Two, two, three. Two, two, three. Two, two, three.

"Fuck it. I know where she is."

My punch misses the bag entirely.

We stand in silence while I wait for Teo to continue. But when I turn to look at him, he's staring at me with crossed arms. He's going to wait for me to ask.

I take a long, steadying breath. "Where?"

"Come to the meeting, and I'll tell you."

"Don't piss me off right now."

"Or what?"

I crack my neck, ready to square up to him if I have to. Teo sniffs, sensing the incoming attack, and matches my stance.

But before either of us can land a blow, Donatella steps between us.

"Enough of this nonsense, you stupid boys!" She gives us both a stern look before turning on me specifically. "You. Let your friends help you, dammit. I cannot spend another day dealing with your sulking, and you will lose everything you've spent five years building if you don't clean up your act. Do you hear me?"

God, if that woman doesn't terrify me.

"And you!" She turns on Teo. "Tell the poor man where Cassandra is. He's literally going out of his mind with worry. Look at the state of him. So don't be such a dick."

Teo murmurs something that sounds suspiciously like an apology as he looks down at his feet.

For a moment, we're just two teenagers again, causing havoc and getting into fights for no reason. Teo must think it, too, because he shoots me a sheepish look.

"I'll meet with them," I declare, a peace offering if there ever was one.

Teo nods. "She's with Mia, staying at her place by the looks of things. Chiavari...senior...has more details."

The relief that floods through me is only a splash of respite in the face of the fire of despair that has consumed me these last forty-eight hours. But it's enough to make the walk to my private study more bearable.

After so long of having her near-constant presence in my life, her absence feels like I'm missing a limb.

It's more than just the overwhelming heartache and depression spiral of having hurt her irreparably. I miss her companionship, her sarcasm, her seemingly unending determination to mess with me. Her laughter haunts this house like a ghost.

But her lips haunt my memories like a parasite, sucking every ounce of feeling and joy from me to the point where I don't know if I even remember what it's like to be happy.

Nothing matters anymore. There's no way to fix this. No way I can atone for what I've done.

And now I'm going to have to figure out how to live with it. Even if living without her means that I'll slowly become a shell of the person I once was.

I shake these thoughts from my mind as I step into the office. These were my friends. Donatella was right. I should at least pretend to let them help me.

"So?" I ask the room, immediately getting to business. "What is it you have for me?"

Marco clears his throat and approaches my desk first, holding a thick file of documents. He dumps them in front of me with an unceremonious thud.

"What am I looking at here, Chiavari?" I ask the older man irritably.

"Loan agreement paperwork," Marco replies as I take a look at the document at the top of the pile.

I tense at the sight of the name signed at the bottom. "Carmine Bellini's loan agreement paperwork."

"The man was many things, but sloppy was not one of them," Marco continues. "Look at the handwriting. The loan he allegedly took out on Lazzaro's behalf wasn't written in cursive."

I massage my temples. "This feels like grasping at straws."

"I knew my friend."

"Not well enough."

Marco's lips curl out slightly. "I knew him better than anyone. Better than the goddamn wife who abandoned him.

Carmine was a good man. If you hadn't caught him red handed with the Cartel, I would never have believed he'd do something like that."

I stare at him. This is a rare rational display of passion for something other than accounting.

"So you're saying he didn't write the loan?"

Marco slams Lazzaro's loan document on the table before me with the flat of his hand. "No. I'm saying he wrote it under duress."

Beside me, Teo quirks his eyebrow. "An interesting theory."

"Boss?"

I look up and motion for Martino to join us.

"That night at the *Candelabra,* I took a look in Lazzaro's office before Cas was due on stage. I didn't understand what it meant at the time, but…" he hands me his phone.

On it is a picture of an unkempt desk. Documents litter every corner. There are so many you can barely see the oak surface beneath. The trash can beneath is overflowing.

I swipe to the next photo. This one is more zoomed in on a crumbled piece of paper, half-burned on top of the trash. I swipe again, and the paper unravels.

"Cage the canary," I read aloud.

"It was still smoking when I found it. Lazzaro did a piss poor job of trying to destroy it."

I keep looking at the handwriting. There's something so familiar about it. "So someone else gave Lazzaro the instruction to kidnap Bellini."

"I have a good idea who it might be."

We turn to look at Dante standing with his usual swagger in the corner. The South African must have been fully briefed on the situation, judging by the look of pity he throws my way before continuing.

"I was in South Africa when the tobacco shipment went out. I helped them load it into the damn shipping containers myself. There was no possibility they could have arrived here empty unless someone intercepted them en route."

"We've been over this already, Dante," I say, already tired.

But Dante shakes his head. "I looked into it. The Cartel don't have their own ships or dock."

"So they hired a civil trawler," Teo counters.

"If they did, the shipment didn't arrive back in Brooklyn."

I lean forward. "You mean the Cartel intercepted the package and took it elsewhere?"

"I'm saying no one arrived in Brooklyn within a seventy-two-hour window of the interception with a load that big. Not at the civilian docks."

"But we know the Cartel has the tobacco right now. They've been underselling us for weeks," Teo adds. "So how the hell did they get it?"

Dante procures his own document and slides it over to me. "There was only one other vessel capable of carrying the shipment, and docked privately within that window."

There, in black and white, is the name of my private yacht.

I stare at it for a moment. Wondering why I ever allowed myself to think anyone else was responsible for this mess. Because, of course, it was. Of course, he would do something like this.

"I'm going to kill him."

I look up at Teo. Never in my life have I ever seen him look so furious.

"We can't," I let authority lace my tone. "If we go after him, the negotiations were for nothing."

"If *you* go after him."

"Vitale," Marco places a hand on his shoulder. "This isn't your fight."

Teo shakes it off. "The hell it isn't. My family's killers are on that damn list. My sister's murderer."

"Stand down, Teo," I snap at him. "Chiavari, Dante. Gather this evidence up to present to the Guild. Take Vitale with you."

"Like hell," Teo all but growls at me. "I'm coming with you."

"No, you're not. You're too emotional. I can't trust you to have my back in there."

Teo sneers. "*I'm* too emotional? You've locked yourself up here for days, Rocco. You've barely eaten, barely slept since she left. Don't you dare come for me, you fucking hypocrite."

I offer him a long, cool look.

"Martino," I bark without breaking his stare. "You're with me."

THE DRIVE into New York is as tense as it is frustrating. Martino keeps glancing in the rearview as if he might say something.

But it doesn't matter whether he approves of this solo mission.

I need to speak with him alone. Need to hear the truth

from his own mouth. Because if I have to kill him, there can't be any question about who did it. I need to shoulder that burden alone.

When we finally arrive, Martino tries to get out of the car. But I shake my head. "Keep it running."

Perhaps it's the dressing down I gave Teo earlier or the sheer ferocity in my eyes, but he doesn't object.

The familiar path to the elevator and the long wait up to the penthouse only serve as fuel for my already explosive fury.

I don't bother declaring my presence. As soon as I reach the apartment, I kick down the doors and storm straight into the room.

"Well, isn't this a surprise," Giuliano Moretti all but purrs. "Two visitors in one day, lucky, lucky me."

"What the hell are you…"

My words catch in my throat at the sight of another figure emerging from the balcony.

Amidst the dense vegetation of my father's solarium, her cheeks now oddly hollow, and her face streaked with tears is…

"Cas?"

28

CASSANDRA

He's not supposed to be here.

No. He can't be here.

But I can't move, can't speak as Rocco's gray eyes hold me in place.

Two days apart, yet it feels like a lifetime. I thought maybe my mind was exaggerating his beauty. I was delusional enough to believe that he would become a distant memory with enough time.

But my body's reaction is instant and relentless. Every fiber of my being is called to him, begging me to approach, to brush his hair from his eyes, to wrap my arms around him. He's like a beacon calling only to me.

Calling me home.

Giuliano approaches me with measured gentleness. "Do you feel alright, Miss Bellini?"

He wasn't what I thought he would be. The ruthless ex-don that Rocco had painted for me doesn't match the man before me.

His hard edges have been softened by time. He has

graying temples, and he was more concerned with cultivating his plants than the schemes of the Guild. And when he spoke to me of how he had spared my mother…

I let Giuliano place a worried hand on my arm and guide me over to the couch, forcing me to look away from Rocco's now terrified expression.

"What the hell is going on?"

I flinch at the bite in Rocco's words, unable to look anywhere but my hands.

"Why don't you take a seat, boy," Giuliano instructs as he sits in the armchair next to me, close enough to give my shoulder a reassuring squeeze.

"Leave her out of this."

Giuliano sighs. "This is a family matter, Rocco. Come join us, please."

Rocco stalks closer but refuses to sit. "She never gave an oath. She is not family. Let her go. This is between you and me."

Giuliano tilts his head in my direction, offering me a sad smile. "Ah. You really haven't told him?"

"Please don't," I implore him, a lump already building in my throat.

"Tell me what?"

Finally, I allow myself to look up at him, at the stubble already growing across his chin, at the dark circles beneath his eyes, and at his bloodied knuckles. I note the way his body is shaking. Is it with anger or fear?

Giuliano leans closer to me. "It is your choice. But he is my son. I think he deserves to know."

"Cas." Rocco seems to choke on my name.

I take a long breath to steady myself, allowing my hand to drift down to my stomach.

"Rocco."

Like a switch, Rocco's shaking subsides to an eerie stillness.

"I'm pregnant."

I can't bear to look at the emotions that cross his face as he suddenly stumbles forward, half crashing into the couch before him.

Everything inside me screams for me to go to him, but Giuliano's gentle hold on my shoulder keeps me grounded.

Slowly, Rocco lowers himself into the couch, his expression emotionless as he addresses me directly. "What have you done?"

His words feel like a knife, burying itself deep between my ribs.

I didn't know how he would react. I couldn't bear to imagine it. Even when Mia and I waited those excruciating minutes for the result of the fifth pregnancy test. Even when we counted back the weeks to be absolutely positive, it was *his*.

But *this*? To respond as if somehow I was to blame? As if this was my fault?

My desire to leave Brooklyn suddenly reignites with a vengeance. I want to get away from the man who would so quickly turn on me. On us.

"Rocco, this is the mother of your child, my grandchild," Giuliano's voice is outraged on my behalf. "I taught you better than that."

But Rocco ignores him. "You went to him? Instead of me?"

"She knew I could offer her something that you would be incapable of doing."

"Shut the fuck up!" Rocco yells at his father. "Answer me, Cas."

His rage ignites my own. It's like a tinderbox, always ready to explode at this point.

"No one leaves the Guild, Rocco. You told me that!" I shout right back.

"You are not a part of the Guild," Rocco growls.

"But my son will be its heir."

The fire in his eyes resides just enough for me to see it—the longing, the hope, the joy he has restrained by pure willpower.

He wants this. He wants my son.

But I can't live in a reality where that's even a possibility.

"I must say, it felt as if I was having Déjà vu when you came here, Miss Bellini. You do resemble Giuseppina. It could have been seventeen years ago if I hadn't been so gray."

I find myself smiling a little at that.

Everyone always said that I look like my mom, although I never personally saw it. I've always idolized her for her beauty and her kindness. Up until these last few weeks, I didn't think she was even capable of doing anything wrong.

I address Rocco directly, "I came to Giuliano to ask for permission to leave the Guild on behalf of my son. The way my mother once did for me."

The silence that follows is almost unbearable.

Rocco seems to have retreated into himself entirely.

Giuliano, however, is more than comfortable filling the silence. "I was just telling Miss Bellini about that day. She doesn't remember, but Giuseppina brought her along to that meeting. You were eight years old, but your mother carried you the whole time. You were fast asleep."

Rocco slowly turns to look at his father.

"She'd packed already," Giuliano continues. "She was dragging a suitcase behind her too. Deceptively strong, that woman. She would have fallen straight to her knees to beg for asylum if I hadn't stopped her."

"But Giuseppina had already made her oath to the Guild. I told her there was no way I could let her leave, but that wasn't why she was there. She was there to beg on behalf of her daughter. After the Vitale massacre, she couldn't bear to see young Miss Bellini grow up in this environment."

Giuliano squeezes my shoulder again. "Of course, being a father myself, I completely understood her suffering."

"You were no father to me," Rocco growls.

"Silence."

The word is chillingly sharp, and I find myself shying away from Giuliano's touch.

"I offered her a deal out of the goodness of my own heart," Giuliano offers me an apologetic smile. "I allowed her to choose between her husband and her child."

This news had almost crushed me when I first heard it.

My mother had always brushed off any questions about my father, always claiming that he abandoned us.

But the picture of us she kept…the fact she never took another lover. —had she loved him? Had she cried for him as she took me away?

Either way, she hadn't hesitated in her choice. Something that, until two days ago, I might have struggled to understand.

But now? Knowing my child is now growing inside of me, I know there is nothing I wouldn't sacrifice to protect them. And if offered the same choice, I wouldn't hesitate either.

"What did he offer you?" Rocco says quietly.

I say nothing.

"What did he fucking offer you?"

"Do not speak to her like that!" Giuliano roars.

Rocco stands, towering over him. "You have no authority anymore, old man. You have nothing to offer us."

"My my, that temper. It's no wonder she came here without telling you," Giuliano tuts. "And for my grandchild? Rocco, I would offer the world."

I can see it in Rocco's face; that pent-up rage is going to explode at any second.

So I stand up. "He wants to be able to visit."

Rocco blinks at me in confusion.

"He will let me go as long as he can visit and offer my son the choice to rejoin the Guild when he turns eighteen," I clarify.

He turns back to his father. "So that's your plan? You're going to slowly turn my own son against me?"

"You think so little of me."

"I think *nothing* of you."

"My offer was more than reasonable, don't you think? Considering the risks I would need to take to ensure that you never found them," Giuliano nods at me. "I was just explaining this when you so rudely barged in."

"I will not allow it," Rocco's intense gaze meets mine. "Cas, we're leaving now."

But I shake my head.

There's no world where Rocco lets me leave. There's no world where I can go anywhere with him, and I don't completely lose all my resolve.

I shake my head because he isn't only the father of my son, he's the murderer of my father and the don of the Italian Mafia. There is no world where my child will grow up safely around him.

Even if, by some miracle, Rocco lets us go. I would live in constant fear that he would come back for us at some point. Or worse, his enemies would discover us and use us to destroy him.

He can't know where we go, can't have any hope of finding us.

"I can't."

Rocco searches my face desperately for another answer, but I don't show him anything. This is the sacrifice I will never stop making.

"As much as it pains me to agree with my son," Giuliano interrupts us. "On reflection, my offer could now be seen as ill-advised, given that Rocco is aware of our plans. Perhaps we could all take a seat and discuss this as adults?"

He gives both of us a pointed look, and slowly, we return to our seats.

"It seems we have the opportunity to discuss a solution that works for us all, to prioritize the protection of the Guild's next heir."

Rocco glowers. "Don't listen to him, Cas. He has no intention of helping you."

Giuliano merely rolls his eyes before addressing me.

"I may be many things, Miss Bellini, but I know how to learn from my mistakes. I now see I was unwise to separate your family. Your father's longing clearly outweighed his rationale, considering he dragged you out of hiding against your knowledge."

"You bastard."

"I am not talking to you."

"Let him finish, Rocco," I snap.

Giuliano smirks a little.

"I'm prepared to make a different offer. Now that my son is here and is aware of the entirety of the situation," Giuliano reaches to take my hand, "I will allow the three of you to leave forever if you can convince Rocco to relinquish the Guild to me."

My heart stops beating.

My traitorous brain immediately fills my head with images of the three of us. A perfectly happy and normal family, somewhere far away from this city. Our child playing in the yard. The child has my dark hair and his father's inquisitive gray eyes.

But it's an illusion, a complete fantasy. The job always comes first.

"She doesn't want me," Rocco hisses.

"Then you can co-parent. Or whatever it is they do these days," Giuliano counters. "I'm sure Miss Bellini can see the sense in keeping a father figure around."

There's no way Rocco would agree to something like that. Not with everything that is at stake. I smile bitterly at the very thought.

"You think too much of me. I would never be able to convince him."

Giuliano's Cheshire Cat smile stuns me. "On the contrary, I think you think too little of yourself. Isn't that right, Rocco?"

We both turn to look at him. He's running his hands together like a man teetering at the edge of his own doom. But that resolve in his eyes, the power it holds...

"I'll do it."

The lump in my throat threatens to choke me.

He would do it, too.

He would give up everything he had built, those five years of excruciating negotiations, to sit on the periphery of our child's life, to watch from the sidelines at my beck and call, only being able to see him at weekends or on alternate weeks.

Never to cross the boundary without my permission, never to insert himself in our lives unless needed.

Never to speak to anyone from the Guild again. To turn his back on Teo and Donatella, and Martino. To let go of his income, his wealth, his cars.

He would give every aspect of his life to me and our son.

But who am I to ask that of him?

"I can't accept."

There's a beat where all Rocco can do is stare at me in disbelief.

"Why not?"

"I...I love him. I can't ask him to do this."

Rocco's eyes fill with unshed tears. The impact of my words has a visible effect on his entire being, tearing him apart before my very eyes.

What am I doing to him? To us?

"That's a pity," Giuliano purrs, closer to my ear than I was expecting. But Rocco's expression is ruining me. I can't look away.

"I was truly hoping you would make this easier for me."

The next thing I know, Giuliano is holding a blade to my throat.

29

ROCCO

"Counter offer: you hand over the Guild, or I kill Miss Bellini and your unborn child."

I can't believe I let myself get distracted.

That I let my guard down in front of my father for even a moment.

But Cas' confession, for the second time, had completely broken me. Her words doomed us both to a lifetime of torment.

All I ever wanted was for her to be safe. To be at peace, to sing and laugh and fucking *live*.

Now Giuliano Moretti's knife is at her throat, and it's my fault.

"Let her go."

White hot fury consumes me at the sight before me. Cas is clutching desperately at my father's arm, as if hoping by some miracle she will be able to push him away.

But I know my father, know that knife.

I know that whatever soft old man act he was pulling has now disappeared into thin air.

This is the true face of the disgraced Mafia don.

"You know the lengths I have gone to," Giuliano growls. "If you think for one second I'm letting this opportunity slip away, you're gravely mistaken."

I slowly get to my feet, keeping my hands up and palms open. But my eyes are on Cas, scanning every inch of her face which is streaked with tears.

"This is between you and me," I say slowly. "Let her go."

"Renounce your claim to the Guild."

Giuliano's grip on Cas tightens, and she winces as the blade presses closer to her skin. A thin line of red appears, a whisper of blood against her neck.

My heart slams against my ribs, each beat a countdown to disaster. I can't let this happen. I won't.

I need more time to think.

"You think they would welcome you back when they realize you're the one who's been selling us out to the Cartel this whole time?"

"I've been cultivating a relationship with Amos Rubio far longer than you've been don, boy," Giuliano sneers. "He's been more than eager to help me out ever since you came to power and cracked down on the activity in *Electrix.*"

"You let the Cartel operate on Guild territory?"

Giuliano laughs. "I would let anyone operate on Guild territory for the right price. There's no prize for taking the moral high ground, Rocco."

"Is that why you put people like Claudio Lazzaro on your payroll?"

I see Cas tense up at the name in my periphery, but I don't look away from my father.

"Lazzaro was a useful asset."

"Lazzaro was an abusive drug addict."

"Which made him easy to control." Giuliano shakes his head. "You know nothing of leadership if it took you this long to figure that out. Control is everything."

Without warning, Giuliano grabs Cas and pulls her off the couch. She yelps as the knife momentarily presses into her skin once more before she can scramble to right herself, her back now against Giuliano's chest.

"Every man has his weakness, Rocco," Giuliano drawls on. "Lazzaro's was drugs. But it seems you and Carmine have something in common."

Cas thrashes against his firm hold.

"It was a stroke of genius, I think, forcing him to smuggle his daughter back into Brooklyn so that she was within arm's reach. It kept him very motivated indeed. So much so that he killed himself instead of sharing my secrets."

He turns his vile face to Cas' ear. "All so I wouldn't have an excuse to seek you out and kill you myself. But it seems fate was just saving you for this exact moment."

I take a step forward, hands twitching with the desire to wring his neck.

Giuliano's eyes narrow, his grip on Cas tightening. "Don't," he warns, pressing the knife harder against her throat.

But Cas isn't just some damsel waiting to be rescued.

She locks eyes with me, and in that split second, I see her determination—she's not giving up, not willing to let her father's death be in vain. Her eyes dart over to my father's makeshift greenhouse, to the rake hanging from the wall.

I take another step, forcing Giuliano back. "Careful now. I would so hate for this to get messy."

Without warning, Cas drives her elbow into Giuliano's

ribs, catching him off guard. It's enough to make him falter, just a heartbeat of hesitation, but it's all I need.

I grab the rake, swinging it in a wide arc. The metal teeth catch Giuliano's arm, tearing his grip away from Cas and knocking the knife out of his hand.

Cas stumbles forward, free but disoriented, and I rush to her, shoving her behind me. I barely have enough time to take comfort in her reassuring warmth, her familiar scent, when Giuliano lets out a scream in frustration.

"NO!"

He's on me in an instant, fists flying. He's fast for an old man, his strikes precise, honed by decades of street brawls and backroom deals. I barely dodge his first punch, but his second catches me in the gut, knocking the wind out of me.

I stagger back, the rake slipping from my grasp. A pair of hands grip my shoulders, holding me steady.

"Rocco!"

Giuliano seizes the opportunity, grabbing a nearby pair of shears, their blades gleaming under the penthouse lights.

"You've always been weak," Giuliano sneers, advancing. "Too soft to lead. Too soft to be my son."

I tear myself away from Cas' comforting embrace. "And you're too desperate to see this is over."

I dart left, and he lunges, the shears aimed at my chest, but I sidestep, grabbing a potted plant from a nearby table and smashing it over his head.

Giuliano staggers, dazed, shards of ceramic and soil cascading down his suit. I kick the shears from his hand, and they go sliding across the cement.

With a frustrated grunt, he launches himself at me.

We're locked in a brutal dance now—blow after blow, some missing and some landing as we grapple for control.

The pain is only secondary to my instinct to fight, to protect. To win.

Finally, I see an opening. I drive my shoulder into him, sending him crashing into the balcony doors. The glass spiderwebs with the impact but doesn't break.

Giuliano is gasping now, his breath ragged. His suit is torn, blood dribbling from his nose and staining the expensive fabric.

But his eyes are still wild, still hungry. "You're nothing without me," he hisses.

I kick him squarely in the chest. It's the final blow needed for the door to crack completely. Glass rains down as my father falls back onto the balcony. Red gashes appear on his arms and face.

"I am everything I am today in spite of you."

Giuliano picks himself up, suddenly, laughing hard. "Yet you're still going to kill me? After five years of refusing to even consider it, wanting so desperately to set a new precedent. You're going to kill me in the same room as your unborn child?"

I stride forward, stepping through the open door. "You threatened my family."

"And now, one day, your son will know exactly who he needs to kill when he wants your job."

I throw myself at him, realizing too late that he was goading me. Enticing me closer, pushing me to attack.

Quicker than I thought possible, he kicks out and pushes hard.

My trajectory shifts, and I find myself launched from the balcony.

"Rocco!"

Cas is all I can hear as I stare down at the fifty-three-storey drop.

My hands scrabble for purchase on anything within reach as I fly over the railing. My palms hit the metal bar running across the top, and I cling to it for dear life.

Giuliano is peering down at me a heartbeat later. He's already laughing heartily, cruelly, as he assesses my predicament.

"I was prepared to wait years for this," he declares. "But I'm glad I'm still young enough to enjoy this properly."

Without warning, he pounds down on my left hand hard enough to break my fingers. I let go of the bar instinctively, the muscles in my right arm straining to hold on.

"You humiliated me for five years, shoved me in this prison in the sky while you ruined everything I had spent a lifetime building."

"CAS!" I scream out. I'm desperate to see her, to hear her voice one last time, but there's no response.

I try to hoist myself back up to grip the bar again with my left hand, but my broken fingers won't respond to my command.

"But today, fate has granted me a reward for my suffering." My father presses down on my remaining right hand. "Your death will be sweet, but not as good as raising my new heir myself."

No. No.

"Don't you dare fucking touch them."

Giuliano merely smirks. "Don't worry, I'll make sure Miss Bellini is very comfortable when you're gone."

Time slows as three things happen simultaneously.

My father increases the weight on my hand, and my fingers begin to slip.

I have the sudden, terrible realization that I never told Cas that I love her.

And a pair of shears pierce through Giuliano's neck.

Blood spurts from his mouth like a fountain of pure death. My brain barely registers what it's seeing as he sags forward and topples head-first over the railing.

But as his body knocks into mine, my grip on the bar fails me.

This is it.

I close my eyes, bracing myself for the sudden rush of wind that will inevitably lead to my crushing death on the sidewalk fifty-three stories below.

My last comforting thought is that at least now, Cas will be free.

"Oh no, you fucking don't!"

Something firm snatches at my wrist, nearly pulling my arm out of the socket.

My eyes snap open with alarm, only to find Teo half hanging off the balcony, face covered in blood spray and clutching onto me with sheer determination. Cas, at his side, anchors him, all the while trying to reach down to me, too.

I rally myself, operating on pure adrenalin, as I reach up to grab Teo's forearm with my broken hand, willing my appendages to lock into place.

Teo pulls with a yell of agony, and then suddenly, another pair of hands are snatching at my shirt and pulling me up, too.

Between them, I make it up inch by bloody inch until they can roll me over the railing and back onto the safety of the balcony, completely and utterly spent.

By the sound of panting, I know the others have collapsed nearby as well.

"Cas? I…"

A small, shaking body slams into mine. Arms wrap around my neck, and I immediately hold her to me, wanting every part of her pressed into me, needing every reassurance possible that she's alive and here and safe.

This beautiful, brave woman who is carrying my baby. Our baby.

"I'm sorry," she sobs in my ear, only making me hold on to her tighter. "I'm so sorry."

"It's okay. We're okay." I bury my face in her neck.

"I should never have come here."

I hold her for another minute before finally looking up to see Teo examining the blood on his hands.

"What happened?"

His eyes flash to mine. "I…might have followed you."

Slowly, I pry Cas from my arms. But I can't bring myself to let go of her hand as I approach my friend.

He watches me with growing alarm. "Don't you dare give me shit for disobeying an order. Coming here on your own was the very definition of reckless, and I…"

I throw my arms around him.

"Oh." Slowly, he relaxes into the embrace.

"You killed him."

"I did."

The feeling is a strange one. On the one hand, I'm glad it was him and not Cas. She already has enough blood on her hands, thanks to me.

But on the other, my father's absence is both a weight lifted and a burden taken. Everything I ever worked for is now being thrown into question. Was there a world where the transfer of power wouldn't end in violence?

I pull away from Teo and offer him a genuine and heartfelt smile. "Thank you."

Teo smiles back before his eyes dart over to Cas at my side.

"I better start on damage control. I'll give you two a moment to sort yourselves out."

With that, he gets to his feet and brushes himself off.

I've never seen a man stand so tall.

With one last glance out at the city skyline, Teo departs.

"It's one hell of a view from the top."

30

CASSANDRA

"I don't even know where to start."

I sniff back another onslaught of tears as Teo closes the door behind him.

Rocco looks back at me, strong and courageous and the father of my unborn child. The man who fought the monster that was Giuliano Moretti, who was willing to sacrifice everything to keep us safe.

Not only had I misjudged him, but I accused him of a crime he didn't commit.

But despite everything I've done, and almost betraying him for his own father, he opens his arms wide for me.

I reach for him in the space of a heartbeat, finding my home against his chest.

"I'm so sorry. I didn't know, I was just trying to..."

"It's okay, Cas. I know. You were only trying to protect the baby."

I swallow hard. "He lied to me. He said he'd help me, that he'd keep me safe."

"I know."

"I should have listened to you."

He pulls away slowly, a solemn expression on his face when I look up at him. "I understand why you didn't. What I did to you, Cas, it's unforgivable."

"Rocco..."

"Please, let me finish," he steps away. "I meant what I said before. I'll give it all up for you. Teo can take my place. I just want to be a part of our child's life. In whatever little way will you allow me to be."

I shake my head in disbelief. "I won't let you do that."

"I will never be able to atone for what I did, but please let me try in this small way."

"Rocco!" I cry. "You didn't kill my father."

Rocco looks away, his jaw clenching. "I may as well have."

"My father was manipulated and used by that monster to the point where he felt his only way out was suicide."

"You weren't there that night, Cas." He swallows back his own tears. "I cornered him, challenged him, pushed him to his limit."

"Would you have killed him?"

His eyes shoot back to mine in confusion. "What?"

"If he had gone with you, would you have killed him, eventually?"

He lets out a bitter laugh. "You know, I was making plans? I knew there would be several who would find the power transition a struggle. I needed a way to move out long-standing members of the Guild if their loyalties refused to shift."

"Setting a new precedent," I nod with a little smile.

He returns it weakly. "I was thinking about exiling them."

"Where?"

"Ohio."

It's my turn to laugh. "So, if my father had cooperated…"

"he'd have finally been able to see you and your mom again." Rocco's smile falters. "But I took that reunion away from you."

"Rocco," I step forward, reaching to hold his face in my hands, "I don't blame you for Carmine's death. I grieve the life we could have had, but that is not your fault."

His eyes flutter closed at my touch. "I won't stop blaming myself."

"Try," I whisper back before summoning all my courage and standing on my toes to kiss him.

At first, he seems entirely frozen in shock. But then his mouth parts, responding eagerly to my desperation. Our tongues clash, passionately expressing every ounce of joy and relief we both feel to be reunited once more.

When I pull away, I feel dizzy. "I don't want to think about the past anymore. I want to focus on the future. Our future, our child."

Rocco rests his forehead against mine as we both look down at my stomach.

"I will do everything in my power to keep him safe," he vows.

"I know you will."

"If there's even the possibility of a threat against either of you, we can leave, take whatever we can and disappear for good."

I smile, finding it impossible to imagine any kind of danger that could even touch us right now. "If that time comes, I trust that you'll be able to protect us."

"I love you, Cas."

His words find the space in my heart I'd unconsciously carved out for them. It's as if everything we went through was just a delay to this inevitable conclusion.

I want to return the sentiment, but he pulls away once more, taking my hand as he goes. "Come on, let's go home and get you cleaned up."

There's no rush as we make our way downstairs.

But when we reach the foyer, red and blue lights are flashing through the windows as the cops cordon off the place where Giuliano fell.

We find Martino stubbornly arguing with an officer who is clearly trying to convince him to move his car. But with little success.

To my surprise, the cop backs away as Rocco approaches.

Rocco ignores them as he opens the car door for me, and within seconds, the three of us are driving away into the night.

"What was that all about?" I ask as I peer out the back window for one last look at the disgruntled officer.

Martino laughs. "The NYPD owes us a favor or two."

My eyebrows raise as I turn back to Rocco.

"You might have been able to forgive me for some of my crimes, *Angioletta*," he replies seriously. "But that doesn't mean there aren't other things that might surface that you don't agree with."

I weigh his words carefully. The memories of Rocco killing the Cartel men in front of me rise to the forefront of my mind.

But my hands aren't exactly clean, either.

"Well, from now on, you should probably let me commit crimes with you, too."

The words sound so childish in my mouth, but Rocco doesn't smile.

"This isn't a life that you want, Cas."

"I want a life with *you,*" I counter stubbornly. "And I'm not going to sit on the sidelines and turn a blind eye to this. If a threat is coming to you or our baby, I want to know about it."

Martino swerves a little at the mention of the baby, and I wince slightly. I guess that particular cat is out of the bag.

"And don't you dare tell me the Guild is no place for a woman. I know Mia is on your payroll."

Rocco's mouth curves up to one side. "The *Candelabra* is in desperate need of a new manager."

I squeal a little as I throw myself at him, pressing his lips to mine in pure gratitude.

THE MOMENT the bedroom door closes behind us, Rocco is on me.

His hands follow the curves of my hips down to my ass, giving it a firm squeeze as his tongue explores every inch of her mouth with careful precision, causing a wave of goosebumps to pinprick across my skin.

"I'm never letting you leave my side again," he declares possessively as he strips me of my clothes.

I giggle as my pants pool at my feet. "Are you going to try and lock me in here again?"

"If that's what it takes."

His lustful eyes soften for a moment as he studies my face. He cups my cheek and plants a soft kiss on my lips.

"You want me to be gentle with you?"

The sudden vulnerability catches me off guard, "Never."

His smirk returns, and suddenly, he's lifting me up. I squeal as he throws me down on the bed and immediately gets to work tying my hands to the backboard.

"Now you can't escape." He leans back, examining his work proudly.

"Has anyone ever told you how possessive you are?"

Those gray eyes meet mine again, insatiably hungry, and my breath catches.

Wordlessly, he lifts up my bare leg and begins kissing and nipping down from my ankle. Each placement of his lips sends shocks of pure desire straight into my veins.

Unable to reach for him, I can only wait with agonizing impatience as he makes his way closer and closer to my throbbing core. His hand grips my ass again as he pulls away.

I whimper as his mouth disappears from my skin.

"You need to promise that you'll stay," his cruel, cruel voice goads from above.

"Anything you want," I beg breathlessly. "I'll stay. Please, don't stop."

He smirks as he pulls on my leg again, bringing my throbbing core closer to his teasing lips. He buries his face in my thigh, teeth teasing the skin before smoothing the twinge of pain with his tongue.

I almost come then and there.

"Please," I beg again. "I'll stay."

I can feel my wetness building, pleading for any kind of friction or pressure. The longer Rocco ignores it, the worse it gets.

Finally, his nose skims across the fabric of my thong. His teeth find purchase on the frilly material, and he pulls it to one side just as my body shudders with a wave of overwhelming delight.

I spread my legs for easier access. "I want you to taste me."

Whatever self-control Rocco was exercising crumbles in that instant.

His tongue licks me up in one earth-shattering movement.

Suddenly, he buries himself within me with his tongue. His fingers bruise my ass as he holds me firmly in place.

My eyes roll back as he sucks harder, deeper, feasting on me as I try to wrench my hands from their restraints to pull at his hair.

Suddenly, he moans, causing delicious vibrations to erupt from his lips directly onto my most sensitive spot.

"Oh, fuck."

The pressure reaches its boiling point. I can see the stars beginning to form around my eyes and...and...

He disappears once more.

"Rocco!" I cry out, desperately wrapping my legs around him to bring him back.

He straightens to undo the buckle and zipper of his pants, chuckling to himself. "So impatient."

I bite down on my lower lip to stop another protest from escaping as I behold his well-endowed cock with heated anticipation.

Rocco roughly strokes himself, eyes turning dark as they ravage me where I'm tied up on his bed and unable to do anything but succumb to him and his pleasure.

I part my lips in invitation and his stroking increases.

"You're so fucking beautiful." His voice is gruff with desire.

"Then fuck me," I plead. "Take me now. I'm so fucking wet for you, Rocco. Please."

He doesn't need to be told twice. The next thing I know, his lips are crashing against mine, his tongue plunging into my mouth desperately.

I can taste myself on his lips, and I groan at the sensation of it all. It will never get enough of this.

I'm so distracted I barely notice that he's lining himself up at my entrance. When he plunges into me, groaning with pleasure until he is fully sheathed inside, the stars return with a vengeance.

"I love you," I gasp.

Because there's never been a moment when that hasn't been more true.

But to my dismay, Rocco stops again. My straining core is struggling with the effort of keeping him within.

A gentle hand tilts my chin upwards, and I meet his endlessly gray eyes. "Say it again."

"I love you."

His mouth meets mine again as he finally, finally begins to move. But this time, his movements are powerful and relentless.

He growls possessively, "Tell me you're mine."

I have to grip onto my restraints to keep myself anchored so that every time he pounds into me, he still hits that delicious mark.

"I'm yours." My tongue dances hungrily with his.

I lose myself to the rhythm of our joined sexes.

My orgasm explodes from me in a violent ecstasy, but he doesn't stop, doesn't offer me any relief until my second has grown to a breaking point, and then he too, shudders with the outburst of our desire.

We cum together, wrapped around each other in an inseparable union. The restraints around my wrists loosen as if knowing that their purpose has been served.

For what feels like hours, we simply lie there, basking in the beautiful joy of each other's bodies.

"Nothing has ever felt so right." Rocco breaks the comfortable silence first.

"I don't think I've ever been this happy," I agree.

He plants a gentle kiss on my forehead. "And soon, we'll have a little one to add to our joy."

I hum noncommittally before I bury my face in his neck. My tongue darts out to lick the sensitive spot I know sends him completely wild. "I guess there's nothing else for it."

Rocco props himself up on his hand, pulling himself away. "What are you talking about?"

"Well, we can't exactly be doing this all the time when the baby is born," I point out.

His eyes twinkle mischievously. "I suppose that means we should go again."

"You took the words straight out of my mouth."

FIRST EPILOGUE

Cassandra, Three Months Later

I'm going to kill Mia Chiavari.

I let my hatred fuel every step back along Bay Ridge toward the brownstone. I need the walk home to calm down before confronting anyone. The last thing I need is anyone accusing me of having baby hormones.

But I think any rational person would be annoyed if they showed up to work only to discover someone else had closed the club already.

My club.

Mia might still work behind the bar some nights, but I'm not afraid to pull rank on her if she tries this shit again.

It's only been three months since we discovered the pregnancy, but if she's already insisting that I need to be coddled, we're going to have a problem.

I shake it off as I reach the familiar brownstone, my house keys jangling as I open the front door.

The walk home begins to bother my sensitive joints, and

I absently rub my little swollen bump as I imagine stepping into a nice warm bath. Mmmm. Yeah, that will take the edge off.

I step into the foyer, kicking off my shoes as I go, and open my mouth to shout for Donatella...

"SURPRISE!"

One second, the two-story entrance way is entirely deserted. The next, about fifty people line the stairs, each throwing confetti and streamers over the railing, revealing a banner that rolls down from the topmost banister.

Written on it, in giant sparkling letters, is the phrase, "Baby Shower".

I blink at the wild display of sound and color, trying desperately to orient myself when another body slams into mine.

"Happy surprise baby shower, bitch!"

I bury my face in Mia's flaming red hair, returning her embrace just as tightly. "I'm going to fucking kill you."

She laughs as she pulls away, dragging me toward the row of my eagerly awaiting friends, all wanting to offer me congratulations.

The vast majority are from the *Candelabra*. The bar and wait staff I've come to know far too well, and some of the regulars who are coincidentally also mafioso are here as well. Even some of Rocco's closest circle are here. I wave at Martino and Teo, who smile back sheepishly.

"Congrats, Bellini."

I'm surprised when my gaze lands on the stunning blonde before me. "Thanks, Danny."

Things had been awkward when I returned to the *Candelabra* as her boss. At first, she was treading on eggshells, trying to avoid me, probably out of fear that I might fire her. But as things settled, a tentative acquaintanceship had blossomed.

Now that I'm temporarily out of commission, she is, after all, our best performer.

"Will you all let me through!" a voice cries out from the back of the gathering crowd.

My brain short-circuits.

"Mom?"

Giuseppina Bellini elbows her way past the line of bodies and stands before me, radiant as ever, the soft lines of her face curving up into a huge smile.

My mother opens her arms for me and I run to her, a child all over again.

"Cassy, Cassy, Cassy!" she whispers into my hair, a near-perfect match to her own. "I missed you so much."

"Mom!"

She pulls back, squishing my cheeks between her palms. "I can't believe my baby is having a baby."

I grin, although the snot and tears leaking from my face must make me look monstrous.

"Honestly," she laughs, wiping it all away with a tissue. "And here I thought you'd forgotten me, now that you have this new fancy life in the big city."

"Never," I laugh right back.

Ever since that fateful day in Giuliano's penthouse, we must have spoken on the phone almost every day.

At first, it had just been a lot of crying. Mom took some time to adjust to the news about my dad, and though I had spared her many of the gorier details, she was terrified by my encounter with Giuliano.

But slowly, we began to rebuild our relationship. She'd share the stories she remembered of being a part of the

Guild while I introduced her to Rocco and all the new branches of my ever-blossoming social circle.

I throw my arms around her once more, not quite believing that she is finally here, standing in front of me. "It's so good to see you."

"Rocco flew me out and set me up in one of the rooms here," she tells me. "We have all week to catch up properly, so go talk with your friends."

I pull away, squeezing her hands once more before letting her go.

I'm about to turn back into the chattering fray, when a familiar warmth encircles my waist from behind, and a head rests on my shoulder.

"Did you really have no idea, *Angioletta?*" Rocco's voice sends shivers down my spine as he whispers in my ear.

"I was a little preoccupied today, actually," I admit.

He kisses my cheek before spinning me around to face him. His strong, tattooed arms never leave their hold on my waist.

"I want to show you something." His charming smile never ceases to cause my heart to flutter. "But if I give you my present first, Chiavari might murder me in my sleep."

"I resent that!" the redhead shouts from the other side of the room.

I roll my eyes, and Rocco's smile turns mischievous as he leans forward to whisper in my ear. "Let's get out of here."

At that moment, music erupts from deeper within the house, and the crowd begins to disperse, offering us the perfect opportunity to slip away relatively unnoticed. I spot Teo wagging his eyebrows at us as we hurry up the stairs.

Rocco leads me right to the end of the corridor toward the room I first stayed in when we arrived.

"I just finished the redecoration of the master suite," I tease. "Do you want to go make the most of it?"

He chuckles. "All in good time."

Then he pushes the door open.

I gasp as I behold what's inside.

Gone is the California king bed and tastefully plain furniture that had once filled the space.

Instead, there now lies a beautiful nursery. Wood and cream tones warm the entire room. A cradle is covered by a draping, sheer curtain which swoops down from the ceiling. A beautifully ornate rocking chair sits in the corner.

I float inside, scanning the bookshelf as I pass, noting the familiar and unfamiliar titles that reside there. My eyes snag on a particularly worn copy of *Beauty and the Beast*, and I pull it from its new home.

"I used to have this exact edition!" I gush excitedly as I open the first page.

There, in blue felt tip, is my childish script, "property of Cassandra Bellini".

"Your mom brought it with her," Rocco explains, reaching over my shoulder to trace over my five-year-old handwriting. "I wanted this space to be filled with everything you love."

I turn to look at him with tears in my eyes. "You've done that already."

His responding kiss is chaste and tender but, nonetheless, sets my heart alight.

"Come on. Let's get back before they realize we're missing," he announces as he takes my hand once more.

When we rejoin the party, most of the guests have gathered in the living room. Donatella seems to have laid out a veritable feast on every available surface.

My heart sings with joy at the happy chatter, the tinkling music in the background, the laughter and teasing as we walk in.

It's not until we reach the far table and Rocco picks up a glass of champagne, that I realize he's been dragging me here for a reason.

"Ladies and gentlemen, if I could have your attention." His voice booms through the room, instantly silencing everyone. "I hope you will join me in a toast to my beautiful Cassandra."

I flush with embarrassment as everyone around us pulls out a glass, tilts it in my direction, and shouts variations of my name before drinking the amber liquid.

"As many of you know, from the moment Cas came into my life, I was completely awestruck by her beauty and angelic singing voice. But what you might not know is that it was the passionate fire within her that drew me to her."

I look up at Rocco, somewhat confused. There was no need for speeches today.

"She has a passion, not just for her career and her interests, but for everyone she cares about. She showed me that love was possible, even in the most dire of circumstances. And I knew, at that moment, that my life would be forever changed."

I glance around our audience nervously. "Rocco," I whisper.

He just smiles back at me as he sinks down to one knee. Everyone around us gasps, or in Mia's case, squeals.

"Cassandra Bellini, I can not imagine a future without you. Will you marry me?"

Happy tears crinkle in the corners of my eyes as he

retrieves a box from his pocket and opens it to reveal the most beautiful engagement ring I've ever seen.

I laugh as I get down on my knee, procuring a nearly identical box.

"Rocco Moretti, will *you* marry *me*?"

At Rocco's disbelief, I open the box.

For a second, he frowns at the folded piece of paper wedged within the ring crease. But it fades the second he flattens it out. Instead, he gawks at the picture.

"We're having a boy? I mean, we kept saying it would be, but...we really are?"

The room erupts around us as Rocco pulls me into his arms. I melt into him. I have never felt more alive than in this very moment.

I'm still laughing when he tugs on my arm urgently.

"Was that a yes?"

I kiss his nose in response.

"Yes, Rocco Moretti. I will be your wife."

SECOND EPILOGUE

Rocco, Two Months Later

I kiss Cas softly on the temple, careful not to disturb her. One hand rests on the swell of her belly, the baby growing inside her. She murmurs something in her sleep, shifting slightly, protective even in dreams. It guts me, leaving them like this, but the call I got minutes ago left me no choice.

"Tobia Natali is dead," I whisper into her hair.

Her eyes flicker open, fogged with sleep but sharp in an instant. "The Prince's Hand?"

I nod. "Harlem's about to fracture. I need to be at the table to assess the damage before someone else tries to make a move."

Cas reaches for my wrist. "Be careful."

"I always am." But we both know I can't promise to stay safe. Even when I'm careful, this life is still a loaded gun.

I press one last kiss to her forehead and slip out.

Martino's already waiting by the car, leaning against the hood like it's just another night. But it's not.

We don't speak until we're on the road, Brooklyn lights cutting through the dark. The streets look calm, but I know better.

"You're quiet," Martino says, glancing at me in the rearview.

I stare out the window, weighing the thought that's been stalking me for months.

"What if I stepped down?"

His grip on the steering wheel tightens. "You're serious?"

I nod once.

"No Don walks away clean," he says. "Not in this life."

"There's always a first."

"The Guild won't like it. Your enemies won't believe it. The city smells weakness fast."

I clench my jaw. "And what about my family? I'm about to get married. Cas? The baby? You think I'm going to drag them through decades of this shit?"

Martino exhales through his nose. "I've never seen you like this."

"Yeah, well, I've never had this much to lose."

We hit a red light, and he turns slightly toward me. "What are you saying? You hand it over? To who?"

"That's the problem." I rub the tension from the back of my neck. "I built this from ashes. Took it from my father's cold hands. And now... it feels like a noose around my neck."

Martino studies me for a long beat. "You really thinking about walking away?"

I glance at him. "Would you blame me if I did?"

"No," he admits. "But I'd say you're walking into a different kind of war."

The silence after that weighs heavily.

Finally, he says, "So who would you trust to hold the reins?"

I look back out the window, watching the city slide by like a slow-moving threat.

"This conversation stays between us," I say.

"Always."

I let the silence stretch, the weight of the question pressing against my chest. There aren't many men I'd trust. Fewer still who could command loyalty and fear in equal measure. Most would crumble under the pressure or bleed out before they even claimed the chair.

But there's one—the closest person I have to a brother. The Guild runs through his veins as much as it runs through mine. Ruthless, loyal, dangerous as hell.

I don't say it out loud, but the answer is already carved into my bones.

There's only one choice.

Teo Vitale.

THE END

Read more from The Prince's Guild bestselling series, exclusive on Amazon:

Sin & Secrets: A Forced Proximity Mafia Romance
(Rocco & Cas)

Revenge & Ruin: An Enemies to Lovers Mafia Romance
(Teo & Isabella)

Deception & Desire: An Arranged Marriage Mafia Romance
(Leon & Mia)

Obsession & Oath: A Forbidden Bodyguard Mafia Romance
(Dante & Carmen)

Printed in Great Britain
by Amazon